Jurassic Jemma and the Trail of Evil

John J. Delaney

Also by John J. Delaney

The Jurassic Jemma Trilogy

A Dangerous Fossil

Jurassic Jemma and the Mysteries of Time

Jurassic Jemma and the Trail of Evil

This novel is entirely a work of fiction. The names, characters and incidents portrayed in it are the work of the author's imagination. Any resemblance to actual persons, living or dead, events or locations is entirely coincidental.

For Ali
1967-2023
A true friend and great supporter.

ICHTHYOSAUR

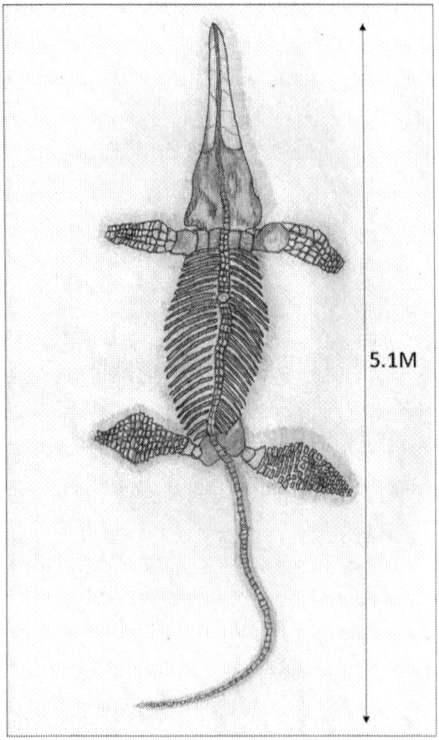

Chapter 1

The early afternoon Cyprus heat was thick with the rhythmic buzzing of cicadas and the fragrant smell of the pine forest that surrounded the villa. Under the shade of a multi-coloured parasol, a tanned woman wearing a gold bikini scrolled mindlessly on a tablet. Her skin had a slight leathery appearance from years of sunbathing but she remained trim for someone in their fifties. She glanced up and smiled as she watched the muscular shoulders of the naked man swimming up and down a blue pool. Reaching the end, he grabbed the side and effortlessly lifted himself out from the water before stepping towards the woman. He was a toned man with olive skin, short dark hair and a neatly trimmed moustache.

'How far today?' she called out.

'Only a kilometre.' He leant over to kiss the top of her head.

'Hey! Don't drip on the screen!' She laughed, thrusting the tablet away.

'Sorry. Fancy a drink?'

'I'll have a gin, please, Malek. Easy on the tonic.'

'OK, gin with a splash on its way.' He wandered over to the alfresco bar while Helen's eyes dipped back to the tablet.

The luxurious five-bedroomed white villa sat on a large plot with no neighbouring properties. Malek returned with two glasses, placed them on a small table next to the sun lounger and nodded at the screen. 'Anything good?'

'Nah, just the usual social media drivel.'

He stood behind her and started gently kneading her shoulders.

'Oh, that's good,' she sighed, 'very relaxing... Shit! The little bitch!'

'What's wrong?'

'I've spotted something on a Lulcombe news site,' she said. 'Something interesting about an old friend.'

'Who?'

She swatted Malek's hands away and sat up. 'Jurassic Jemma and her bitch of a daughter.'

'You've not mentioned her in months. Just forget her.'

'Ah, yes, I'll forget the woman who murdered my brothers and drowned my sons. Why didn't I think of that? Such a simple solution. Look at this!' She shoved the tablet into his hands.

She ignored the fact her brothers had tried murdering Jemma when she opposed their purchase of the site of Lulcombe Museum, after which Jemma had killed them in self-defence. Her sons had then tried to kill Jemma in revenge for their uncles' deaths, except instead she had led them into a dangerous mudslide on the beach where they perished.

Malek squinted at the screen, 'I need my sunglasses.' She passed him the pair of Raybans and he slipped them on before perching on the edge of her lounger. 'A wedding. Whose?' he asked.

'Looks like Jemma has married Brad Jones.'

'That bitch really isn't worth your thoughts, you know. We should be making the most of siesta time.' He tried to hand the tablet back.

She pushed it back at him and frowned. 'Check this out. The bridesmaid is holding a baby girl.'

He shrugged. 'Who is it?'

'That young lady, my bronzed Adonis, is Ellie Thorne, Jemma's daughter, who might be the mother of my grandchild.'

Malek peered closer. 'Your grandchild? I didn't know you had a grandchild.'

'Nor did I until a couple of minutes ago. I'm not totally sure but the timing is about right.' She took the tablet back and zoomed in on the child. 'Can you remember I told you about my sons, Zak and Gary?' Her fists clenched. 'My beautiful boys were murdered by that cow, Jemma. Her daughter went out with my Zak just before he was killed, so that baby must be his.'

'How can you be sure it's his?'

Helen started counting in her head. 'Zak died in August, eighteen months ago. That baby looks the right age to be his.'

'Can you find out for definite?'

'I'm sure I can. My old friend Vincent might be able to help but I'll do some more delving into the depths of the internet first. I need to find out more about the bloody Thorne family.' She continued scrolling.

Malek stood and scrutinised his fingernails. 'Did you do anything else about the new Porsche you promised to buy for me?'

One side of her mouth curled into a sly smile. 'Don't worry, you'll get your car. I've got one of my contacts looking into how easy it is to import one to Northern Cyprus.'

He leant over and tried to untie her bikini. 'Now, shall I carry on earning my Porsche?'

She pushed him away. 'Not now, you animal. I've got to find out some more about my new grandchild.'

* * *

Three thousand miles away in a wet and miserable Dorset, Vincent Lawrence was sitting in his favourite armchair positioned by the picture window of his bungalow, staring at the heavy, dark clouds blowing in from the Channel. The spacious property occupied a prime location in Lulcombe overlooking the sea. With current seaside house prices and his meagre pension, he wouldn't have been able to afford it now, but neither would he consider moving as there were too many happy memories of life with his late wife, as well as the incredible views.

Vincent had a distinguished appearance with silver grey hair and a salt and pepper moustache. After a spell in the army many years ago, he still maintained his military poise. Although he had retired five years earlier, he was still a trustee at Lulcombe Museum where he often clashed with fellow trustee, Jemma Thorne, about the site. He also enjoyed fossil hunting in the area.

'Bloody weather.' He tutted and looked down at his yellow Labrador, Monty, who lay on the cosy bed Vincent had commissioned in navy blue fabric to match the armchair. The dog, snout resting on the edge of his bed to see out of the window, exhaled a deep sigh which Vincent took as agreement.

He gave Monty a quick scratch under the ear before wandering through to the lounge to check the tide clock which told him it was almost low tide. The best time for fossil hunting on Lulcombe Beach was from an hour before low tide to an hour after. He checked his watch. 'I suppose I ought to get ready if I'm going. At least this rain will keep the holiday makers off the beach. Are you coming, Monty?'

He heard the gentle repeated thump of the dog's tail hitting the sofa, which became more rapid with growing anticipation. Vincent smiled, appreciating how they both needed some time to gather their enthusiasm to leave in this weather, knowing that once they were on the beach they'd be in their element.

'That's a yes then.'

As he reached for his phone from the oak sideboard it began to ring. It was Helen Fletcher.

He huffed. 'What does she want?'

He'd once supplied information about the museum to Helen's criminal brothers, Keith and Reggie, and Helen still occasionally contacted him for information.

He answered. 'Helen, hello, how are you?'

'I'm well, thank you.'

'How can I help you?'

'I'm after some information.'

He sighed. 'Sorry, I don't have any of that these days, I'm afraid, unless you're interested in the state of the tide here.'

'I'm sure a man of your local knowledge will have lots of juicy gossip.'

'Gossip? That's not my style at all.'

'Don't worry, it's not much,' she reassured him.

He sighed and picked up a pad. 'Fire away.'

'I've recently seen a photo of Jemma Thorne's wedding.'

'And?'

'Her daughter was standing next to her. Ellie, isn't it?'

His eyes flicked up. 'Yes, that's right.'

'Well, Ellie's holding a baby in the photo. Is it hers?'

Vincent licked his lips. 'Yes, but Jemma won't talk about it.'

'Interesting,' Helen replied. 'No boyfriend on the scene?'

'No, it seems that Ellie is a single mum with no husband or any indication as to who the father is.'

There was a pause. 'When was the baby born?'

'I'm not sure. I'll have it in my diary as we needed to move a trustee meeting because her daughter went into labour and Jemma cancelled at the last minute.' He reached for his old diary and flicked through it. 'Here we are. The meeting was the thirty-first of May last year, so it would have been around then.' Vincent imagined Helen counting on her fingers.

'Right. Thanks so much. I'll send a little something extra to your bank account this month.'

'Helen, I'm extremely grateful for everything your family has done for me in the past. However, it was quite worrying to be questioned by the police after the episodes with your brothers at the quarry, and your sons on the beach.'

'You didn't get into trouble, did you?'

He frowned. 'No, but the detectives found my number on your brother's phone and asked me why I was sending information to him.'

'Don't worry, Vincent. I've got a tame lawyer who would have sorted things out if they'd got difficult for you.'

'It's not that. It's just that I feel I shouldn't be in contact with your family anymore.'

'Family? I'm the only one left now, thanks to Jemma Thorne. The last of the Fletcher bloodline.'

'Of course, I'm sorry to mention it.'

'I'm used to it now. Don't concern yourself. Everything's fine. Could you keep me in the loop about Jemma?'

'OK, Helen.'

'Bye, Vincent.'

He cut the call and stared at his mobile. His hands shook as he reached for his coat. 'Come on, Monty, I need some fresh air to clear my head.'

* * *

Helen returned the phone to its cradle and stepped out onto the patio.

Malek was back in the pool powering up and down with his muscular arms while barely making a splash. When he reached the end, she was standing at the edge staring down. He squinted upwards, her body mostly blocking out the sun. 'Did you learn anything?'

'Oh, yes,' she replied, 'something very interesting.'

'Tell me more, but you should come in here, it's far too hot to stand in the sun.'

Helen removed her bikini and climbed down into the pool.

Malek reached out for her and wrapped his arms around her waist. 'You are still so fit.'

'I suppose so, not too bad for a granny.'

Malek laughed. 'You sure you're a grandmother?'

'Oh yes, I'm sure.' She kissed his lips, slipped her hands around to his buttocks and pulled him into her. 'You know you said that one day you'd like a family?'

'Yes.' He raised his eyebrows. 'But... aren't you too old to have children?'

She grinned. 'Yes, but I've had an idea.'

Chapter 2

'Jurassic' Jemma Thorne lay on the floor with her daughter, Ellie, as their children played together on a colourful play mat. Jemma's son, Rocky, was three. A dark-haired youngster who loved being outside and always wore shorts. Ellie's daughter, Kira, was eleven months old with fair hair and a gorgeous smile. Jemma's cottage sat on the hill overlooking the sea at Lulcombe on the coast of West Dorset. It was an old semi-detached house with lovely views of the woods leading down to the Beach Car Park. Beyond the trees in the distance, the blue expanse of the English Channel shimmered like glitter on a Christmas card. The lounge with its sofa and two large armchairs, would probably be described as cosy by an estate agent but Jemma loved the whole place and had no intention of ever moving. After they married, Brad had partially knocked out the wall between Jemma's cottage and his adjoining property to make the home larger and to allow Ellie to live next door. That way she could have some space of her own without being under her mother's feet.

Both Jemma and Ellie were tall and slim. Jemma had shoulder-length brown hair with some blonde highlights to obscure the odd grey strand that had recently started appearing more frequently. Ellie had longer hair that changed colour from its natural auburn whenever the mood took her, though now it was a darker brown.

Ellie grinned. 'This is still a bit weird, Mum, our kids playing together.'

Jemma put her hand on Ellie's arm. 'You wait 'til they're teenagers and Kira realises her Uncle Rocky is only two years older than her.'

'I love that we can all have some time together,' Ellie said. 'I'm so glad you went part-time at uni. You're not getting bored yet, are you?'

'No way!' Jemma replied. 'It's given me a chance to get Spiny finished and ready to be sent to the Isle of Wight. I know Vincent would like it to be on display in Lulcombe but it feels right it should be on show nearer to where it was found.'

The previous year on the south coast of the Isle of Wight, Jemma had discovered the first complete specimen of a Spinosaurus ever found in the UK, and had decided to offer it to a dinosaur museum near the clifftop meadow where she'd found it.

'When is the new museum in town due to open?' Ellie asked.

Jemma thought for a moment. 'I bet it'll be another month or so until it's ready for the first visitors.'

Ellie frowned. 'Are you OK now with the move from the old museum?'

Jemma shrugged, reminded about the fight she'd put up against the sale. 'I suppose so. I'm happier now that it's increased in size from the first few designs. There'll be plenty of room for all of the displays from the old museum and some new ones as well. I'm not happy that the mega-bucks from the sale of the whole hotel site ended up with Helen Fletcher though.'

'No further news about the police claiming criminal funds back then?'

'Nope,' Jemma said. 'After she scuttled back to her lair the trail went dead. Evidently, there's no extradition treaty with the Turkish Republic of Northern Cyprus.'

Ellie handed Kira a bottle of juice. 'At least Helen'll never set foot in the UK again, what with the warrant and all. Amrik said immigration will be on the lookout for her. There's a cell with her name on it just waiting for her.'

Rocky climbed up onto Jemma's knee and she pulled him closer for a hug. 'Hopefully, we'll never have any dealings with her again.'

Jemma had a torrid past with that family after she'd killed Reggie and Keith Fletcher, Helen's brothers, while they were attempting to murder her. The following year Helen's sons, Zak and Gary Richards, had kidnapped Rocky and tried to kill both Jemma and Ellie. Jemma had only managed to overcome them owing to her knowledge of the dangerous local geography, and a great deal of luck.

Helen had been the mastermind of a plot seeking revenge for her brothers using her twins to do the dirty work. When things started to unravel she fled back to Northern Cyprus beyond the reach of UK police.

Jemma passed a beaker of milk to Rocky, who snuggled down next to her, making contented noises as he drank. 'By the way, Ellie,' Jemma remembered to ask, 'are you still OK for a day's filming on Wednesday?'

Ellie glanced over. 'Yes, that's fine. I've got a school reunion on Friday night but Wednesday is clear. I'm looking forward to a day back in front of the camera. Will it be on the Isle of Wight again?'

'Yes, the producer wants to have another day in the field where we found Spiny. There were some interesting GPR results from the opposite side.'

The team on the TV show used ground penetrating radar

to shoot electronic waves into the ground and measure what came back. They hoped that the results would reveal fossilised bones with a different density from the surrounding rocks.

Ellie grinned. 'Do you think we'll find another Spinosaur?'

Jemma thought for a moment. 'I don't think the readings we got were for anything that big. The area to dig is around two metres long so it could be a part fossil or something smaller.'

'It's exciting either way.' Ellie looked at the two children. 'Is Brad still enjoying his life with these two?'

Jemma smiled. 'He loves looking after his son and granddaughter. Do you think you'll ever start calling him Dad?'

Ellie paused. 'No, I don't think so. Brad will always be Brad to me. Liam was Dad for twenty years so it wouldn't feel right to call him anything but that.'

She had found out a couple of years before that Brad was her real father after Jemma's fling with him twenty years before. Until that time Ellie had always thought Jemma's ex-husband, Liam, was her father.

'What time will he be home?' Ellie asked.

Jemma checked her watch. 'Around six, he said. He's in London buying some fossils.'

'That man loves a good shopping trip, doesn't he? He's still wheeling and dealing then?'

'Oh yes, he seems to make money with it so I'm not complaining. He's got loads of contacts so has sold a lot of my surplus specimens.'

'That's good. I hope they're all above board.' Ellie sighed. 'I've had enough excitement with stolen fossils and dodgy dealers.'

* * *

At the villa in Cyprus, Helen stretched out on her lounger and applied more sun cream. Malek climbed the pool ladder to lay on the sunbed next to her, closing his eyes in the warm sun and sipping his bottle of Double-O Beer before letting out a contented sigh.

Helen sat up. 'Malek, I've been doing some thinking. As I haven't got any family left alive, we should start our own.'

He stretched out an arm to find his sunglasses, slipped them on and turned to face her with a frown on his face. 'You want to adopt?'

She grinned. 'Sort of.'

'We might struggle with the agencies here as you're a bit old and you're not a Turkish resident.'

'I was considering an English child.'

Malek frowned. 'What? How would that work?'

Helen reached over to hold his hand. 'I was thinking of getting my granddaughter to come over and live with us. I might need to get somebody in to help look after her though. I don't want to ruin my nails.'

Malek was silent for a moment. 'Would the British courts allow that?'

'Who mentioned anything about going through official channels? I just want to look after poor Zak's daughter and bring her here to Cyprus.'

'And how will you get her?'

'Go and fetch her,' she said.

'But won't you be arrested if you return to England?'

'There is that slight problem, but I might be able to find another way.'

He frowned again, deeper. 'How?'

'You remember telling me about that cousin you have who has a trawler and works in the Aegean and Med?'

'Yes, Ozlem. I worked for him for a few months.' He glanced down at his hands. 'It was very hard work, lots of... *kabarciklar*. I think that is blisters in English.'

She held his smooth hands and her face softened. 'Well, I was wondering if Ozlem might be interested in a little trip.'

'I'm sure if the money was right, he'd go anywhere.' He glanced downwards. 'If it was a successful trip, wouldn't the British Police come after you for the child?'

Helen shrugged. 'I need to work out some of the details. I'm still in the planning phase. Harry Collins is going to ring me this afternoon about the hotel site sale, so I'll ask him then.'

Malek squeezed her hand. 'Sounds exciting.'

Several hours later the villa phone rang. Helen donned her robe and padded inside to answer it.

'Hello, Helen, it's Harry.'

'Hi, Harry, tell me about my money.'

'The funds should be in your company's account within two weeks but I need some forms signing.'

'Can't you post them?' she snapped.

'I'd prefer to pop over and sort them out in person. That way, I know they've all been signed and witnessed in the right place.'

'Fine,' she said. 'When are you coming?'

'I can grab a flight at the weekend.'

'Surely there's one tomorrow?'

'There are several, but they cost more.'

'Just get your ass out here and sort out my money.'

He paused. 'OK, I'll see what's available. I'll have to stick them on the bill.'

'Just do it. Let me know when you want picking up from the airport. I'll send Malek.'

Harry chuckled. 'Have you found him a Porsche yet?'

She pinched at the skin above her nose. 'No, it's not that easy to buy one here.'

'Poor bloke, having to suffer like that.'

'He has a good life. Oh, has the POCA case gone away?'

The authorities had been trying to use the Proceeds of Crime Act to claim some of the money she'd inherited from her brothers, suspecting it had come from criminal activities.

‘I’m sure it has.’ Harry finally broke the silence. ‘For a claim to succeed, the funds have to be confiscated within six years of the date of the criminal activity. I’ve managed to come up with a trail of legitimate property deals covering the last six years, so they shouldn’t be able to stop the funds being sent overseas.’

‘Excellent, Harry. Thanks. Just what I pay you for. Another question. Could you talk to one of your colleagues in family law? If someone reunites a small child with their rightful family in Northern Cyprus, can the UK authorities force them to be returned to Britain?’

Again, Harry fell silent for a while. ‘Would one of the child’s parents be involved in the process?’

‘One parent is deceased and the other is based in England. The repatriation would be organised without parental consent.’

‘Hmm,’ he replied. ‘I’ll see what I can find out. Could be tricky but I’ll check the position. What’s the timescale?’

‘If you could take a look before you fly over, that would be perfect.’

‘OK, Helen. Will do. See you.’

‘Bye.’ She ended the call and padded back to the pool.

‘Good call?’ Malek asked.

‘Possibly,’ she replied. ‘I need you to have a word with your cousin. I fancy a cruise.’

Chapter 3

On Wednesday, Jemma and Ellie left at five-thirty am to drive to the Lymington ferry terminal for the half-hour crossing to Yarmouth on the Isle of Wight. Brad had been left in charge of the two youngsters and was looking forward to a day with his son and granddaughter. He was over six feet tall with brown hair. With a trim build, he kept himself fit, and despite having lived in England for three years, his American accent hadn't softened.

By seven, Brad had dressed the children and given them breakfast, so they were ready for their own day out. They stood in the kitchen where a camouflaged rucksack sat on the large wooden table. Brad clapped his hands. 'OK, you two. Kira, we'll get you in the carrier and Rocky, you're good to walk down to the beach today, aren't you bud?'

The three-year-old grinned. 'Yes, Daddy.'

Brad high-fived his son and pointed him towards his little rucksack 'Bag check time!'

Rocky ran to his bag, unzipped it and held it open for his father.

'Have we got some juice for Rocky?'

His son pulled out his favourite bottle, the mouthpiece covered in bite marks, and gulped enthusiastically before dropping it back inside the bag.

Brad nodded. 'A drink for Kira?'

A carton of milk appeared and was ticked off the list.

'Snacks?'

'Loads!' Rocky's eyes glowed with excitement at the pieces of fruit and bag of cheesy crisps packed with the bottles.

Brad pointed at the bag. 'Let's zip it up then, we've got a beach to go and patrol.'

'Daddy, poo bags for Dino!'

Brad extracted the small black bags from his coat pocket with a flourish, rustling them towards Rocky's face and making the toddler giggle. 'But of course!' He couldn't help beaming at the two youngsters in their coats. When he'd returned to England three years before he hadn't thought about having a family. Within that time, he'd discovered he had a daughter in her twenties and a young son. The previous year, Ellie had presented him with a new granddaughter.

They finished their preparations, attached the lead to Dino and made their way out of the door with the dog's tail wagging as he strained at the leash. Dino was Jemma's Border Collie, black with some white patches, who'd shared many of her adventures over the last few years.

* * *

Jemma and Ellie arrived at the terminal, checked in and joined the short queue ready to board the ferry. Other than some delivery vans and a scattering of tourists it was quiet, and they were quickly able to park their vehicle inside before making their way to the restaurant.

'Why do we have to arrive so early, Mum?' Ellie asked. 'Surely the TV company can run to a hotel on the island for one night?'

'Not in the budget, I'm afraid.' Jemma shrugged. 'This is just a follow-up episode, after all, whether we get another proper series or not depends on what we find today.'

'So, you're saying if we don't come up with something interesting there's no third series?'

'Probably, although I have an idea for a drone exploration of the cliffs behind Lulcombe near to the place where Plessie came out of the rock fall.'

Prior to finding the first complete Spinosaurus ever discovered in the UK, Jemma had found a massive plesiosaur in a nearby landslip.

'Could be exciting,' Ellie scanned down the menu. 'Mind you, if you do find any fossils in the cliffs, won't they be difficult to dig out?'

'I'll cross that bridge if we spot anything.'

It was a short crossing with a calm sea. They leant on the rail at the edge of the deck to watch the Isle of Wight appearing through the morning mist. Gannets cried over the drone of the engines, following the boat and gliding along without flapping. It didn't seem long before the passengers were called to return to their cars.

They disembarked from the ferry and drove across the island to the south coast meeting point at Compton Bay where the filming crew were waiting. The car park was near to the edge of the cliffs and looked out over the blue expanse of the English Channel. A broad sandy beach with some chalk cliffs towered to the west. Behind it gorse-covered slopes climbed towards the centre of the island. There were several tents and gazebos in the field near the carpark, but Ellie headed straight for the catering van.

Jemma laughed. 'You've just had breakfast.'

Ellie checked the time on her phone. 'Yes, but that was nearly two hours ago! You don't want me looking all frail and underfed on camera, do you?'

Jemma rolled her eyes. 'You! Underfed? That'll be the day.'

One of the TV crew wandered over. 'Ready for the production meeting, Jemma?'

She nodded to the red-haired woman. 'On my way. Back in twenty minutes, Ellie?'

A muffled reply came from her daughter, who'd already managed to find a bacon sandwich from somewhere and was eating it as if she hadn't been fed in two days let alone two hours.

Jemma approached the tent where the crew were waiting and stepped through the flap. 'Morning all.'

Inside was a long wooden trestle table surrounded by folding chairs. Three other tables were spaced along one of the sides and were covered in screens, keyboards and a mixing desk. An assistant was on his knees taping down cables to avoid trip hazards while the director and cameraman were sitting with clipboards ready to plan the day's shooting. Two other crew members were peering at maps on a computer screen.

They discussed what they were hoping to record before leaving to watch the initial works. As they were trying to finish filming within a day, the TV company had hired a small digger and a driver to remove the top three feet of turf and soil. The yellow excavator soon moved the first layer ready for the human diggers to move in.

* * *

Back in Lulcombe, Brad reached the beach with his entourage and sat with Kira on his knee as Rocky played with some stones. The tide was on its way out, but the sandy area hadn't been exposed yet. Gentle waves washed the loose shingle with no hint of the sea's ferocity that was often unleashed during winter storms. The sun threatened to break through the thin clouds but a breeze blowing from the east kept the temperature cool.

Rocky focused on his task. 'I'm finding fossils.'

Brad laughed. 'I knew you'd start early.'

'Quite a little family group you've got there, Brad.' A voice made him jump.

He twisted around to see Vincent Lawrence standing behind him with his dog on a lead. Dino, who was running about as usual, raced towards the Labrador, touching noses before rushing off, as if to brag about his status as a free dog.

Brad nodded. 'Hey, Vincent. How are ya?'

'I'm fine, thanks.' He put on a pair of glasses and peered at the children. 'And who do we have here?'

Brad pointed at Rocky. 'This is my son, Rocky. As you can tell from his fossil hunting exploits, he's also very much Jemma's boy.'

'Ah yes, he's grown a lot since I last saw him. He must be what, at least two years old by now?'

'Three. It flies by, doesn't it?' Brad lifted up Kira to stand her on his leg. 'And this is Ellie's daughter, Kira. She's nearly one.'

Vincent reached over and held the little girl's hand. 'Lovely to meet you. Who's her daddy?'

Brad's face became stern. 'I'm afraid he's not around.'

'I'm sorry, I didn't know. I bet Ellie's glad of your help. Does she live close?'

'Next door to us.'

'In the cottage you inherited from Chrissie? Nasty business, wasn't it?'

Brad's then girlfriend, Chrissie, had been pushed off a cliff by one of the Fletcher brothers who had mistaken her for Jemma. As she had no other family, Chrissie had left her house to Brad.

'Yes, it was.'

After the silence stretched out to the point it became

uncomfortable, Vincent turned to leave. 'Anyway, I better be off. I'm going for a scout along the low water mark to check if anything has washed out from the latest rockfall. Goodbye to you all.'

'Bye. See ya later.' Brad watched the older man pick his way down the beach.

'Old man gone,' said Rocky.

'Yep, he's gone,' Brad replied. 'Your Mom doesn't like Vincent. They argue a lot about the museum.'

'Fossil!' Rocky picked an iron pyrite ammonite off the shingle.

Brad ruffled his son's hair. 'Great spotting, kiddo, Mom will love that one.'

'Fossil for Mummy,' Rocky nodded triumphantly as he stuffed it in his pocket.

* * *

On the southwest coast of the Isle of Wight, Jemma and Ellie made their introductory piece to the camera in which Jemma explained the nature of Compton Bay's Cretaceous rocks before giving a recap of the exciting discovery of a complete Spinosaurus the previous year. Ellie then talked about the principles of using ground penetrating radar, GPR, to survey the field in search of anomalies that might be fossils.

The grassy meadow led into a steep-sided valley that curved down towards the sea. The local population of jackdaws complained about the intrusion onto their patch and a lone rabbit peered out from beneath a hawthorn hedge. After the mechanical digger removed in thirty minutes what would have taken the team several days, the manual digging commenced. With the top layer now removed, five students from Southampton University worked their way along the newly exposed soil with trowels and scrapers with the excited enthusiasm of the start of a dig.

After an hour of digging and filming, one of the students called out, 'got something!'

Jemma and Ellie dashed to the spot where the girl was kneeling and watched as she gradually removed the dirt from around a hard, white object.

Jemma shouted, 'stop!'

The girl jumped back. 'What is it?'

Jemma stepped into the hole and brushed away more of the loose soil. 'It's not a fossil. I think it's a human skull.'

The director, Jackson Carter called, 'cut!'

He was a thin man in his forties with brown hair and a worried expression. He wore jeans, boots, white shirt and a black leather jacket that seemed too large for him.

Jemma swore under her breath as the cameras were turned off and the team looked to her for guidance with wide eyes.

'Sorry guys,' she said, 'we have to call the police. They'll organise a forensic archaeologist to come in and rule whether the bones are ancient or modern.'

Jackson shook his head. 'Well, that's today's schedule bollocksed, isn't it?'

Jemma frowned. 'Afraid so. It's over to the police now. The bones seem modern to me but I'm definitely no expert.'

'What would that mean?' he asked.

She rubbed her chin. 'I think they're classed as modern if they're post Second World War. As I said though, it's really not my area. If they're modern, it will be a crime scene and their forensic people will take over. That means we won't be back here for a while.'

'So, we're hoping for old bones then?' Ellie asked.

Jemma shrugged. 'Not really. If they're ancient then we'll have to hand the site over to the archaeologists, as it's not one of our targets for *The Rock Detectives*.'

The director sighed. 'OK, everybody, let's go back to the production tent.'

Jemma placed her hand on his shoulder. 'OK. I'll tell you my backup idea for the next series.'

* * *

At her villa in Northern Cyprus, Helen had finished reading the English papers. Although they were two days old, she liked keeping up to date with the news back home. Malek had gone into Kyrenia to have a puncture repaired on his old Toyota and would be away for the morning. It was relaxing to have some time on her own without a shadow always following her around.

Her mobile buzzed. She checked the display and answered immediately. 'Vincent, good to speak to you again. What have you got for me?'

'Helen, I've got some more information about Jemma's family. I suppose she must be Jemma Jones now, although I'm not sure if she still uses Thorne.'

'One moment.' She made some notes on her tablet. 'OK, continue.'

'Brad and Jemma have a son, Rocky, who's three. Jemma's daughter, Ellie, has a child called Kira, who's one. There seems to be some confusion about Kira's father. I'm not sure if he's left or if he's not known, though he's certainly not involved anymore.'

There was a pause as Helen finished tapping. 'And where does Ellie live?'

'Next door to Jemma on Seaton Road in a house Brad owns.'

'Happy families. Lucky for them.' Helen sneered. 'Thank you so much, Vincent, that's incredibly useful. You've earned a bonus.'

'Thanks, Helen. I don't know if I'll find out anything else so that might be it for a while.'

'Don't worry, Vincent, if I need any more information, I'll ask. Bye for now.'

'Goodbye.'

She cut the call and checked her notes. 'Well, it would seem I have a granddaughter. I'd better find a local nanny to help out when she joins us. I bet she can't wait to meet her Gran.'

Chapter 4

The following morning, Jemma and Brad managed to lie in past eight-thirty while Rocky played in his bed before coming to their room. The sun peeked in through a gap in the beige curtains and bounced off the mirror on Jemma's dressing table to flicker on the ceiling. Jemma had two lectures to present at Swanbourne University but the first didn't start until two so she could look forward to some free time.

At nine o'clock her mobile vibrated on the bedside cabinet. She unwrapped Brad's arm from around her neck and answered. 'Hello.'

'Mrs Jemma Thorne?'

'Speaking.'

'I'm calling from the Hampshire and Isle of Wight Constabulary. I have some interesting information about the bones you unearthed while filming your TV show.'

She gripped the phone tighter. 'OK.'

'I know you stopped when you found the skull but our forensic team has now uncovered a complete adult male.'

'Are we talking ancient or modern?'

'It's definitely modern.'

'So that's the dig shut down then?'

'I'm afraid so as it's now a crime scene. However, the amazing news is that, following examination of the items found with the body, we think we have the identity of the deceased. It appears to be Cornelius Marsh, who we believe was your grandfather.'

* * *

Vincent Lawrence had just finished breakfast at his seaside bungalow when Helen Fletcher rang. *What does she want now?* He let it ring a few times before answering. 'Morning, Helen.'

'Hello, Vincent. I need another little job doing.'

He sighed. 'What now?'

'I'd like you to apply for a copy of the birth certificate for Ellie Thorne's daughter, Kira, and post it to me as soon as you can.'

'And why do you want that?'

'Don't worry why. I just want one.'

'I'm sorry, I can't help you out anymore. I spoke to Brad yesterday and he reminded me of the damage your brothers did. I feel guilty because I gave them the information about Jemma that may have contributed to Chrissie's death. Also, applying for a birth certificate would leave a trail that could lead back to me.' He heard a sigh.

'I'm afraid my brothers, and my sons, for that matter, were loose cannons who went off and did their own things. All Reggie and Keith wanted was to acquire the museum but they went about it in totally the wrong way.'

He gripped the phone tighter. 'My mind's made up, Helen. I won't help you anymore.'

'Wait a moment, Vincent, I fully understand where you're coming from, I do. Don't worry about the birth certificate, I'll ask my solicitor to sort it out. I'd like to do one thing though.'

He rubbed his face. 'What?'

'The sale of the whole hotel and old museum site is about to complete, and I'd like to make a one-off substantial payment to you as a token of my gratitude.'

He squirmed in his chair. 'I'm not sure it would be wise of me to accept it.'

'Don't be silly. I'd also like you to have a slap-up meal at the Cliff House Hotel with a night's accommodation in one of their luxurious suites.'

He sighed again, deeply. 'That's very generous of you, Helen, thank you. If I accept your gift, this is all done with, isn't it? I've finished?'

'OK. You enjoy your evening and I'll send the money.'

'Thank you, Helen. Goodbye.'

'Bye, Vincent.'

He ended the call. *I'll finally break free from the Fletchers.*

* * *

Ellie entered the kitchen holding Kira and was about to hand over her daughter when she noticed Jemma sitting still, staring at her mobile phone on the table.

'You OK, Mum?' Ellie asked. 'You're really pale. What's up?'

'I'm a bit shocked.'

'Oh God, what now?'

'That skull we found during the dig...'

'Yeah?'

Jemma's eyes were glazed over. 'The police think it's Cornelius.'

Ellie's eyes widened. 'Who, the time traveller?'

'Don't start that again. No, for real this time.'

One of Jemma's colleagues, Sally, had played a prank on her when she discovered a Spinosaur in another part of the Compton Bay field. Sally had hidden a replica of Cornelius's gold ring in the fossil's mouth and Jemma had made an offhand joke about her fossil-hunting grandfather being a time traveller. The statement had gone viral and for some time Jemma was the laughingstock of the scientific community. One of Helen's sons, Zak, later murdered Sally and had tried framing Jemma for the killing.

Ellie touched her mother's arm. 'Why do they think the bones are his?'

'The body was wearing army dog tags with his name on, and they also found his field notepad in the inside pocket of his jacket that has survived all this time.'

Ellie whistled. 'That's incredible!'

'Oh, and the skeleton is wearing the actual gold ring that grandma gave to him as a wedding gift.'

'What's next?' Ellie asked. 'Have you got to identify the remains?'

'No,' Jemma replied. 'They've asked for DNA samples from your grandad and me to confirm, but they're sure it's him.'

'Did they say how he died?'

'They think it was blunt force trauma to the head. His skull was fractured and he was buried in the field.'

Ellie paused. 'I can't believe he was murdered. Poor Cornelius. What a horrible way to go. Who could have done it?'

'I don't think they have a clue. After all this time, they probably won't be able to find any forensic evidence.'

Kira started crying to tell them it was time for a drink, so Ellie took her back from her mum while Jemma warmed some milk.

'Have the TV company decided whether to go ahead with the drone filming at Lulcombe?' Ellie asked.

Jemma handed Ellie the bottle. 'Sorry Els, I meant to tell you as soon as you came down but got slightly distracted. They're happy to make a new single programme using the drone to do the searching if I think there's anything worthwhile in the cliffs. It will make a change from people walking up and down with the GPR units.'

'That's great, so will we get paid for another episode even if they don't go for the next series?'

'Yes,' Jemma replied. 'The only thing is that they want us to have a practice run on the cliffs first, so we look like we know what we're doing.'

Ellie sat on a wooden chair by the table and held the bottle for Kira who grasped at it as she drank. 'That's cool. When do you want to do it?'

'How about early next week? I'm not at uni on Monday or Tuesday so we can have a go then. There'll be fewer folks on the beach than if we tried at the weekend.'

'Have you got to supply the drone?'

Jemma shook her head. 'No,' she said. 'It's coming out of the show's budget and being delivered on Friday.'

'So, we just have to learn how to fly the thing,' Ellie grinned.

'I thought you could do the flying. I'll watch the stream on the laptop and try my best to guide you in if I spot anything interesting.'

Ellie's eyes sharpened. 'You're only after someone to blame if it gets broken.'

Her mother responded with an over-exaggerated shrug.

'Where's Brad?' Ellie asked. 'I haven't noticed him clomping around upstairs.'

'He went out for a run.' Jemma glanced at the clock on the wall. 'He'll be back soon. Do you fancy visiting Grandad tonight? I haven't been for over a week. I hate missing visits.'

'Yeah, I'd love to go with you if Brad's up for babysitting again, unless Kira can come along too.'

'I don't know if the care place is happy with young children visiting, but I'll ring them and check. I'll be leaving around sixish.'

'That works for me. Come on Kira, let's get you dressed. We can take Dino for a walk into town.'

Hearing his name, the dog pricked his ears, stretched and padded towards the back door of the house.

Ellie scratched behind his ear. 'Give us ten minutes, Dino, and we'll be ready.'

* * *

As Jemma had expected, the receptionist at the long-term care and rehabilitation centre was not happy about children under two being brought in on visits, so Brad stayed at home with Rocky and Kira while Jemma and Ellie went together.

Jemma's father, Bernard, had been in a coma for almost two years after being poisoned by carbon monoxide. His boiler had been tampered with by Helen's son, Zak, posing as a gas service engineer and Jemma had discovered her parents unconscious at their home. Carol had recovered quickly but Bernard hadn't fared so well, and had been in hospital throughout most of the period until recently when he was moved to a long-term care facility.

As Jemma finished her call to the care centre, a very sweaty Brad came in through the back door. 'There are too many damn hills around this place. I start running faster and bam! It's like hitting a brick wall.'

She kissed him. 'Judging by the colour of your face, you've had a good run.'

He checked his running watch. 'Yep, ten miles today and the leg's feeling stronger.'

It had taken Brad several years to get over his injuries after he'd been hurt in a hit-and-run incident with an old boyfriend of Jemma's.

'Are you OK to have the kids tonight if I take Ellie to see Dad?'

'Yeah, that's cool.' He clapped his hands together. 'Right, I need a shower first. Any sign of Bernard coming round?'

'It's pretty unlikely.' She swallowed. 'I'm just dreading the inevitable conversation about turning off the life support.'

'They won't do that, will they?' Brad asked.

'Hopefully not.'

'Is your mom still going every day?'

'Yep,' Jemma sniffed. 'She goes to talk to him each morning after breakfast.'

'Hey.' He looked her in the eyes. 'I'm sure he's fighting his hardest to get back to you guys.' He brought her in for a hug.

'Oh, God! Emotional moment over, you stink!' She laughed and pushed him away.

He sniffed his armpit and pretended to gag. 'You're quite right, ma'am, I'm gonna go clean up. How about you join me? I could do with a bit of help with my dodgy leg.'

Jemma grinned. 'I'd love to but Rocky's playing in his room and we both know he'd be demanding to be let in too.'

'OK, rain check 'til later?'

'We'll see,' she said.

He hugged her.

'Yuck! You're dripping! Get off for your shower.'

He grabbed a glass, filled it with cold water and headed upstairs with laboured steps. 'I'm getting too old for this.' he smiled at Jemma. 'Although it's not the years, it's the mileage.'

* * *

Jemma and Ellie strolled into the brightly lit reception of the long-term care and rehabilitation centre. Jemma still wasn't used to going there instead of the intensive care unit her father had been in before, but it was a nicer place without the anti-septic smell of the hospital.

Ellie gazed around. 'It's so much better in here. I just wish Grandad would wake up.'

They signed in on the visitor computer screen and walked down the corridor to room five. The sign on the door read *Bernard Marsh*.

Bernard was lying on an intensive care bed with an array of wires and tubes keeping him alive. A monitor attached to a stand was displaying in numbers his precarious hold on life. The room was brighter than most in a hospital and had lots of colourful paintings. Jemma had been told that some coma patients responded to different sounds and colours, if they ever opened their eyes.

Before the incident, Bernard had been a healthy man with a complexion that matched his love for the outdoors but, lying motionless, he now looked pale and drawn. Loose skin hung from his arms, which had lost all of their muscle.

Ellie and Jemma squeezed his hands, careful not to dislodge any wires, and sat on the chairs beside the bed. For the next thirty minutes, they alternated between telling him what had happened recently, asking him questions and chatting between themselves.

The door opened and a nurse entered. 'Hello, Jemma, Ellie,' she said, her smile gentle and warm. She had grey hair and wore a two-piece blue uniform.

'Hi, Sarah.' Ellie glanced at Bernard. 'Any changes?'

The nurse checked his chart. 'Nothing really, although we have recorded a few flickers on the brain wave activity monitor so he might be listening away to what you're telling him.'

Jemma smiled. 'Well, that's something positive at last.'

The nurse touched her arm. 'It may be nothing but it's better than a completely flat line.' She hung up the chart and left the room.

Ellie squeezed Bernard's hand. 'Come on, Grandad, I know you're listening. It's about time you woke up. You've got a great-granddaughter who's desperate to meet you.'

A tear ran down Jemma's cheek as she watched Ellie with her grandfather. She held her hand. 'One day, Els, one day.'

Chapter 5

The following day the tide was out and Lulcombe Beach basked in its full glory, a mix of sandy patches and rocky shingle. The sun tried to peep through the fluffy clouds but a light breeze off the sea made it feel cool. Waves lapped the edge of the sand as two figures peered at a small electrical device.

Jemma giggled as Ellie stared at the controller in her hand and the drone on the stones.

'What do I do next, Mum?'

'Try pressing the levers and see what happens. According to the video, it works like a joystick. Imagine it's a game on your PlayStation.'

Ellie wiggled the levers frantically. 'Nothing.'

Jemma stared into her phone. 'Have you turned it on?'

Her daughter showed her the controls. 'Yes, look, the switch is up and the green light is on but it's not moving.'

'What about the switch on the drone itself?'

'What?' Ellie asked.

Jemma rolled her eyes, walked over to the dormant drone and picked it up. 'This one!' She flicked a switch. 'Don't touch any knobs until I'm out of the way.' She gingerly laid the machine on the stones and stood behind her daughter. 'And activate!'

Ellie tried again and this time the rotors started whining as the machine lurched up into the air. 'It's flying! Now what?'

'Try the controls and see what it does,' Jemma responded.

Her daughter wiggled the lever and the drone jerked upwards before landing with a thud on a patch of sand.

'Gently!' Jemma warned. 'You'll smash it!'

Ellie persevered, tongue peeking out slightly between her lips as she concentrated, and this time it lifted more smoothly and flew towards the cliffs.

Jemma moved closer to her daughter. 'What's on the screen?'

Ellie peered at the display. 'A lot of rock.'

'OK then, fly it sideways across the cliff face and then move it up and scan another line.'

* * *

Further down the beach, Brad was sitting with Rocky as he played with the stones.

Brad pointed. 'Look buddy, Ellie's got it flying.'

Rocky stared at the drone moving backwards and forwards along the cliff face with an annoying mosquito-like whine wafting down the beach. 'Mummy and Ellie have heli-copter,' he said.

Brad stood. 'Do you want to go and watch?'

His son shook his head. 'Got to find fossils.'

Brad grinned. 'OK, Jurassic Rocky!'

* * *

Jemma squinted into the small screen. 'Stop. Can you go back a bit, please, where the lighter line cuts across the cliff? There's something interesting sticking out.'

Ellie frowned in concentration as she manoeuvred the drone back a few feet. 'Here?'

'Yes, perfect, can you zoom in a little?' Jemma asked.

Ellie gazed at the controls. 'I've no idea, but I can move it in closer.'

Jemma clenched her fists. 'Be careful, won't you? We don't want to hit the cliffs. I don't think it would do it much good to crash from that height.' The display showed the section Ellie had honed in on. 'That looks interesting,' Jemma said. 'Can you bring it back down?'

Ellie carefully brought the drone back down onto the beach.

'Great work, Els, handling it like a pro at the end.'

'I'll be getting my pilot's licence next. What do you reckon you saw?'

'I don't know, it could be part of an ichthyosaur's skull but I need to double-check the footage. Let's go home and I'll load it onto my PC.' Jemma glanced around. 'Quick, some people are coming over. Let's skedaddle before they start asking questions.'

Ellie picked up the drone and they wandered over towards Brad and Rocky who were on their knees closely examining the surrounding stones. Rocky ran over with something grasped firmly in his fist.

He gave them a huge grin. 'Mo nite, Mummy!'

'Ammonite,' Jemma corrected. 'That's lovely!'

'A nomite.' Rocky mixed the sounds up in his tongue so he tried again, 'A. Mo. Nite.'

'That's it! Good job. Now, who wants some lunch at the pub?'

'Great idea,' Brad said. 'I'm starving!'

* * *

The sun beat down relentlessly and, apart from the cicadas, it was quiet and peaceful as Helen lay on her sunbed reading a paperback after having retreated out from the direct glare to a shady spot under a colourful parasol. The sound of tyres crunching on her gravel driveway disturbed her concentration, so she sauntered inside to put on a robe and sandals.

A car door slammed, closely followed by a second, and then Malek approached along the path trailed by a middle-aged man who, despite the sun, was wearing a black suit. He was balding and tugged a wheeled carry-on case behind him.

Helen stepped outside to greet them. 'Harry! Good journey?'

The man dragged a hand across his forehead and flicked sweat beads over the gravel. 'Not too bad, apart from this heat.' Despite his discomfort, he held out a hand for her to shake.

She pretended not to notice his hand and instead plucked at her robe. 'Hot day for black. In Cyprus, it pays to dress accordingly.' She pointed to a shaded terrace with a table and chairs. 'Looks like you need to sit. I'll fix you some cold lemonade.'

He checked his watch. 'Bit early for a G and T, I suppose?'

She had to force a smile. 'Let's get down to business and we'll have a drink with dinner. Are you staying tonight?'

Harry dropped into the wicker chair and sighed. 'Yes, if that's OK? My flight leaves Ercan at eleven forty-five tomorrow. I can book into a hotel if it's not convenient.'

'That's no problem, the guest room is always made up.' She looked him up and down and raised her eyebrows. 'You can shower before we eat.'

He opened a side pocket in his case. 'I've got the final transfer documents for the sale of the hotel and museum site in Lulcombe. Once they're signed, we can complete the deal and the six million will be in your company account, after I've deducted my fees, of course.'

'Of course.' Helen pursed her lips. 'Where do you want my autograph?'

Harry passed the papers across the table, and, after she signed them, he witnessed her signature.

She checked her watch. 'OK, onto the next matter. Did you have a chance to speak with your family law colleague about my question?'

The solicitor shuffled his papers. 'Ah, we have a slight problem with that.'

Helen yawned. 'Go on.'

He consulted some notes. 'In theory, a grandparent can seek permission from the court to adopt a grandchild if its parents have died or if it's somehow in danger.'

'Sounds good,' she said.

Malek returned, placed a tray on the table and poured a glass of iced lemonade for Harry and Helen.

Harry sipped the drink. 'A written request needs to be made using form C-100, setting out the reasons for the application for which permission is sought. However, the main issue is that you have an outstanding warrant for your arrest on a charge of incitement to murder, as well as other charges.'

'All fabrications.'

He smiled. 'I'm sure they are but as you don't want to come to the UK to dispute the charges, we have no way to get them struck off.'

She frowned. 'But that's your job.'

'You give me some evidence that you didn't send the messages they found on your sons' phones and I might be able to get them quashed, though I don't know if that'll be enough.'

She checked her freshly manicured nails. 'Oh well, I can't locate any evidence at the moment.'

A frown flashed across his face. 'In that case, then, you have zero chance of receiving permission through the courts.'

She shrugged. 'I guessed as much. If I was successful,

though, and brought my grandchild here, would the police or other UK authorities be able to extradite the child or come and fetch her?'

Harry shook his head and sighed. 'I hope you're not considering anything illegal. The position is that the Turkish Republic of Northern Cyprus has not signed up to the international treaty on child abduction and there is no official extradition agreement. It also hasn't signed up to the Hague Convention on the civil aspects of international child abduction.'

Helen stared at Harry. 'Sorry, I got lost halfway through that. Please summarise in a few words.'

He sipped his lemonade. 'There is no international mechanism to return abducted children. However, Northern Cyprus does not want convicted criminals and occasionally cooperates with the UK authorities to extradite high profile criminals.'

Helen drank from her glass. 'Interesting. I'm sure with my special relationship with the local police and judiciary, which costs me a number of fancy meals and expensive bottles of wine, nobody would ever come looking for me here.' She waved an arm towards the surrounding forest. 'We're quite secluded in this place. I love the privacy.'

Harry glanced at the pool. 'I wouldn't have thought looking after a child would fit in with your current hedonistic lifestyle of drinking and lounging around the pool.'

She set down her drink. 'It will be a little different but Malek will be happy to help.'

Malek spluttered in his beer. 'I will?'

Helen frowned. 'You will! And I can always get a girl in from the village if it gets too much. I'll ask my cleaner if she knows anybody.'

'That's it!' Harry held up his hand. 'I don't want to know any more and I certainly don't want to be involved in any of your more outrageous plans. I've helped the Fletcher family with all of their property deals for over twenty years. Some were more legitimate than others but recently you've started to worry me.'

She slammed her hands on the table. 'With what I have on you, Harry Collins, you will do what I ask. Remember, I have several videos both your wife and the Law Society would be very interested in. Kelly is such a lovely girl and so young!'

He flushed and returned the papers to his case. 'Look, I didn't know how young she was. I was stupid and I know it. I'll have a shower now, please, if I may? I need to clean up.'

Helen smirked. 'It will take more than a shower to do that, Harry.'

* * *

Ellie lay sweating in bed as a nightmare plagued her night's sleep. In her dream, she grinned at Zak as he passed her a glass of orange juice. She took a swig. 'This tastes strange.'

'Get it down you,' he replied. 'You don't want to get dehydrated.'

She drained the glass, lay down and gazed at the ceiling.

Zak's hands moved over her naked chest. 'Now, where were we?'

As she turned towards him everything went fuzzy, and then...blackness.

Chapter 6

Several days later, Jemma took Rocky to visit her Mum, Carol. It was only a five-minute drive through Lulcombe to the white-rendered bungalow on the Highfields Estate where her parents had lived since they returned from Spain three years before. When Jemma arrived, her mother was already standing at the opened front door.

'How does she always know when we're about to pull up, Rocky?'

He stared at her with an expression that said *does what Mum?*

They parked on the drive and Rocky ran straight to his gran's arms. Jemma followed them into the kitchen.

Carol stood by the table and smiled at Rocky. Her hair was now totally silver as she'd stopped colouring it, and she'd also lost weight. She'd once been very house proud but Jemma noticed a pile of unwashed dishes on the worktop. Her mum's priorities had changed with a comatose husband. Over the last few years, she seemed to have aged considerably from the strain of visiting Bernard in hospital and then in the long-term care facility.

'My, you're getting heavier, young man.' Carol groaned. 'I won't be able to pick you up soon.'

Rocky frowned. 'I'm not heavy, Daddy's heavy.'

'How was Dad yesterday?' Jemma asked.

'No change, love. There have been no more spikes on the brainwave chart,' Carol replied with tears in her eyes.

'That's a shame.' Jemma hugged her. 'He'll wake up one day.'

'Oh, I keep hoping that but I'm so worried that soon they're going to ask me for permission to turn the machines off. I dreamt the other night that one of the cleaners unplugged your father to use the vacuum cleaner and then forgot to plug him back in again.'

'You are silly, Mum. You're paying for the room, or at least Dad's pension is.'

'You're right, love. When are you next going to visit?'

Jemma thought for a moment. 'Wednesday, I think. Ellie wanted to take Kira in but they weren't keen when I rang.'

Her mum shrugged. 'I wouldn't worry what they say, just take her. It might do Bernard good. After all, we're paying their wages so they should be beholden to us.'

'I suppose so.'

'Have you heard anything else about finding Cornelius? I was amazed when you rang and told me about him.'

'No, nothing,' Jemma replied. 'I took a cheek swab from Dad and sent it off with mine, but they haven't come back yet. They did say it could take a few weeks as it's not a priority case.'

'It's so weird his body turning up after all those years.' Carol touched her daughter's arm. 'That's if it is him.'

'I think it is, Mum. It all ties in with where and when he disappeared.'

Carol put her head in her hands. 'Oh Jem, when is life going to get back to normal?'

'I don't know. It all went haywire after I found Plessie. Nothing's been the same since.'

'Look, love,' her mum replied, 'don't forget that you've now got a husband, a young son and a new granddaughter. You've got lots to be thankful for.'

'I know but I just want Dad to be home again.'

* * *

Vincent frowned as he scanned the front page of his newspaper. 'Bloody world's going mad,' he grumbled.

His ageing Labrador padded over to check if any food was imminent.

He rubbed the dog's hackles and was about to return to his paper when the phone pinged. 'Now what?' He snatched up the mobile. 'Oh, Helen.' He read the message.

As a thank you for your consultancy there is now an extra twenty-five thousand pounds in your bank account. Also, as a special treat, a room and a meal are booked at the Cliff Hotel for Thursday night with a little surprise.

'Wow, Monty. That's nice of her, although I hope she's not up to something. Maybe it is just generosity, after all. Whatever it is, that's it then. I'm not doing anything else for the Fletcher family.'

* * *

Ellie bit her lip as she stood outside the entrance to her old school. It was only five years since she'd left but it seemed like an age. She'd spent a while getting ready for the reunion disco before selecting a knee-length red dress with a high neck. Stylish but not too sexy was the look she was aiming for. Her long brown hair had been taken up and was held in place with two clips. As she was quite tall, she was happy to wear flat comfortable shoes.

'You going in or staying here all night?' Ellie jumped as a voice from behind pulled her from her thoughts.

She turned to see one of the lads from her year. 'Hello, Dan. I'm building up my courage to go in.'

He went to kiss her cheek, but she reached out to shake hands instead. 'How are you doing, Ellie?' he asked.

'I'm alright. You?'

He was nearly six feet tall with a mop of unruly brown hair. His skinny teenage frame had since filled out into a more solid appearance.

She couldn't help grinning. *He's fit.*

He smiled. 'Penny for your thoughts. You're zoning out.'

'Sorry, I was miles away. You've changed a lot since sixth form.'

'You haven't. You still look eighteen.'

She played with her hair. 'Charmer.'

'I heard through the Lulcombe grapevine that you'd had a baby. How's life with a little one?'

Ellie grimaced. 'It has its moments, but I wouldn't change it for anything. Kira is so demanding, but I love her to bits.'

'Are you coming back on the telly?' he asked. 'I saw you with your mum on *The Rock Detectives*.'

'Yeah, we're doing some filming soon.'

'What are you after this time?'

She leant towards him. 'Sorry, top secret. I'm not allowed to say.'

He nodded. 'Is it like *if I told you I'd have to kill you?*'

'Not that bad. They keep the locations secret so nobody turns up while we're recording.'

'The life of a TV star.'

She grinned. 'Not quite but it's a lot of fun and I get paid a bit.'

'OK.' Dan held out his arm. 'Want any moral support going in?'

Ellie's eyes flicked up. 'Better not, people might think we're a couple.'

His smile faded. 'I suppose so. Come on then. Let's meet the old crowd.'

The sports hall had been decorated with balloons and banners welcoming the *Class of 2018.*

There was a hubbub of conversations all competing with a disco. The deck was manned by an over-enthusiastic DJ with a disregard for how many people were actually dancing to the tracks he was laying down.

Ellie and Dan bought some drinks and headed in different directions. 'Catch you later. I'm off to find the footie team.' Dan turned to go.

'Cheers, Dan. Thanks for the support.' She smiled as he walked away. *Well, he's still a nice lad.* She strolled over to a group she'd been friends with at school.

'Hi Ellie, love what you've done with your hair,' one of her friends said.

'Hi Shannon,' Ellie hugged her and worked her way around the rest of the old gang. 'Well, where have those years gone?' she asked.

Shannon giggled. 'It's not that bad. At least we've been out a few times. Not that we've seen that much of you since you decided to have a baby.'

Ellie grinned. 'It's a full-time job with a little one.'

'Still not revealing who the father is?' Penny asked.

'Nah. No big deal. It was a fleeting thing and he's not on the scene anymore,' she said.

'I hope he's paying his share,' Shannon said.

She shrugged. 'Enough chat about me and babies. What's everybody been up to?'

The night flew past and Ellie enjoyed herself, even though she was only drinking Coke, though later she declined the chance to visit a nightclub as she didn't want to be home too late. Before the slow numbers began, she put down her glass and headed for the exit. On the way she bumped into Dan.

'You off?' he asked.

'Yep. I've got a baby to put to bed.'

'Do you miss the drinking and clubbing?'

Ellie looked back towards her friends. 'I thought I might, but, to be honest, I love being around Kira and looking after her so much it doesn't bother me.'

He smiled. 'Do you fancy a drink sometime? If you can get a babysitter, that is.'

She froze and her hands went clammy. 'No, sorry, I really don't have time, what with Kira and everything.'

He nodded. 'OK. Keep in touch. I'm sure we're still friends on Instagram.'

'Yes. Cheers Dan, see you.' Ellie turned and rushed off without any hugs, kisses or sweaty-palmed handshakes. All she could think about was her unfortunate encounter with Zak Fletcher when a passionate weekend had almost led to her death.

* * *

Jemma and Brad were sitting together on the sofa in her cosy living room with a glass of wine and a Rolling Stones CD on the player.

'This is perfect,' Jemma said, snuggling down with Brad's arm around her shoulders as *Fool to Cry* played in the background.

'Sure is. Both kids asleep and the place to ourselves. Ready for bed?'

She checked her watch. 'In a bit. I won't settle until Ellie gets home.'

He chuckled. 'She's twenty-three, you know.'

'I still like to know she's back safely, especially after what happened to her a couple of years ago.'

Ellie had gone home with Zak Richards, one of Helen Fletcher's sons, after a night out and had ended up being drugged and left for dead in a countryside carpark. She had only survived due to being found by a birdwatcher.

'I get that.' He sipped his wine. 'You're a great mom, you know. To both of them.'

'It's hard work but it's lovely, and I'm definitely ready for a holiday. I can't wait until we go to Florida.'

'Are you looking forward to meeting my parents?'

She snuggled tighter against him. 'Yes, it will be wonderful, and I bet they can't wait to meet their new family. Two new grandchildren and a new great-grandchild. How cool is that?'

'They're excited. Even Pop thinks it's awesome and it takes a lot for him to get excited about something.'

There was a scratching sound and Ellie opened the back door. 'Evening, you two. I thought you'd be in bed.'

'No, we were chilling,' Jemma said. 'Had a good night?'

Ellie shrugged. 'It was OK. Anyway, I've got a headache so I'm straight off to bed. Is Kira asleep?'

'Yes, she's settled so might sleep right through.'

'Thanks. Night, Mum. Night, Brad.' She gave them both a hug and stepped through the door to the stairs.

Jemma jumped up. 'Something's the matter.'

'She's certainly edgy,' Brad replied. 'I wonder what happened.'

Chapter 7

Ellie stretched out on the lounge carpet playing trampolines with Kira and Rocky. Unfortunately, she'd been assigned the role of chief trampoline and three-year-old Rocky was getting quite heavy to be jumping on her. Every time Rocky landed, his niece cried with laughter. She doted on her Uncle Rocky, a title that, with only a two-year age difference, might make them laugh in the future.

Ellie finally called time on the exhausting game and flopped into an armchair as a message came through on her phone. It was from Dan.

Hi Ellie. Enjoyed the reunion. I'm still after a date. How about a drink sometime? Dan

She stared at the display. *I can't go out with him. I don't feel safe after what happened with Zak.*

Her hands shook as she started to type the words, *No thanks,* but instead she threw down her mobile and sobbed.

The back door opened and Brad entered. 'Damn traffic's awful.' He looked at Ellie. 'You OK? What's up?'

'Nothing,' she said.

He knelt next to her chair and put his arm around her shoulders. 'Come on, tell me what's up.'

She burst into tears again. 'Oh, I'm just broken. There's this guy called Dan who seems really into me, but I don't want to let him near me because of what Zak did to me last year.'

He squeezed her shoulders. 'Don't worry. It'll take time to get over what happened. When somebody you trust treats you like that, it's bound to have an effect on you and put you off new relationships. That bastard took advantage of you, but it'll get easier. I promise.'

'Thanks, Brad.'

'How about you get together with this Dan and explain the problem. If he's a decent guy, I'm sure he'll be happy to take it slowly with you.'

'He wants to meet up for a drink but I don't think I can go. I'm so scared.'

Brad held her hand. 'Why don't you meet up in a busy place and just have a chat.'

She sobbed. 'I could, I suppose. As long as we weren't alone.'

'Perfect. Dan sounds alright. At least he didn't run away when he found out you had a kid.'

The back door opened again and Jemma burst into the lounge. 'Put that kettle on. I'm parched. No bloody tea at our meeting as the fuse had blown in the kitchen. I've had to drink water to keep me awake.' She plonked herself down in a chair. 'Well, have I missed anything exciting?'

Ellie looked at Brad and grinned. 'I've been bounced on by my very heavy baby brother.'

Jemma grabbed Rocky from the floor where he'd been playing with Kira. 'Have you been jumping on poor Ellie?'

Rocky grinned. 'Ellie boing, Ellie boing.'

Kira started crying.

'Sorry,' Jemma said. 'Here, have him back.'

Kira's tears stopped and she smiled as Rocky joined her again on the carpet.

Jemma glanced at Ellie. 'You OK, Els? You look pale.'

'I'm great.' Ellie rubbed her eyes. 'Just tired after going out last night. I don't know about anybody else but I'm ready for some Florida sunshine.'

Brad frowned. 'Has Kira's passport come through yet?'

Ellie pointed at the sideboard. 'Yes. I've had it for a few days. We just need the family ESTA now.'

Jemma checked her phone. 'The email said it should be here today.'

Brad picked up his son. 'Of course, if you had proper American passports like me and Rocky, you wouldn't need an ESTA.'

Ellie wrinkled up her nose. 'I'm fine with my British passport. Anyway Rocky, it's greedy having two nationalities.'

Jemma stood. 'It would be much easier if your mum and dad would just jump on a plane and come visit us here.'

Brad shrugged. 'Pop said he'd never get back on a plane after Vietnam. If they wouldn't come over for the wedding, I can't see them coming over just for a visit, even with grandchildren to meet.'

'I'm happy to go if it means some warm weather,' Ellie said. 'I've wanted to go to the Keys ever since I watched Bloodline on Netflix. It will be nice to meet your Mum and Dad for the first time.'

* * *

Vincent parked at the Cliff Hotel, slipped on his jacket and headed towards the entrance tugging his small-wheeled suitcase. The hotel stood on an elevated plot with fantastic views of Lulcombe Bay. It was an old-fashioned place with a reputation for quality service and prices to match. As he approached the front door, it was opened by a concierge in a smart blue uniform.

'Good evening, sir. Let me take your bag while you check in.'

Vincent strolled towards a highly polished mahogany counter where a young lady in an elegant dark suit smiled at him.

'Good evening and welcome to the Cliff Hotel,' she said.

He gave her his name and, as she checked him in, he handed over his credit card.

'Oh, there's no need for that, Mr Lawrence.' A small grin crossed her face as she gave him a key on a heavy wooden fob. 'All extras are included. You have a table reserved in the restaurant for 8 pm and you are in our most luxurious suite on the fourth floor. All courtesy of Mrs Fletcher. Have a wonderful evening.'

'Thank you.' He retrieved his case and turned towards the lift.

It arrived with a ping, the door groaned open and he wheeled his case inside before hitting the number for his floor. He'd had meals in the hotel before but could never justify the cost of a stay in such an expensive place.

As the lift slowly crept up to the fourth floor, he smiled at himself in the mirror. 'I'm going to enjoy tonight,' he said to his grinning reflection.

The lift stopped and the doors opened. He exited with his case, peered at the numbers on the wall and headed for room four-one-one. He found the door and tried to open it with the key, which didn't work, but when he tried the handle the door swung open. He stepped inside and dumped his case on the bed, removing his jacket. The room was decadent with white and gold wallpaper, plush gold sofa, chairs and bedspread. A massive picture window offered incredible views out over the English Channel.

On a side table, a bottle of champagne sat in an ice bucket with a small silver envelope attached. The envelope opened easily and contained an elegantly written note.

Thanks for your help. I hope you enjoy the whole experience. Helen.

He jumped as he heard a splashing sound from the bathroom.

Oh, is the cleaner still here?

He tiptoed to the door and nudged it open. The bath was overflowing with bubbles but the bigger surprise was the young lady lying in it covered in suds.

'Hi Vincent. I'm Kelly.'

Chapter 8

A kestrel hung in the breeze over the field behind Jemma's cottage. Ellie squinted at it as she lay on a reclining chair on the patio trying to stay warm in the weak spring sunshine. May had been wet and now she was desperate for some warmth. The garden was peaceful as it faced down towards a small wood and, beyond that, the blue expanse of the sea. The buildings deadened any traffic noise from the road on the other side of the houses.

In the house's shade, Kira was fast asleep in her pushchair so Ellie was taking advantage of a rare opportunity to read her paperback. After a few chapters, she put down the book and checked her mobile. *I should reply to Dan. I ought to respond.*

She typed a reply to Dan's latest text. *OK. I'll come for a drink but it's not a date.*

Her finger hovered over the send button before she gulped and tapped the screen.

* * *

Vincent stood open-mouthed as he stared at the unexpected vision in the large bath.

‘Oh…I think you’ll find you’re in the wrong room, young lady.’

‘Kelly.’

‘Er…yes…Kelly.’ He glanced around the spacious bathroom and spotted a pile of neatly folded clothes on a chair with some red lingerie on the top. ‘Wait a minute. How do you know my name?’

She giggled. ‘Oh, I know a lot about you, Vincent.’

He took a step backwards. ‘I don’t know what your game is but I think you should get dressed and leave.’

She smiled. ‘Nothing to worry about. I’m a friend of Helen’s and she asked me to come along and make your evening more memorable.’

‘Memorable?’ he stammered.

‘Oh yes. A night to remember. Helen was pleased with all the help you gave her when she was selling the hotel site.’

He ran his hands through his hair. ‘That’s a lovely gesture but…’ his eyes narrowed, ‘how old are you?’

‘I’m nineteen.’

He tried to smile but it turned into a grimace. ‘Nineteen. Oh, I suppose that’s something. You look so young.’

‘You should count yourself lucky. I bet you don’t often get the chance to share a bath with a nineteen-year-old.’

His eyes widened. ‘Share a bath…’

‘Oh yes. It’s lonely in here on my own and there’s some champagne in an ice bucket on the table. How about opening it for us?’

He turned back into the bedroom and took the bottle of Dom Perignon from the ice. ‘Very nice.’ He opened it with a loud pop.

A voice came from the bathroom. ‘Don’t spill any.’

His mind raced as he tried to process what was happening. *Things like this never happen to me.* His hand shook as he picked up a glass and poured out some of the sparkling liquid. He filled the second glass, took a sip, and set both glasses on the tray along with the silver bucket and bottle before bringing everything to the bathroom.

Kelly pointed to a stand beside the bath. 'Leave them on there and let me try some.'

He put the tray down and handed her a glass.

She took a sip and passed it back to him. She slowly stood and his mouth dropped open as the suds slid down her body to reveal her pert figure. She held out her hands, unashamed by her nakedness. 'Now slip out of those clothes and come join me. I need someone to scrub my back and afterwards, I've got something interesting I'd like to show you with an ice cube.'

Vincent hadn't moved since the suds started descending. 'Ice....' he gulped. 'Oh, sod it, you only live once.'

He tore off his watch, wrenched off his clothes, strewing them to the tiles and climbed in.

* * *

Brad and Jemma strolled up to the door at the long-term facility where her father was being cared for before pressing the button on the Intercom.

'Jemma and Brad, for Bernard,' she said. The door clicked. She pushed it open and entered with Brad.

A nurse wearing a blue uniform was sitting behind the desk. 'Hi Jemma, hi Brad.'

'Hi, Sarah. How is he?' Jemma asked.

'No change, I'm afraid,' she replied.

Jemma nodded. 'Oh well, we can always hope.'

The nurse handed them two visitor lanyards and they stepped down the corridor to room five. It always seemed so quiet in Bernard's room, the only noise being the bleep of the life support machine and the rhythmic whooshing of the respirator.

Brad pulled up two chairs and they sat and started chatting to the comatose patient lying motionless in the bed.

* * *

Vincent lay contently back in the huge bath holding a glass of champagne, the naked girl snuggled tightly against him.

'That was very good, Vincent,' Kelly said. 'How about we dress and go down for dinner? We can always try for an encore when we return.'

'An encore? I'm not a young man anymore.'

'Funnily enough, I happened to bring along a little blue tablet that should do the trick. After all,' she gestured out towards the room with its decadent furnishings and extravagant features, 'Helen paid for the whole night and I'm sure she'd want us to have our money's worth.'

He stood, grinned and reached for an enormous fluffy white towel. 'Well, now you mention it, I am a little peckish.'

* * *

Brad and Jemma had been chatting to Bernard for twenty minutes and were now trying to get comfortable on their hard plastic chairs.

Brad stared at his pale father-in-law. 'It's such a shame he hasn't seen Kira yet.'

A tear dribbled from Jemma's eye as she squeezed her father's hand. 'Did you hear that, Dad? You've got a beautiful great-granddaughter who'd love to meet you.' She twisted towards Brad. 'It's not fair. He's a lovely man who never hurt anybody and he's lying here because of the Fletchers. He hardly had any time back in the country before this happened.'

Brad held her hand and smiled. 'How long have they been back from Spain?'

Jemma's eyes flicked up. 'It must have been 2022.'

They both jumped as a dry, cracked voice from the bed beside them croaked.

'2021.'

Chapter 9

Vincent opened his eyes and stretched out his legs. He reached over to the other side of the bed, which was empty but still warm. There was a heady scent on the pillow, which he inhaled as he remembered the events of the previous night.

'Kelly,' he whispered and then much louder, 'are you there?'

He threw back the sheets and picked up a plush white dressing gown from a chair before padding through to the bathroom. That was empty as well. Daylight peeped around the edges of the curtains, and he squinted as he slid them open to let the sunlight stream in. It was a beautiful day with a clear blue sky. He stepped out onto the balcony to take in the views of Lulcombe Bay and the English Channel.

Sauntering back inside still grinning, he noticed a single red rose on the side table. Beneath it there was a note on hotel headed paper.

Morning Vincent. Thank you for last night, it was lovely. Sorry to dash off but I have work to do early this morning. I hope you enjoyed Helen's little gift. Kelly XXXX

He closed his eyes, inhaling her perfume from the small

piece of notepaper. 'Oh, Kelly, I never got your number,' he whispered.

A ping from his phone alerted him to an incoming message and brought him back to the present. He checked and saw it was from Helen.

Vincent. I hope you had fun with your new friend. Check your emails for a little surprise. H

He tapped in a reply.

Thank you, Helen. I had a wonderful night. Kelly was most enthusiastic. V

After responding he sat in an armchair and checked his emails before selecting one from Helen containing the subject *Surprise.*

His mouth went dry as he read the contents.

I see that you had a rather energetic night last night. There's life in the old dog yet. It's amazing what occasions a mature gentleman can rise to with the assistance of some modern pharmaceuticals. Please see the attached video and await my next email.

His eyes widened and his finger shook as he opened the MP4 file attached to the email. It showed him lying on his back as the lithe, young Kelly bounced up and down, apparently enjoying herself whilst expressing her feelings raucously.

'Oh no.' Vincent whispered, returning to his emails where a second from Helen had come through. He hesitated and then opened it.

What an interesting recording. Well done you. You did a brilliant job and should consider a career in the adult film industry. Isn't Kelly delightful? I'd kill for a body as pert as that. She's certainly good at what she does and can make a quality video as well. However, she does have her faults, one of which is that she doesn't always tell the truth. When she told you she was nineteen, she wasn't totally accurate. She should have actually said fifteen. Now, if the recording was to fall into the wrong hands it could make things very awkward for you. A lot of prisoners don't like gentlemen who interfere with young girls. Reflect on that for a few moments before you open my final email.

He closed the email, held his head in his hands and sobbed. 'What have I done? I've been so stupid. I should have known it was too good to be true.'

The phone display lit up as another email came in.

Please don't think I'm being ungrateful, because I'm not. However, I'd like to continue with our mutually beneficial arrangement and in future, whenever I ask you to do something for me, you will do it without question. Understood?

He composed a brief response and sent it.

Understood.

The reply came back immediately.

Good man, Vincent. Now go and have a nice breakfast and build up your strength. I can imagine a night like that must be quite exhausting at your age. Don't worry, everything is paid for.

He threw his phone on the bed, lay beside it and sobbed.

* * *

Helen sipped her orange juice as the Cypriot sun blazed down from a cloudless sky. Although it was only ten o'clock, the temperature had already hit thirty-five degrees and was forecast to reach forty by mid-afternoon.

'Another hot day today, Malek.'

Her tanned companion peered up from his handheld games console, his eyes hidden behind his Rayban sunglasses. 'Is it?' he replied.

'Yes, it bloody is. I know you've grown up in this place, but it is way too hot today.'

He removed his sunglasses. 'Have you thought about how hard it will be to keep a child cool?'

She slammed down her drink. 'Of course I have. We'll just have to keep her in the air-conditioned rooms.'

He dropped his console and held up his hands. 'I was only asking.'

Even the local birdlife had silenced, a sign their efforts at feeding and singing had finished until things cooled down later.

Malek sat up on his lounger. 'Everything go OK with Kelly and Vincent?'

Helen smirked. 'Oh yes. The old fool fell for her, hook, line and sinker. I could almost feel his jaw drop from over here when he read she was only fifteen.'

'*Is* she fifteen?'

'Nah, she's twenty-one but looking young is how she makes her living. However, Vincent doesn't know that so he'll be much more compliant in future and boy, will I test his new-found loyalty.' She ran her hand over his muscular chest. 'You know, watching Kelly's video has got me all hot and bothered. Let's go back inside and crank up the aircon. We can watch her in action and re-create some of the scenes. I've got an itch that needs scratching.'

His eyebrows lifted. 'What?'

She took his hand. 'Come on. I'll show you.'

* * *

Jemma and Carol were sitting beside Bernard's bed with tears in their eyes as they held his hands. Ever since the previous day, when he'd briefly stirred and tried talking to Jemma and Brad, he'd been drifting in and out of consciousness.

A white-coated doctor made notes on a tablet as he checked the readings on the various monitors connected to his patient. After finishing his deliberations, he pulled up a chair to sit with Carol.

'He seems to be sleeping normally now. It's incredible he's

come round after so long, very unusual but not unheard of. Over the next few days, we'll assess his capabilities and decide on the next stages of his rehabilitation.'

'OK.' Jemma said.

'We have to establish how we're going to progress. As he is now breathing for himself, we've removed the tubes. We may have to re-insert the eating tube if he struggles to swallow.'

Carol smiled. 'I bet he won't like that if he's awake.'

The doctor nodded. 'We'll start eating therapy, speech therapy and physical therapy to try help him regain muscle strength. His muscles will have atrophied after so long without being used. Any movement will drain him physically.'

'Will he eventually return to normal?' Jemma asked.

'That's difficult to predict,' he replied. 'We'll need to check if he's confused, depressed, angry or resistant to therapy. He'll need to be dedicated to getting better.'

Carol reached for Jemma's hand. 'I'm sure he will. He's always been a fighter.'

The doctor stood. 'It will be a long, hard journey, but he's made a start over the last twenty-four hours. We'll just have to make sure he doesn't get too impatient to be out of here.'

* * *

Helen was lying on the sofa in the air-conditioned lounge at the villa, stroking Malek's hair as he leant up against her. 'Thank you. My itch has been thoroughly scratched.' She checked her watch. 'What time is your cousin getting here?'

Malek turned to peer up at the clock. 'He'll be here in half an hour. He's very reliable.'

She stood and snatched up her robe from the tiles. 'We'd better get dressed then. Don't want to scare the poor guy.'

At twelve o'clock, a white van pulled up on the drive and a short, dark-haired man with a full beard climbed out. He wore blue overalls and looked like he'd driven straight there after a week of fishing. A cigarette hung from his mouth and he gazed around the garden before dropping the butt end on the gravel and grinding it in with his boot.

'Ozlem,' Malek shouted. They hugged. 'This is Helen.'

The weather-tanned boat owner moved to shake Helen's hand, spotted how dirty his hands were and nodded instead. 'Merhaba, Helen,' he said.

'Hi, Ozlem. Thanks for coming,' she replied. 'Would you like a beer or a coffee?'

He nodded. 'Coffee please.'

Helen beamed at Malek. 'Will you do the honours, please? I'll have a gin and tonic.'

Ozlem grinned as his cousin left the room. 'You have him trained well. Unusual in a Turkish man.'

She smiled. 'He knows his position here. Now, down to business. I need a boat to take two people to England, collect a very young family member and then return here. The rest of the family won't be very happy, so we'll need to be careful. Is this something you can help with?'

He ran a hand through his hair and sucked in a breath. 'That sounds risky. I don't know...'

Helen sipped her drink. 'Of course, I will be happy to compensate you fully for the level of risk you will be taking.'

He rubbed his chin. 'If I do agree then I won't be able to fish for at least a month, so it will be expensive.'

Her lips narrowed. 'How much?'

He shrugged. 'I'll have to go away and find out who is available to crew this thing. I'll also need to work out how much fuel I'll need. Will it be a short stay in England?'

Helen thought for a moment. 'A week? Two weeks? Might be a little longer.'

'OK,' he replied. 'I work out boat hire, fishing time lost, wages, fuel and food. I think this won't be a legal journey so I need to include some bribes. Is that right?'

She looked him straight in the eyes. 'A few bribes might be useful.'

Malek returned with a tray of drinks. 'Here we are.' He glanced at Ozlem. 'All sorted?'

His cousin took a tiny coffee cup and sipped from it. 'I know the task. Right, Malek, how's my uncle?'

* * *

Ellie drove into the main car park in Swanbourne, reversed into a space and dried her palms on the duster she kept for wiping the windscreen. 'I'm going on a date,' she said to her reflection in the rearview mirror. 'Dan is a nice guy. He likes me. He is not a homicidal maniac out to drug and kill me. I can do this.'

She stepped out of the car and locked the door. It was still light, but she knew the carpark would be well lit if it was dark when she returned. There were also a few couples walking hand in hand around the town and enjoying the last of the evening sunshine. An elderly pair gazed through an estate agent's window at some of the local seaside properties.

The warm night meant that drinkers spilt onto the pavement outside the pub, laughing and talking while holding glasses. Several stepped out of her way to let her through and she thanked them as she hovered by the door. Through the glass, she could see Dan standing by the bar chatting to the barmaid.

She froze.

I can't do this. I just can't do it.

She turned away, brushing past the alfresco drinkers. One grinned at her.

'That was quick, love.'

She tried to return a smile. 'Forgot something.'

The walk back to her car rushed by in a blur and once back

in the driver's seat she put her head in her hands and sobbed. 'What's wrong with me?'

Chapter 10

Vincent arrived home at ten and let his Labrador, Monty, out for a walk around the garden. His neighbour had agreed to feed the dog and take him for a walk while Vincent was at the hotel. After the dog had finished watering the shrubs they both went back inside where Vincent made a coffee and sat on the sofa staring out to sea. 'I wish I'd never agreed to help the Fletcher family, Monty. It feels like I've sold my soul to the devil.'

The elderly dog padded over and rested his chin on his owner's leg.

Vincent stroked his head. 'You won't let me down, will you? I'm worried about what Helen is going to ask me to do. I've been so stupid, but I'll have to do what she says. I didn't realise Kelly was only fifteen. She lied about her age, you know.'

He picked up a couple of envelopes his neighbour must have left on the table. One contained a bank statement and his hand shook as he saw the balance, boosted by a deposit of twenty-five thousand pounds marked *International Transfer Cyprus*.

'Oh, Monty, what will she want next?'

* * *

Jemma had just washed the breakfast pots and sat down with a cup of tea when her mobile rang.

'Hello, Jemma Thorne.'

'Good morning, Jemma. This is DS Smith from Hampshire Police. I have an update on our latest findings in connection with the discovery of the bones.'

'Thanks for ringing. What do you know?'

'Well, we've analysed the DNA samples from yourself and your father and can confirm that the remains are definitely your grandfather.'

Jemma wiped her palm on her trousers. 'Wow. It still feels strange, especially now you've confirmed it.'

He continued. 'We're also sure we've retrieved the murder weapon. We found a large geological hammer buried with the body and our forensic tests have shown that it matches the wounds on his skull.'

She felt herself go pale. 'What a horrible way to die.' There was a pause as Jemma contemplated Cornelius's last few moments alive.

'The other news is that we've recovered a fingerprint from the hammer. Obviously, with the length of time since the murder it may be difficult to find any matches, but we'll give it a go.'

'It's amazing you got a fingerprint at all. Good luck with finding a match. Anything else?'

'No. That's it. I thought you'd be interested.'

'Thanks, DS Smith. Bye.' She cut the call and placed her phone on the table. *Anybody would think my family is cursed. So many bad things have happened over the years.*

Jemma and Ellie drove to the care centre with Kira and Rocky.

Ellie unbuckled her daughter from the car seat. 'I don't

know about you, Mum, but I'm a bit nervous about introducing Kira to Grandad.'

'Don't worry. He'll love her. He seems so grateful to be alive. We've just got to be careful not to overwhelm him with stimulating stuff.'

After signing in, the receptionist smiled at them. 'It's so lovely to see Bernard awake. Your Mum's like a new woman.'

'It's incredible,' Jemma said.

The four of them entered Bernard's room where he was sleeping. With his hair brushed and his face shaven, he had some colour in his cheeks at long last, and now looked much better than he had for the previous two years.

Ellie took his hand. 'It's great to see him without the breathing and feeding tubes. More like the old Grandad.'

Rocky pulled on Jemma's sleeve. 'Grandad awake?'

'Not at the moment, Rocky. Let's wait for him to wake up. I've brought something for you to read.' She held up a colourful book.

'Bear Hunt,' he shouted.

Bernard's eyes fluttered open. 'We're gonna catch a b-big one....'

Rocky dropped the book and ran to the bed. 'Grandad. You remembered.'

'Hello, Rocky.' Bernard's voice was still croaky and quiet. He smiled at the others. 'Jemma, Ellie...who's that?'

Ellie stepped forward holding her daughter. 'This is Kira, your great-granddaughter. She's been waiting to meet you for ages.'

Bernard gritted his teeth as he lifted his arm and gently touched Kira's cheek. 'Hello, Kira.' Exhausted by the effort he closed his eyes and laid his arm back on the bed. 'Nothing works properly yet,' he said.

Jemma touched his forehead. 'That's alright, Dad. The doctor said it's going to take a while to build your muscles back up.'

'So tired,' he said.

'You're bound to be. Don't worry, go back to sleep,' she replied.

There was no reply, and he closed his eyes.

Ellie hugged her mum. 'It's wonderful he's breathing on his own. Have they said how long he'll be in for?'

Jemma shook her head. 'They don't know. They want to keep him in for observation while they try to build him up. Luckily, the staff here have worked hard moving him around in bed so he didn't suffer from back rashes and bed sores.'

'They've been fantastic with him, Mum,' Ellie replied.

'Grandad's lazy.' Rocky said and picked up his book. 'I'll read him a story.'

Jemma watched with a tear in her eye. 'This is wonderful, Ellie.'

* * *

Later that evening, Ellie waited to be picked up by Dan. He'd been understanding about being stood up in the pub and was persistent in trying to persuade her to come out for a meal with him. She'd finally relented and agreed to go.

Now, she stood in the corner of the kitchen checking her makeup in the mirror.

'Give us a twirl,' Jemma said. 'We don't often see you in a dress.'

Ellie gave a theatrical twirl and her white sundress lifted up.

'Steady on, girl,' Jemma laughed. 'I wouldn't do that too often unless you want to flash those long legs of yours and let the whole restaurant see the colour of your knickers.'

Ellie blushed. 'Mum! I thought I'd dress up for a change. Dan's taking me to The Cliff Hotel for a meal tonight.'

'The Cliff Hotel?' Brad whistled. 'He must have a well-paid job. What does he do?'

'He's a trainee accountant so I doubt he earns a lot, but he said it's a special treat.'

There was a knock at the door and Ellie walked over to open it. Dan was standing on the doorstep nervously stepping from one foot to the other.

His eyes immediately widened. 'Wow, you look stunning.'

She smiled and hugged him. 'Thanks. It's just an old thing from the wardrobe.' She twisted around. 'Come and say hello to Mum and Brad or I'll never hear the last of it.'

Dan stepped inside and straight into a hug from Jemma and a handshake from Brad. 'Hi Jemma, Brad,' he said.

'Hello, Dan,' Jemma replied. 'Looking smart.'

He glanced at his white button-down shirt, dark green chinos and brown shoes. 'Thanks, I tried.' He touched his neck. 'To be honest, I didn't know if I was supposed to wear a tie, but I've got one in the car in case.'

'I wouldn't worry,' Brad said. 'Your money is as good as anybody else's. They're happy with smart casual in the restaurant.'

Dan reached for Ellie's hand. 'Come on then, Miss Thorne, your carriage awaits.'

They said their goodbyes and left.

* * *

At around ten-thirty, the door to Ellie's cottage opened and closed. Jemma stopped the film she was watching with Brad and waited for Ellie to come through. After a couple of minutes, she heard footsteps on the stairs and shouted through the door that connected the two properties.

'Ellie, you OK?'

When there was no answer, she got up, shoved her feet inside her slippers and shuffled next door. Treading up the stairs, she began to hear sobbing from the bedroom.

She knocked. 'Ellie, can I come in?'

There was no reply, so she opened the door slowly and peered inside.

On one side of Ellie's tiny room was a sloping ceiling waiting to concuss the unwary or careless. With a double bed and a wardrobe, there wasn't much extra space, but Ellie still managed to fill every available gap with cuddly toys and discarded clothes. She was lying on the bed in her crumpled sundress and Jemma sat beside her, slipping her arm around the sobbing girl.

'What's up, Els? What's happened?'

'Nothing.' Ellie sniffed. 'It's just me.'

'Why the tears? Have you fallen out?'

'No, I had a lovely night. Dan's been really nice and understanding.'

'And?' Jemma asked.

'We were sitting in his car outside and he went to kiss me.' She spluttered tears. 'I tried, Mum, I really tried but as he leant in all I could see was Zak coming towards me. I burst into tears and scrambled out.'

'Had you explained to Dan what happened with Zak?' Jemma asked.

Ellie rubbed her eyes. 'I wanted to, Mum, but I just couldn't bring myself to tell him.'

Jemma hugged her. 'Don't worry. You'll get over it eventually. How about trying some counselling?'

'I don't want counselling. I just want to be able to kiss Dan without seeing Zak's face. He's bloody dead; he can't hurt me anymore. I'll never see Zak or his family again.'

Chapter 11

Jemma tried to concentrate on Vincent's monotonous ramblings. He'd spent twenty-five minutes explaining the timescale for moving the exhibits from the old museum to the new building five hundred yards away. The town hall was warmer than at the previous meeting but that, and the fact Vincent had such a boring voice, induced her yawns. Finally, he breathed, so she seized the opportunity to jump in.

'So, to paraphrase the last half hour, the move will be done by professional movers but some of us need to be there to supervise?'

He scowled. 'That's the gist of it. Thank you, Jemma.'

She smiled sweetly. 'You're welcome, Vincent. I'd like to personally supervise the movement of Plessie as she would be easy to damage.'

'We are using trained professionals, you know.'

'How many of them have moved a sixteen-metre plesiosaur fossil before?'

He blustered. 'Probably not many but I'm sure they'll do a good job. Anyway, if there's no more business, I can see the refreshments are ready.' The secretary, Wendy, had organised a tray of tea and biscuits, and Vincent now moved towards them.

Jemma's eyes locked on the chocolate digestives, mentally dividing the number of biscuits by the number of people in attendance. She smiled as she calculated there'd be sufficient for one each unless anyone committed the unspeakable act of taking two.

She took her mug to a small table and rolled her eyes when Vincent slid into the seat beside her.

'Family all OK, Jemma?' he asked.

'They're all good, thanks, and the youngsters are growing quickly. How about you? Do you see much of your daughter?'

He frowned. 'Not much. She's busy with her life in London. We chat occasionally...' His voice trailed off as he took a mouthful of tea. 'How's the latest arrival doing?'

'Kira? She's lovely. On the verge of walking.'

'That's nice.' He glanced around and leant in before whispering. 'Is Ellie managing alright as a single mum?'

She brought down her cup and twisted around to face him. *Why so many bloody questions?* 'Of course, she is. We all help her. Brad is chief babysitter while we're filming the new show.'

'Oh yes,' Vincent replied. 'How are the plans coming along? I heard you had to wrap up on the Isle of Wight.'

'We're filming in Lulcombe but it will involve ropes and abseiling, so it's a bit more complicated than I hoped.'

He puffed out his chest. 'Well, if you want any help, I was a keen mountaineer for many years and would be qualified to act as your rope leader.'

Jemma's face softened. 'Now, that might be useful. Ellie and our cameraman will have to be lowered down alongside me, and we'll need to send parts of the fossil back up the cliff.'

'That would be easy. I'd recommend a session on the climbing wall at the leisure centre to get you both used to abseiling and using your equipment.' He touched his chin. 'Unless you already have climbing experience?'

'No, none at all, so I'll take you up on that, please. We've earmarked part of the show's budget for any kit or advice we might need so we could pay you a bit.'

'Not necessary,' Vincent said. 'I'd be delighted to pass on my expertise. I could abseil down with you to keep an eye on the ropes and equipment.'

'Brilliant.' She turned her mug. 'I'll check my diary and come back with some suggestions.' She glanced at her watch. 'Oh, I'd better go. I've got a meeting with Amrik and a Hampshire policeman about my grandfather's murder.'

His eyes narrowed. 'Do they know who killed him yet?'

'That's what they're coming to tell me.'

Jemma wriggled into her jacket and walked back up the hill to her cottage. The town was getting busier and she had to dodge a number of ice cream-wielding tourists, guarding their multi-coloured trophies while watching out for seagulls intent on a smash-and-grab. As she strolled along, she reflected on Vincent's new found interest in her family. *What's he up to? He's never shown any interest before, though the offer of help is appreciated. Maybe he's trying to be nice after all the arguments about selling the museum. Unless he has an ulterior motive.*

Jemma arrived home with a bag of fresh rolls she'd bought from Lulcombe's tiny bakery. As she spread the contents on a plate on the kitchen table, the smell of hot bread worked its wonder. Brad, Ellie and Rocky suddenly appeared to check out the glorious odour that had permeated through the whole cottage within a minute of the bag being opened.

Conversation ceased while the bread was demolished and the table was soon covered in crumbs and empty plates.

Ellie licked her lips. 'Good call, Mum. I couldn't decide what to have for lunch.'

Brad topped up his coffee. 'Anything interesting at the meeting?'

Jemma's eyes flicked up. 'No, it was just hearing about the plans for the move. Oh, and Vincent has volunteered to help with the ropes for the cliff filming of *The Rock Detectives*.'

He glanced over. 'Are you OK with going down on a rope, Jem? You used to be scared of heights.'

She shrugged. 'I'm fine now. It helped when I held Ellie after the Fletchers caused the cliff collapse.'

Keith Fletcher had detonated some quarry explosives while Jemma and Ellie were recording an early edition of the programme. He'd hoped to kill them both, but the old explosives hadn't worked properly and Jemma ended up saving Ellie from a potentially fatal fall.

After they'd finished eating and cleaned the table, Brad took Rocky, Kira and Dino for a walk. There was a heavy knock on the back door, prompting Jemma to check her watch.

'That'll be Amrik and his colleague.'

Ellie stood. 'I'll leave you in peace.'

'No need,' Jemma replied. 'It's not private.'

Her daughter sat down again. 'Good. At least I'll get to hear what's going on.'

Jemma opened the door and let in the two detectives. She and Ellie shook their hands as Amrik introduced the other detective.

'This is Detective Sergeant Steve Smith from Hampshire Police.'

Amrik was a British Asian of Pakistani descent with a swarthy complexion and a full beard. He'd been involved in most of Jemma's dealings with the police and had protested her innocence when she was wrongly charged with the murder of her workmate, Sally O'Keefe. He'd been at Swanbourne for ten years and had worked his way up through the uniformed section to detective constable and then D.S.

His colleague, Steve, was taller with fair hair and appeared almost too young to be a sergeant.

Jemma poured them both a glass of orange juice. 'OK. What do you know?'

DS Smith took out his notepad. 'Well, you know we managed to lift a print from the rubber-handled hammer used to kill your grandfather?'

'Yes, incredible after so long.'

He continued. 'Well, initially we couldn't find a match on any of the police databases but when I contacted Amrik he had some ideas.'

Amrik joined in. 'The automated fingerprint recognition system we use was only set up around 2001. The previous one was the National Automated Fingerprint Identification System, or NAF for short, and prior to that they used the PNC, Police National Computer.'

She frowned. 'Sounds complicated.'

'It is,' Amrik replied. 'Nothing was kept in digital format until the nineteen eighties. Before then fingerprints were compared manually with prints on file. The early systems weren't cross-referenced very well but I spotted details of an entry in Cornelius's notebook.'

'Right,' she said. 'How did that help?'

Amrik brought out his own notepad. 'He had written; *I am becoming increasingly annoyed by the presence of Ronald Fletcher. He always seems to turn up at my dig sites and feeds off my discoveries like a parasite. He has been digging in the northern part of the Compton Bay field and we had words earlier.'*

The blood drained from Jemma's face. 'Fletcher! I don't like that name.'

Amrik nodded. 'I'm afraid so. I carried out a search of the old records and found a print on the PNC for a Ronald Fletcher. He was convicted in 1986 and served twelve months in prison for assault occasioning actual bodily harm. When I checked his fingerprint to the one found on the murder weapon, it turned out to be a match.'

'So,' DS Smith tried to take back the limelight, 'the good news is we know who killed your grandfather.'

She responded to the pause. 'And the bad news?'

'Unfortunately, Ronald Fletcher died in 2010, so will never face trial for the murder.'

She frowned. 'Is he related to the Fletchers who caused all the problems after I discovered Plessie?'

Amrik and his colleague made eye contact. 'Yes, he was the father of Keith, Reggie and Helen, grandfather to Zak and Gary.'

Jemma slammed down her glass, spilling orange and making everybody jump. 'Murdering bloody family.'

Ellie put her arm around her mum's shoulders. 'They've gone now, Mum, there's no need to think about them anymore.'

'Helen got away though, didn't she?'

Ellie glared at Amrik. 'Are you any further forward with extraditing her to face trial here?'

Amrik shook his head. 'The Turkish authorities in Cyprus don't cooperate with anybody other than Turkey, so no chance, I'm afraid. The warrant for her arrest on the charge of incitement to murder will stay on her record forever so at least it will stop her ever returning here.'

Chapter 12

A lone skylark took off in the field adjacent to the farm track, twittering up until it disappeared from view.

Jemma, Ellie and Vincent picked their way along the dirt and stone bridleway that joined up with the South West Coast Path. As they neared the clifftops, they spotted Jackson Carter from the TV company following them, so they waited by the final galvanised five-bar gate for him to catch up.

Jackson was in his forties with eyes that constantly darted around as though he was constantly checking the vista for camera shots. He'd been the director of *The Rock Detectives* from its first episode.

'Hi Jemma, Ellie, stunning views,' he remarked after finally catching up. They all shook hands and Jemma introduced Vincent.

'Vincent has agreed to be our rope master for the cliff work.'

'Thanks, Vincent,' Jackson said. 'Have you done any fossil removal from cliffs before?'

Vincent glanced at Jemma. 'Well, I've been involved in a lot of fossil collecting and mountaineering so it's just a matter of putting them together.'

'Right.' Jackson paused. 'OK then, Jemma. What were you thinking?'

Jemma pointed to a bright yellow gorse bush near the clifftop. 'If we bring a couple of tractors down to this point, we can attach the ropes to one of them and use a winch on the other one to drag up the parts of the fossil. We've borrowed a metal cradle to keep the bones safe as they're pulled up.'

Jackson wandered to the edge of the cliff. 'How stable is this section?

'Not too bad,' Jemma replied. 'The rocks are a bit flaky, that's why the skull has been exposed. The ichthyosaur could be lying along the line of the cliff, so we won't have to dig far into it to remove the pieces.'

Jackson looked at Vincent. 'Would you be happy using a tractor as an anchor point for the ropes?'

He nodded. 'Yes. That'd be plenty of weight to hold four people on ropes.'

Ellie counted on her fingers. 'Four?'

He glanced at her. 'You, your mum, me and the cameraman.'

'Oh,' she replied. 'I'd forgotten about him.'

'How long do you think filming will take?' Jackson asked.

Jemma thought for a moment. 'It might take a week or more but with decent weather and, assuming the rock isn't too hard, we could hopefully extract it in three full days.'

'That's good,' Jackson said. 'We have to keep an eye on the budget for filming. We'll need to include the cost of hiring the tractors and climbing equipment. If we use the winch to pull up the fossil, how will the four people...' he paused to find the right word, 'dangling down get back up?'

Vincent moved his arms up and down. 'We can pull ourselves back up using rope clamps.'

Ellie frowned. 'How easy is that?'

'Oh, it's not difficult. The clamps do most of the work,' Vincent replied. 'It's all down to technique. I've already mentioned to Jemma that I can take you to Swanbourne Leisure Centre to practice on their climbing wall.'

'Any other questions, Jackson?' Jemma asked.

He checked his phone. 'No, I think that about covers it. I'll get some quotes for hiring the tractors but we'll be good for three days' filming. I'm hoping to end up with six episodes if all goes well.'

* * *

Jemma had agreed to go down to the museum that afternoon to lend a hand with the removal of the exhibits to the new building. As she approached the famous old building, there were two large vans parked outside with a stream of workers wearing overalls carrying boxes up the ramp.

She peered around the panelled main hall, now largely empty of the display cabinets, stands and exhibits that had been such a feature of life since she was a little girl being shown around by her grandfather Cornelius.

Tears formed in her eyes as she thought of the plans for the historic building: a pile of bulldozed rubble as the foundations for a modern hotel. She wiped her face on her sleeve and wandered through into the newer extension that housed Plessie, the fossilised plesiosaur skeleton she'd uncovered on a stormy morning at Lulcombe Beach three years earlier. A vivid flashback raced through her mind of the night soon after when she'd discovered the unconscious form of Anna, the museum manager, who'd been viciously assaulted by the Fletcher Brothers as they stole Plessie.

Jemma shook her head to try clearing the unhappy memories and stepped over to where several of the removals team were sitting on upside-down packing cases drinking teas and coffees.

'Are you Jemma?' one of them asked. He was a solidly

built middle-aged man with a beer belly trying to force its way through his polo shirt.

'Yes.' She moved to shake his hand but he ignored the gesture.

'Thank Christ for that, we can finally get started with moving this bloody beast.'

She frowned. *What a rude man.* 'What's the plan?' she asked.

'We're basically going to take down the display, stuff it in these boxes and dump them in the new place for you and your colleagues to rebuild like a giant Lego model.' He peered closer. 'Does the skull come to pieces?'

'No,' she snapped, 'it's all one piece and it's important it stays that way.'

'That's a shame. It's bigger than our biggest box. We'll have to trundle it on a trolley.' He put his hand behind the skull. 'How is it attached to the wall?'

Jemma's nostrils flared as she stood between him and the skull. *I'm losing my patience with you.* She breathed out. 'There are brackets all around it. I can remove it for you. That might be safer.'

'Sorry, no can do,' he said. 'We've been contracted to shift all the pieces and deliver them to the new museum. We have to do all the moving ourselves or it invalidates the insurance.'

'Well, please be gentle,' Jemma pleaded. 'It's priceless.'

'Right, if you could just stand to the side, love, we'll get a move on.' He checked behind the skull. 'That's good. I've spotted that each bone has a code on it so if it does come to bits you can reassemble it at the other end.'

'Yes,' Jemma replied. 'There's a master diagram on the computer that shows which pieces go where.'

'OK. Why don't you go and make a cuppa for yourself and we'll have this jigsaw back in the box and ready to go in no time. Mine's a strong tea with three sugars while you're at it.'

Jemma clenched her fists. 'I'm contracted to observe the

move and I don't think making tea is covered by *my* insurance.'

The removals man shrugged. 'Suit yourself, but don't get in the way.'

Jemma watched for a few minutes but heard Vincent calling her from reception. She sauntered back out from the extension and found him holding an ammonite.

'Hi Jemma, can you remember which one this is, please? They've got a bit confused and the label has come off somewhere.'

She tutted. 'That doesn't bode well. It's an Asteroceras, so should go in the box with other Jurassic Coast fossils.'

He handed it back to the young mover and pointed to the correct box. 'How are they getting on with Plessie?'

Jemma grimaced. 'I don't think I can watch any more. I'm not convinced they know what they're doing.'

He frowned. 'They're supposed to be the leading museum removal experts in the south. I'm sure they'll be fine.'

There was a sudden loud crashing noise from the new extension.

Jemma glared at Vincent and shouted, 'Plessie!'

Chapter 13

The following morning, Vincent washed his breakfast pots and, for the sixth time in the past hour, stared at the mobile on his kitchen table. His Labrador padded over and nosed up against his hand.

'Oh, Monty, I don't want to ring her ever again but she threatened me. Who'd look after you if I went to prison?'

Two big eyes gazed back at him as if to say, 'don't leave me on my own.'

Vincent rubbed the dog's head, picked up the phone and scrolled through his contacts before pressing the call button. A strange ringing tone signalled the recipient was overseas.

'Hi Vincent. I do hope you're well and have built up your energy after your recent exertions. Do you have anything interesting to tell me?'

'Not a lot,' he replied. 'I've found out a bit more about the plans for Jemma's new TV programme.'

'Go on,' she said.

'The next series of *The Rock Detectives* is going to be filmed on the cliffs in Lulcombe. Jemma spotted a skull protruding from the stone whilst filming with a drone. She thinks it could be an ichthyosaur so they're going to attempt to remove it by using a team to abseil down to it.'

'Mmm. Interesting. Who will be abseiling down?'

'I think it will end up being Jemma, Ellie, me and a cameraman. I sort of volunteered to be in charge of safety as I have some mountaineering experience.'

'That sounds fascinating. How high up will they be?'

'Probably twenty-five metres but it should be safe. The ropes will be anchored to a tractor and a second one will be used to winch up the bones.'

Helen giggled. 'And you're in charge of safety?'

'Not all of it. I'm only the rope master.'

'Thank you for that gem, Vincent. I'll have a think and come back to you.'

He gulped. 'Oh, one other thing.' He checked a note by the phone. 'You know that Jemma unearthed her grandfather's body on the Isle of Wight?'

'Yes,' she paused, 'you told me he'd been murdered a long time ago.'

'Well, Jemma told me that the police believe the murderer, who is now deceased, was none other than one Ronald Fletcher.'

This time there was another, more prolonged silence on the other end. 'What? As in my father, Ronald Fletcher?'

'Yes.' He checked his notes. 'It says here, "Father of Helen, Keith and Reggie Fletcher".'

She started cackling. 'Oh, that's so funny. The old devil. I knew he had a bit of a violent streak but I never took him for a killer. That's brilliant news, Vincent. Our families are destined to cause each other pain. Jemma hasn't got a clue what's going to hit her.'

'OK. Bye, Helen.'

He cut the call and flopped back into his armchair cradling his head in his hands.

* * *

Jemma stood by a bench in the workshop at the new museum and stared at the pieces of plesiosaur skull scattered in front of her. The jagged shapes had been rearranged into roughly the correct position in preparation for the attempted repair, and now she wiped away a tear as she assessed the damage.

The workshop had only recently been installed and equipped, so the surfaces were pristine and the tools unused. It had a rectangular wooden workbench with adjustable lighting overhead and several heavy-duty vices at one end. She had selected half a dozen assorted clamps and held a tube of clear glue as she assessed the damage.

The unpleasant leader of the removal team was beside her moving his considerable weight from one foot to the other, wringing his hands. 'I blame that bloody new lad. He obviously overestimated his own strength.' He grinned nervously. 'It will superglue back together again, won't it?'

'It might,' she sighed, 'but the important thing about this,' she glared at him, 'was that I had discovered and prepared the only complete, unbroken, plesiosaur skull in the world. That is what gave it a priceless valuation.'

'Yes, but the bits will go back together quite easily, won't they?' He reached for one of the pieces.

'Don't touch!' Jemma shouted and he jumped backwards like a scalded child. 'You've done enough damage already,' she said. 'I think you'd better go and finish off the rest of the move while I work out how I can repair this negligent destruction of a unique piece of scientific history and assess the cost of the damage. Just don't break anything else.'

He gulped and slunk back to his van.

* * *

Ellie steered Kira along the bustling pavement in her buggy. The sun had brought out the tourists, good for the local businesses but not for a young mother trying to navigate the narrow pavements.

She peered in through the window of Molly's Teashop and saw Dan wave at her. After she'd stood him up at the pub and they'd had their meal at the Cliff Hotel, he'd tried a *tea and cakes* approach and she'd agreed. She took a deep breath and pushed the door open with her back, pulling the buggy in behind her. As she turned, Dan stepped over, pecked her on the cheek and touched her arm.

'Hi, Ellie.'

'Hello,' she said, nodding down at the buggy. 'If I lift her out, can you fold it and put it over there by the coats, please?'

'Will do.' He pointed to a table. 'I reserved that spot with a child seat. I'm glad I did as it's getting busy.' He battled to fold the buggy, eventually parked it and joined Ellie as she slid Kira into the brightly painted wooden seat. He reached over and took Kira's hand.

'Hello, Miss Kira.'

Kira smiled and looked down. 'Hello,' she said.

Ellie bit her lip. 'Anybody would think she likes you.'

He winked at her. 'I have that problem with all the girls.'

'I bet you do.' Ellie grinned as she scanned down the menu.

'What do you fancy?' he asked.

'Hot chocolate and a piece of rocky road, I think.'

He stood. 'Sounds good. I'll go and order. Anything for Kira?'

'No, I've brought her some milk and she can try some of my cake.'

He wandered off and joined the queue.

Ellie leant down towards her daughter. 'Dan's nice, isn't he?'

'Dan,' Kira said proudly.

'Yes, Dan.' Ellie smiled as she stared over at the tall young man at the counter. 'Very nice.'

The object of their mutual admiration returned carrying a tray with two mugs and two slices of a chocolate creation with bits of white and pink mixed in.

'Copycat,' Ellie laughed.

'I'd already decided. Honest.'

They chatted whilst demolishing their cakes, and it turned out Kira liked rocky road and kept asking for more of Ellie's rapidly shrinking slice.

'I should have asked for two pieces,' she said.

Dan started to get up. 'I'll fetch another.'

Ellie put her hand on his. 'No, it doesn't matter. I'm glad she likes it.' She realised she was still holding his hand and snatched it back before blushing.

He jumped. 'I don't bite.'

'I know you don't,' she replied. 'It's just...'

'Look, whatever the problem is, I can try to help you.'

'Oh, it's just me.' She wiped her eyes. 'There are a few things you ought to know about me.'

While Kira played with the spinning blocks on the front of the child seat and drank her milk, Ellie gave him a potted history of the events of the couple of days she'd spent with Zak Richards, only leaving out most of the more intimate details.

He sat quietly as Ellie described being drugged and dumped at a deserted nature reserve to die. He held her hand again. This time she didn't snatch it back.

'So that's why I'm nervous about responding to anything physical. Damaged goods. That's what you keep trying to go out with. Bloody damaged goods!'

'Don't worry.' Dan squeezed her hand. 'I'm good at mending damaged things and I'm very patient.'

'You'll need to be.' Ellie glanced at her daughter. 'You don't know what you're trying to get involved with.'

Chapter 14

The new museum building was a steel fabrication with ground-floor brickwork and numerous windows which gave it a light, airy feel. Even though Jemma had fought against the move from the traditional museum in the centre of Lulcombe, she had to admit the replacement building was well-designed and spacious.

The wall that faced all visitors who came through from reception was now adorned with the incredible sixteen-metre plesiosaur fossil, Plessie, that Jemma had found three years before.

A voice startled her. 'You've done a fantastic job of repairing the skull.'

She looked up. 'Oh, hello, Vincent. It's not too bad, is it?'

He peered closer. 'If you didn't know where to look, you'd never spot the joins. Oh, I've received a message from the removals firm. If we don't sue them for the damage, they'll give us a fifty per cent discount on the cost of the move.'

She brushed a fleck of stone from the bones. 'I'm still tempted to sue those unprofessional cowboys but I suppose it did go back together pretty well. I hate to admit it but this is a very impressive building now all the exhibits are in place.'

‘I’m pleased as well,’ he said, ‘and we’ve got lots of storage space upstairs plus the workshop where you repaired Plessie. The other good thing is we have some capacity for new displays.’

She smiled. ‘I’m hopeful the ichthyosaur from Lulcombe Cliffs will turn out to be complete and worth displaying.’

Vincent pointed. ‘There’s a free wall on that side that would be perfect for it.’

‘Fingers crossed we can extract it all,’ she replied.

‘Has the owner of the cliff given his permission for the extraction to go ahead?’ he asked.

‘Yep.’ Jemma held up her thumb. ‘All good to go. He just wants us to limit how far we dig into the cliff to two metres so it doesn’t risk taking too much out of the field at the top.’

‘Will that be enough?’

She chewed on her lip. ‘I hope so. It appears to be lying parallel to the cliff so we might manage with around a metre.’

Vincent moved to go but turned back. ‘I’m looking forward to it. Bye, Jemma.’

She watched him leave and smiled. *Maybe he’s not too bad, after all. At least his heart’s in the right place.*

* * *

Later that afternoon, Brad and Jemma walked into the long-term care facility, signed in and wandered down to Bernard’s room. As they approached the room, they could hear an argument in full swing.

‘But I want to go. I’m ready.’

‘Look, Bernard, you’re not fit enough. You can’t walk yet…’

‘I nearly can, I could borrow a wheelchair,’ he interrupted.

Carol sighed. ‘You need to be a bit more mobile first.’

Jemma knocked on the open door. ‘Hello. Mum, Dad we’re here.’

Carol stood and hugged them both. 'Can you tell this stubborn old fool that he's not ready to go home?'

Bernard folded his arms. 'But I want to go home. I'm already fed up with the food in here and I want my own bed.'

Jemma stepped over and hugged her father. His ruddy complexion was a big improvement on the pale, motionless face she'd been watching for two years. 'Hi, Dad.'

'Hello Jemma. Can you take me home?'

Jemma sat by the bed. 'Sorry, Dad. What does your consultant say?'

Bernard tutted. 'He says I need to stay here for another six weeks.' He leant over towards Jemma. 'I think he just wants the money. It's bloody expensive in here, you know.'

'I know it is.' Jemma glanced across the bed at her mum. 'Oh well, it's a sign he's getting better if he's reached the argumentative stage.'

Carol rolled her eyes. 'Tell me about it. Being in a coma had its advantages.'

Brad laughed. 'You know you don't mean that, Carol.' He pulled up his seat. 'Anyway Bernard, how's the memory going?'

'Bloody mattress.' Bernard shuffled to make himself more comfortable. 'I suppose I've started remembering some things. I can remember that bastard of a gas man who nobbled our boiler and nearly killed us. I'd love to get my hands on him.'

'Don't worry about him, he's dead,' Jemma said.

'What?' Bernard's hand went to his forehead. 'Did you kill him?'

Jemma made a rocking motion with her hand. 'Not exactly. He followed me on to the beach and ended up sinking in a deep mud flow along with his murderous twin brother.'

Carol tutted. 'That wasn't your fault.'

Her daughter shrugged. 'I may have forgotten to go and fetch help.'

‘Good girl,’ Bernard said. ‘I hope the bastards suffered.’

‘Forget about the Fletcher family,’ Brad said. ‘They can’t hurt you anymore.’

Chapter 15

Jemma parked her silver Ford Fiesta in the Swanbourne Leisure Centre carpark. She rubbed the back of her neck and grinned at Ellie. 'Right. Are you ready to dangle on a rope?'

Her daughter drew a breath. 'As ready as I'll ever be.' They grabbed their kit bags from the boot and headed inside.

The leisure complex had been extended ten years before and the original 1970s concrete block now had a newer tall section that housed some squash courts and a climbing wall. The girl on reception took their payments and guided them to the stairs leading to the second floor where they'd be starting their abseiling lesson. Jemma's hands were sweaty as they ascended.

At the top, they spotted Vincent inspecting a pile of ropes and equipment.

'Hi, Vincent,' Ellie shouted.

The older man glanced up and waved. 'Morning, ladies. Over here. I'm organising what we need.'

They wandered over and watched while he explained about the baffling pieces of kit.

'OK. Have you got all that?' he asked.

Jemma nodded her head. 'I think so.'

He clapped his hands together. 'Right. Let's get you harnessed up.'

The next ten minutes were spent attaching the belts and straps, until finally they were all trussed up and ready to go.

Jemma twisted her trousers. 'I wish I'd worn leggings like you, Els. My jeans are giving me a right wedgie in this harness.'

Ellie giggled. 'I'm fine.'

'Trouble is you look good in leggings. I always look like an anorexic chicken.'

'Here, Mum. Let me help you.' Ellie grabbed the back of Jemma's belt and hoisted her trousers.

'Oi, stop that.' Jemma tried to twist free. 'I'd just got them straight.' She stuffed her hand inside her jeans and struggled to straighten her knickers.

'Having fun, ladies?' Vincent strolled over. 'Come on then. Let's abseil. If we all stand by the edge, I'll start you both on a descent and then I'll join you. You first, Jemma.'

Jemma seized the rope and hesitated before shuffling backwards towards the vertical drop. She peered over and gulped. 'I'm not sure that I can do this.'

Vincent touched her arm. 'You need to relax and tilt back like I showed you. Don't worry, I've got you.'

She swallowed. 'I'm not sure about this. Can't Ellie go first?'

'Breathe deeply and lean into it. Don't forget to lift the rope a little with your right hand so it passes through the belay device. You can take it a step at a time to start with. Don't try to bounce yet.'

Jemma leant back out over the edge and took a few tentative steps while feeding the rope through the mechanism. Rather than look down she fixed her gaze on the joists holding the roof up. She edged further down.

'Come on, Mum, you've got this,' Ellie said.

Jemma lifted the rope again but overdid the movement and dropped a metre before the safety rope stopped her downward progress. She screamed, her legs left the wall and pointed towards the ceiling as she hung in the air dangling and spinning.

'Not quite that fast yet.' Vincent grinned. 'You need some more practice. Tell you what. Put your feet back on the wall and keep your legs horizontal without moving. I'll send Ellie down and then join you both.'

As Jemma righted herself she observed the other groups of abseilers. To their right was a party of six teenagers all climbing up the wall with the agility of monkeys. She tutted and peered at the group on their left, four lads in their twenties abseiling down with large bouncing steps. 'Look at them. They're doing in seconds what's taken me five minutes.'

Vincent's voice drifted down. 'Practice, Jemma. It takes lots of practice.' He gestured at Ellie. 'Go on then, off you go, and remember what I told you.'

Ellie leant out, taking several small steps before starting to bounce, and within a few seconds she was level with her mother.

Jemma tried to raise a grin. 'Show off.'

Vincent peered over the top. 'That's brilliant, Ellie, perfect synchronisation of steps and rope release. You're a natural. I'm coming down to you now.' After a couple of deft bounces, he was level. 'OK. Let's bounce together, shall we?' He grinned at Jemma. 'Or just walk down to the bottom.'

Jemma continued with some tentative small steps while Ellie bounced her way straight down to the ground.

'You need to coordinate your steps or bounces with lifting your right hand to free the rope, Jemma. Try pushing yourself out from the wall, release some rope and reconnect with the surface.'

Eventually she managed something that resembled a bounce and within a couple of minutes joined her daughter at the base of the wall.

'Brilliant.' Ellie ignored the tangle of ropes and harnesses in an effort to hug her mother. She grinned at Vincent. 'Again.'

He wiped his forehead. 'In a bit. I want you to have a go at using rope clamps and foot ascenders to climb back up again.'

He explained how the clamps and sliders worked to lift each foot in turn, locking one in place so the other could ascend. It took them fifteen minutes to return to the top, by which time Jemma was panting.

Vincent patted her on the shoulder. 'That's not bad for a first attempt. Have a rest for a few minutes and we'll go again. Next time, I want us to stop halfway down and stay locked in place. You can pretend to be digging on the cliff face without spinning around and getting dizzy.'

Jemma took a deep breath. 'I didn't realise this would be so tiring.'

He laughed. 'Wait until you wake up tomorrow morning. You'll find aches in places you didn't know existed, but at least you won't have to ascend so often while you're working on the cliffs. You've got to work on your technique and fit in lots of practice. Don't worry, we've got some time before we have to do it for real.'

Ellie stretched. 'I'm glad I'm not doing this with heavy camera equipment.'

'I spoke to Trevor,' Vincent said, referring to the cameraman. 'He's done quite a bit before so is happy to just turn up when he's needed.' He rubbed his hands. 'Come on then, let's go down again, we've only got two hours booked.'

Jemma's eyes widened. 'Two bloody hours! It feels like twenty already.'

After they'd showered and changed, the café menu was calling so they met with Vincent for cups of hot chocolate and pieces of flapjack. The room was busy but they managed to secure the last vacant table. Judging by the number of children running around in a hyper-excited state swinging balloons and party bags, there'd been a birthday party at the Leisure Centre.

Jemma's head tilted. 'Thanks for that, Vincent. I'm a lot happier now. I reckon a few more hours and I'll be raring to go over the edge of the cliff.'

'You're welcome,' he said. 'I'll book another session on the way out. Ellie's a natural though.' He twisted towards her. 'Are you sure you haven't done any before?'

She beamed. 'No, never. It's great fun, and it was good of you to give up your time to train us.'

'That's not a problem,' he replied. 'Time isn't that important when you're retired and live on your own. Other than taking Monty for a walk, I haven't got a lot to do.'

'That sounds like heaven.' Jemma's gaze drifted off to the view through the window.

He frowned. 'It was pleasant for the first few years but then Rita died and life became somewhat lonely.'

Jemma touched his arm. 'How long has it been now?'

'Over twelve years,' he said, glancing away.

Ellie frowned. 'That's quite a while to be on your own. Have you ever thought about dating again?'

He laughed bitterly. 'Who'd want an old codger like me?'

'I'm sure there are lots of dating sites for old...' Ellie paused, 'I mean more mature people looking for company.'

He shook his head. 'I don't think I'm quite right for Grindr.'

Ellie grinned. 'I think you might find that it's called Tinder, unless there's something you're not telling us.'

'Grindr, Tinder, it's all the same.'

Ellie glanced at her mum who tried not to guffaw. 'Well, there are some differences but we won't go into those today.'

He sipped his drink. 'Anyway, Jemma, are all the arrangements in place for the filming?'

'Yes,' she replied, 'it's all coming together nicely. The director wants the three of us working on the cliff face with a cameraman alongside. They will also use a drone camera to take some aerial shots from a distance. That will show how high up we are, which I don't want to even think about.'

Vincent thought for a moment. 'Have they got the tractors arranged?'

'Sorted,' she said. 'We've got two tractors, one with a winch and also a large green cover for the work area to deflect any rocks that might tumble down. We've also borrowed a metal sledge to bring the skull and bones up to the top after we've removed them.'

Ellie finished her piece of cake and licked her lips. 'It should be so exciting. Fingers crossed for dry weather and no high winds.'

Vincent stared at Jemma until his eyes glazed over. 'I'm sure it will all go to plan.'

Chapter 16

The first day of filming was greeted with a beautiful blue sky and no wind. The sea was incredibly calm and a couple of sailing boats out in Lulcombe Bay crept along with their sails flapping as they tried to catch a breeze.

Jemma parked in the makeshift carpark by the track which led down to the clifftop area where the team would be based for the next few days. As they walked down the path, two gulls were circling over the sea watched by a lone buzzard high above.

'Are you looking forward to this?' Ellie asked her mum.

'I think so. I'm a bit nervous about the abseiling and working at height, but Vincent's lessons helped. I feel much more confident about the equipment than I did before he showed us the ropes.'

Ellie shook her head. 'Was that supposed to be a joke?'

Jemma winked. 'Sorry.'

'Oh Mum, that's awful.'

Jemma shrugged. 'OK. I won't use that one on camera.'

Two enormous red tractors were parked well back from the edge with a network of ropes leading over the clifftop and down towards the sea. A line of folding tables was covered with equipment and Jemma could see piles of ropes, clamps and digging gear, while a further table contained two drones with their controllers. A large tent was filled with TV monitors and electrical instruments all powered by a generator chugging behind.

Ellie scanned the scene and frowned. 'Where's the catering van?'

'Oh, I meant to tell you,' Jemma grinned, 'they decided that, as there wasn't such a big crew this time, they didn't need a full food wagon.' She pointed. 'They've got some flasks of tea and coffee, and some packs of biscuits in the tent.'

Ellie tutted. 'No bacon sarnies then? I'm not happy.'

Jemma held up her rucksack. 'I've got a couple of packs of crisps in here, if you're on the verge of collapse.'

'Thanks, Mum, that's better than nothing.' Ellie shrugged. 'I have to watch that I don't waste away and look really gaunt on camera. You got anything else good in there?'

'Not much.' Jemma opened it and peered inside. 'Tin foil, bags of plaster and some superglue in case we need to hold any of the bones together as we remove them.'

After they were both equipped with radio headpieces and microphones, they joined the team on the clifftop. The director, Jackson Carter, was standing with Vincent and another man.

'Have you met Trevor Kennedy, our cameraman?' Jackson beckoned Jemma closer. 'Trevor's experienced in filming at heights and has worked on several mountaineering documentaries.'

'That's good to hear,' Jemma said. 'I'm afraid we're novices but we'll do our best. We've had a few lessons in dangling and climbing from Vincent so hopefully, we'll be able to abseil down and climb back up again.'

Vincent rolled his eyes. 'Dangling! Have you forgotten all the terminology already, Jemma?'

‘Fraid so, Vincent. I can just about remember what to do but not what everything is called.’

Jackson spoke into his headset. ‘Yes, OK. I think we’re about ready.’ He turned back to the roped-up team. ‘The gang in the tent are all set up to receive the live streams from your helmet cameras and from Trevor as well.’

Jemma gulped and grabbed Ellie’s hand. ‘This seems a lot higher than the climbing wall.’

Her daughter squeezed her hand back. ‘Don’t worry, it’s all the same principles but with a slightly longer rope.’

‘I believe you,’ Jemma replied.

Vincent watched Trevor clip onto his rope and lean effortlessly out over the edge before bouncing down and setting up his camera angle ten feet below the top, ready to shoot the ace fossil hunting team.

‘And action,’ Jackson called.

Vincent reached for his rope. ‘Come on, Jemma, let’s get you attached and you can go over the top.’

Jemma donned her hard hat and watched as her harness was attached to the safety rope. After Vincent had passed it through the clamp, she took the other rope and pulled it tight.

Vincent stepped back. ‘Right. Off you go.’

Jemma shuffled backwards over the edge and tried not to look down towards the beach where the waves were crashing against the shingle.

‘Go, Mum,’ Ellie whispered. ‘You can do this.’

Jemma loosened the rope and leant out. As she moved, the lessons from the leisure centre cut in and she performed a couple of double-footed jumps down towards the cameraman as a huge grin stretched over her face. He finished filming, held up his thumb and pointed his camera back towards Ellie waiting to descend.

‘Next,’ he said into his headset.

Jemma jumped as a massive buzzing insect flew into her

peripheral vision, causing her to spin, but then she realised it was only the drone coming in for some close-ups. She rolled her eyes, regained her footing, and was joined by both Ellie and Vincent.

Vincent gave them both the OK sign and they responded in turn before he commenced his descent to the part of the cliff containing the skull. Both Jemma and Ellie followed suit, their every movement tracked by Trevor's camera.

Jemma managed to descend like an experienced abseiler and had some fluidity to her movements. When they were all set up, Trevor descended and manoeuvred into position ready to record the extraction. Once everybody was in place with their feet against the rock, the team at the top lowered a green tarpaulin to cover the higher part of the cliff so that any loose stones and rocks would be prevented from falling onto people below. Finally, the team removed the trowels and brushes from their rucksacks and the dig began.

Jemma gave a running commentary through her headset whilst trying not to look at the drop beneath as they dug. 'Luckily, the layer of mudstone holding the fossil is quite soft so I'm hoping it won't be a difficult job extracting the bones from the rock. The only downside is that this part of the cliff face could easily collapse so we'll need to carefully monitor the stability of the worksite.'

Vincent dug into the cliff where they thought the tail of the ichthyosaur might be and Ellie worked alongside her mum.

Jemma brushed at a jagged piece of rock. 'With the position of the skull, I'm hopeful the whole ichthyosaur could be lying parallel to the cliff face. That would be perfect as we want to keep the depth we dig into the cliff down to a minimum. We only have permission to dig to a maximum of two metres at any point. If the fossil lay perpendicular to the face, we would only be able to extract the skull but not the body.'

As the three diggers revealed more of the skeleton, Jemma

realised it looked reasonably complete and in very good condition. Ichthyosaurs were the same shape as modern dolphins, just with much larger teeth. This specimen appeared to be about five metres in length.

Ellie scraped away some mud. 'What's the plan for extraction now you can see the completeness and size of Icky?'

Jemma squinted. 'I think we should spend most of today exposing as much as we can and then aim to extract it all tomorrow. The weather forecast is dry for today but there's a chance of some heavy showers in the morning.'

'What will happen if it rains?' Ellie asked.

Jemma frowned. 'Unfortunately, as its name suggests, mudstone turns into a slippery, claylike mess when it gets wet. It'll be too dangerous to be down here if it rains so I want to keep working today for as long as we can and aim to finish it off tomorrow before the nasty stuff moves in.' She stretched out her arms and scanned the horizon. 'What a beautiful day. We couldn't have asked for better weather.'

A lone oil tanker moved along the Channel on its way to deliver its valuable cargo. Closer to the shore, a brightly painted fishing boat chugged from one set of lobster pots to the next, each rope hauled up with the hope of a bumper catch.

Vincent stopped digging to change his position. 'Will we be able to fit the whole of the fossil into the metal sled?'

Jemma turned back to face the cliff. 'No, I think it would be too heavy, so it may take two or three loads to send it all up.'

* * *

Down on the beach below, Brad was walking with Rocky and pointed up to the place with the activity beneath the green cover.

'Look, buddy, can you see Mom and Ellie hanging off the cliff?'

His son used a hand to shade his eyes, trying to make out what was going on. 'Hope Mummy doesn't fall,' he said.

'Nobody will fall,' Brad replied. 'Vincent's in charge of safety.'

Chapter 17

At six in the morning, Jemma was roused by her alarm. Brad stirred beside her, rolled over and snuggled back down under the duvet. Rocky had slept through, so they'd had no disturbances until the radio came on. She padded over to the window and poked her head through the curtain.

'Oh no, it's bloody raining. That wasn't due to start until later.'

'What?' he said with his eyes clamped shut.

'Nothing. I think the weather might stop today's filming.'

'Mmm.' He gave a little snore before going back to sleep.

She turned on her phone and, as she did, it pinged with a message from Jackson Carter.

Rain stops play. Try again tomorrow.

She slipped on her dressing gown and slippers before pottering downstairs and through to Ellie's cottage. Although it had been two cottages they all regarded it as one large house. Jemma tiptoed upstairs and, tapping on the bedroom door, she heard a grunt through the closed door of Ellie's room.

'What?' the muffled voice asked.

Jemma pushed through into the room where a shaft of light was sneaking in through the partially opened curtains, and only a tousled head of hair sticking out from the duvet betrayed her daughter's presence.

'What is it, Mum?'

'It's raining so we won't be going to the dig site today as there's no filming.'

The covers flew back. 'Are you serious?'

'Yes, it's all cancelled.'

'Not that. I mean, you've woken me up to tell me I don't have to wake up.'

Jemma rubbed her eyes. 'Oh, I suppose it sounds a bit crazy when you put it like that.'

'Totally crazy!'

'Sorry, Els. I thought you'd want to know you don't have to get ready for a day out.'

'Thanks for nothing, Mum. I'm going back to sleep.'

'OK. See you later.'

Jemma closed the door a little louder than intended and the resultant bang was followed by the sound of an infant waking and wanting attention.

'Shit, I'll be in big trouble now,' Jemma groaned and rushed back to her own cottage. She made a cup of tea for Ellie before tiptoeing back upstairs with her peace offering.

* * *

Carol had arrived early at the high-dependency long-term unit. Since regaining his appetite, Bernard had complained a number of times about the quality of food, despite his consultant being concerned about him having a rich diet, but he'd begged his wife for something "proper" regardless. Eventually, she'd relented and was now bringing him a grilled English breakfast.

She sat and smiled while her husband savoured the plate of bacon, eggs and sausage, relishing every mouthful with a contented grin. 'It's lovely to watch you eating again. Well, it's lovely to see you doing anything after the last two years.'

Her husband nodded but didn't stop chewing long enough to talk. He sipped his tea and wiped his mouth with a serviette. 'Delicious,' he said, reaching out for Carol's hand.

'I'm so pleased you enjoyed it,' she said.

'Same again tomorrow?'

'Oh no. I promised the doctor I wouldn't bring in more than one a week to start with.'

He winked at her. 'I won't tell him if you don't.'

'Let's see,' she replied. 'How's the memory coming along?'

'I've been trying but I can't remember anything from when that bogus workman turned up right up until I woke up with you in here. Bloody gas man. That bastard tried to kill us both.'

She nodded. 'That's the one.'

'I'm glad Jemma drowned him in the mud. Bloody deserved it.'

'She didn't really drown him. She just left some tracks heading towards the mud. He and his brother are the ones who followed the footprints into the dangerous part and sank.'

He frowned. 'Still the right result in the end. Especially now you're telling me their grandad killed Dad.'

'That's a weird coincidence, isn't it?' she asked.

'The Fletcher family have always been trouble.' He shook his head and clenched his jaw. 'I'm just happy they've all gone now.'

'Apart from Helen in Cyprus but she'll never return to England unless she wants to face the music.'

* * *

Jemma and Brad sat up in bed holding their drinks and a shared newspaper.

'I can't remember the last time we lazed about this late,' she said. 'I feel strangely guilty.'

He finished his coffee. 'You need to learn to relax a bit more.'

She yawned. 'It's hard with a three-year old and a baby next door.'

'Hopefully, we'll all get to relax a bit in Florida in a couple of weeks,' he said.

'I'm really looking forward to it.' Jemma set down her teacup. 'You know, we don't have to work today.'

'Yes...'

'Well, it appears that Rocky is still fast asleep.'

'Yes...'

'Get your boxers off, sunshine, you've pulled.'

* * *

Vincent returned from taking his Labrador for a walk and hung up his wet coat.

Helen had asked him to keep her updated about the progress of the dig in the cliffs but he kept putting off making the call. He didn't know why she wanted that information and was worried about what she was planning.

His mobile rang, making him jump. It was Helen.

'That sodding woman. I'm sure she's got a camera in this house somewhere.' He looked at the dog. 'Unless you're a spy, Monty, feeding her snippets of information?'

The yellow dog looked up expectantly from his bed but once he realised there was no food on offer, he turned around three times before flopping down and closing his eyes.

'I'll take that as a denial. You sure you're not the mole?' He answered the call.

'Oh hello, Vincent. I thought you were avoiding me.'

'Now why should I do that, Helen? Why would I want to miss the delight of one of our conversations?'

‘That’s more like it. You can’t beat a bit of enthusiasm. What have you got for me?’

Vincent spent the next ten minutes giving her a detailed account of the events so far in the quest to remove the marine reptile. After finishing, there was a silence.

‘Helen?’ he said.

‘Yes, give me a few minutes and I’ll ring back.’

The call ended and Vincent shook his head before filling the kettle with water. Before it had a chance to boil the phone rang again. He answered. ‘Yes, Helen, what now?’

‘Have you got a pen and some paper, Vincent?’

‘Yes. Why?’

‘This is what I want you to do.’

Five minutes later, Vincent ended the call, stared at the note on the A4 pad and burst into tears.

Chapter 18

The schedule for the following day's filming was curtailed as the cliffs needed some time to dry out after the rain that had affected the site the previous day. By lunchtime, the team decided it was worth having a go to see how easy it would be to descend and ascend the cliffs.

As they gathered on the meadow at the top of the cliffs, the birds sang lustily as they do after a prolonged wet spell. Everywhere glistened in the sunshine and wisps of mist rose from the damp grass. Eventually, Vincent checked the ropes and declared they could go ahead, deciding he would go down first to check how slippery it felt underfoot.

Jemma stood with Ellie waiting for the go-ahead.

Vincent shouted up. 'OK, we're good to go.'

The cameraman descended next followed by Ellie and Jemma, who was now an old hand at abseiling. Ellie smiled as they made it down with several smooth bounces. 'We'll have you joining a SWAT team yet.'

'Shush,' Jemma yelled. 'I'm concentrating.' She estimated they had another couple of hours of digging before they were ready to send up the first set of fossilised bones. They had two days remaining within the filming schedule before the team had to fly to Iceland for a travel show, so she knew there was immense pressure to finish the extraction quickly.

After ninety minutes, they had made steady progress so Jemma asked for the metal cradle to be lowered so they could attempt to load some bones.

Jemma spoke into her headset. 'Is the sled on its way?'

'We're waiting a few minutes.' Jackson replied. 'There's a black thundercloud out at sea that we're watching in case it heads this way.'

'OK,' Jemma said. 'Let me know what you want to do.'

Vincent glanced over his shoulder. 'That might be nasty, but it should miss us if the wind stays as it is. We can keep going for a bit longer but if it comes our way, we'll have to get off the cliffs immediately.'

After another fifteen minutes of digging, there was a sudden shout from Jackson on the radio. 'The wind has changed and the storm is heading this way. Everybody up. Now!'

'OK,' Jemma said. 'We need a few minutes to secure the site and cover the fossil or else there's a risk it could be washed out and smashed up by the sea.'

'Quick as you can then. The rain might start any minute.'

At that moment a flash of lightning made everyone jump, and it was closely followed by a rumble of thunder.

Vincent flinched. 'Bloody Hell. That was close. We'd better get back now.'

The wind suddenly swung Jemma about. 'Help me with the cover,' she shouted. 'Can't we go down instead of climbing up?'

Vincent peered down. 'No, the tide's coming in. We'd never get off the beach before we were cut off.'

The team above them lowered the large green sheet so that it would cover the six-metre length of the dig.

'Everybody ascend now,' Vincent shouted.

As they started to clamber up over the cover there was

another flash of lightning and enormous raindrops splattered onto the plastic. Almost immediately afterwards, the rain became a deluge that poured off the cliff and over the cover. Instantly, the water had turned the mudstone into a slippery mess, so they couldn't place their feet on the rocks without them sliding straight off.

'Switch to vertical climb using the foot clamps only,' Vincent shouted. 'It's slower but the cliffs are too slippery to touch. Keep calm everybody. Everything will be OK.'

They started the laborious task of pulling themselves up one step at a time. Jemma and the cameraman slowed and Ellie yelled down at her.

'Come on, Mum, you can do it.'

As the rain poured down, Jemma tried to visualise what she had learned on the nice, dry wall at the leisure centre but her mind went blank. She wiped her face, reached up and locked a clamp in place before trying to push herself up using only the strength in her legs. Nothing happened.

'I can't, Ellie,' she replied. 'I'm struggling.'

* * *

Jackson peered over the edge of the cliff as the team battled to ascend and barked into his radio. 'Jemma, are you OK?'

A few seconds later a reply came back. 'I'm struggling to get back up. It's too slippery. Trevor's with me. Vincent and Ellie are nearly at the top.'

Jackson's eyes darted around. 'I'll tell you what, Jemma, when Vincent and Ellie are here, I'll use the tractor to pull you and Trevor up.'

'OK,' she replied. 'I'll hang and try to get my strength back until you're ready.'

Vincent reached the top, clambered over the muddy section and helped Ellie over the lip.

Jackson pointed at the large, powerful vehicle. 'Vincent,

can you watch over and I'll use the tractor to pull up the last two ropes?'

Vincent frowned. 'Slowly, I hope. We don't want them pulled over the wooden guide too quickly. They might hit the hard edge.'

Jackson jogged to the production tent, grabbed the keys and rushed over to the cab. As he scanned the bewildering array of knobs and switches, he tried to recall what he'd been told.

'Ready to go when you are,' Vincent shouted.

'OK,' Jackson replied. 'Nearly there.' He inserted the key, pressed the clutch and turned it. The engine revved and the cab shook as the tractor backfired. A cloud of black diesel smoke belched from the exhaust and the engine cut out. He tried again and this time the engine ran. He eased the lever into first, released the handbrake and gently lifted his foot from the clutch. As he pushed the accelerator, the tractor inched forward, and he turned back to Vincent who was holding up his thumbs.

Steering along the track away from the cliff, two pheasants took off in a panic as he disturbed their grassy snooze. He held his breath as he persisted, inch by inch, twisting around to view Vincent's signals. After he'd covered around ten metres, Vincent dropped his arm and moved his hand across his throat.

Jackson cut the engine, thrust the gear lever into neutral and applied the handbrake. Jumping out of the cab, he rushed back to the clifftop as Vincent and Ellie helped Jemma and Trevor over the slippery mud on to the safer grassy area away from the edge.

Unfastening her harness, Jemma threw her arms around her daughter. 'Oh, Els, that was a bit close.'

Chapter 19

Helen sipped her gin and tonic, yawning as she relaxed on her sunbed while the sun blazed down from a clear blue sky. It was still early so the cicadas hadn't yet started their deafening chorus. She removed her sunglasses and rubbed her eyes. 'What time is it in England?'

Malek checked his sports watch. 'Eight o'clock, I think.'

She stood and went inside. 'I'm sure Harry will already be at his desk. He's a workaholic, that chap, or just plain greedy.'

'I'll go for greedy,' he shouted after her.

In the cool of the kitchen, she called her solicitor.

'Good morning, Helen. You're up early.'

'Hello, Harry. Don't forget it's not that early here.'

'Oh, yes. How can I help?'

'I have a bit of a shopping list I need some help with.'

There was a pause. 'A shopping list?'

'Yes. There are a couple of things I want organising, please,' she said.

'And what are they?' he replied.

'The first item is a house.'

'A house.'

'Am I talking to a parrot, Harry? Yes, a house. I want a

month's rental on a two or three-bedroom property somewhere in West Dorset. It needs to have a garage and be in a secluded spot.'

'You're not thinking of coming back to England, are you?'

'As if I'd do such a thing. No. It's for an associate of mine who wishes to visit the southwest for a bit of sightseeing.'

'OK. What's the other thing?'

'I'd like a dark-coloured Range Rover for the same period.'

'They're expensive to hire, you know.'

She pinched at the skin on her nose. 'I'll tell you what. I'll send twenty thousand pounds to your bank account. Use it to pay for the house rental and the car. Anything that's left you can keep as your...finder's fee. Fair enough?'

'That's very generous. I'm sure I'll be able to provide what you require. What's the timescale?'

'I need them in approximately three weeks. I'll text you the exact date and time. I'd like the Range Rover to be parked in the Marina Car Park in Brixham, Devon. The keys for the vehicle should be hidden behind the front nearside tyre in a waterproof bag. Leave the house key in the glove box. Oh, and it needs a child seat.'

'A child seat? Bloody hell, Helen, what are you planning?'

* * *

Brad carried a tray with some cereal, toast and tea up to the bedroom. 'Come on, sleepy head, I made breakfast.'

Jemma rolled over in a panic. 'What time is it?'

He checked his watch. 'It's nine o'clock. You said you were meeting at the site at midday, so I turned off the alarm and let you sleep in a bit. I thought you might need it after your ordeal yesterday.' He leaned over and kissed her.

'That's great, thanks.' She yawned and stretched. 'My poor muscles. I feel like I had a full-on arm day at the gym.'

'I'm not surprised with what you ended up doing.'

She sighed. 'I didn't like trying to climb back up the cliff with the water pouring down. I nearly didn't make it.'

'Are you sure you're happy to go back down today?' Brad asked.

'I'm not,' she replied. 'Vincent and Ellie are going to load the cradle while I stay up top and supervise like a conductor.'

He grinned. 'That sounds safer.'

* * *

Later that day the team at the dig prepared to winch up the first cradle containing the skull and some of the other pieces. Vincent, who was in charge of loading the bones, had decided they'd do it in two loads as their window for filming was rapidly closing. They had the remaining few hours of the afternoon session and potentially a full day following before they needed to clear everything away and close down the site.

The session had gone well. Although the previous day's rain had been heavy, it hadn't been prolonged, so it had run off and not soaked into the field.

Jemma stood with Jackson in the production tent and watched the live feed that came from Trevor's camera fifty feet below them. 'I'm a bit lost up here,' she said. 'It's frustrating watching Vincent and Ellie working on the cliffs while I'm winch man.'

'Don't worry Jemma. If you feel up to it and it stays dry then maybe you can go back down tomorrow and we can get some more film in the can.'

She listened to the voices in her earpiece. 'Yes, OK, we're ready to lift. I'll tell you when you can operate the winch, Jackson. I'll lean over and guide the rope as the cradle comes up.'

'Right,' he replied. 'Just shout when I need to press the button.'

Jemma stood by the apparatus that had been erected to keep the rope away from the edge of the rocks and peered over.

Jackson smiled. 'The old Jemma wouldn't have done that.'

'I'm a lot braver these days,' she said into her head mic. 'All good to go down there?'

'Send her up,' Vincent replied.

'OK, Jackson, winch on,' she said.

He pressed the button and the cradle started inching up the cliff, the rope straining under the load.

Jemma touched the rope. 'I think the cradle's too full. The rope is really tight.'

All went well as the cradle neared the top but, just as she thought it would reach them smoothly, they heard an ominous crack and the bar holding the rope to the top of the cradle bent away from the rest of the structure. With a lurch, it dropped back down the cliff towards the three people hanging helplessly below.

Jemma waved her arms and yelled over the edge. 'Watch out.'

Chapter 20

At three-thirty the following morning, a hooded figure wearing a dark coat picked its way down the rough track towards the dig site. As the thin torch beam danced on the gravel, a tawny owl hooted in the distance as the waves broke noisily on the beach below. A break in the clouds allowed the moon to shine through and momentarily illuminate the scene. In the brief brightness there was the flash of a knife and then the figure shrank back into the shadows until the moonlight disappeared and the darkness returned.

Ten minutes later, the light bobbed back along the track from the cliffs and the dig site returned to being occupied by wary rabbits, who would never sense the approach of the owl's talons until it was too late.

* * *

Jackson and Trevor were first on site at five-thirty and they stood, hands in pockets, staring out to sea as the sky gradually brightened from the east.

'Thanks for coming down so early, Trev. I need some more

shots of the partially dug-out cliffs, but without the ropes and diggers.'

'No problem, mate. If you move the ropes out of the way, I'll fire up the drone and get it airborne.'

Jackson pulled up the four ropes one by one and coiled them on top of the green tarpaulin. He then dragged up the rest of the cover so that it wasn't hanging over the edge. As he did, some stones that were underneath it came loose and hurtled down to the beach below.

Trevor grinned. 'I can see why they suggested having that. I wouldn't like being showered with rocks.'

Jackson grimaced. 'After yesterday's accident with the cradle I don't want any dented skulls.'

'Yeah, it was a bit frightening down there seeing it drop when we were hanging beneath it,' Trevor said. 'I'm just glad everyone was OK.'

Jackson shook his head. 'My heart was in my mouth when the top bar gave way. We're lucky the one at the bottom was stronger and held by two heavy-duty ropes.'

The cameraman nodded. 'Tina got some brilliant drone shots of the moment the bar came away and the whole thing dropped six feet. It will add to the drama of the programme.'

'Yes,' Jackson agreed, 'although I reckon I aged ten years watching it. We need an uneventful last day of filming today, please, no more drama.' He checked his watch. 'I'm hopeful we can be finished within a few hours if the cradle repairs hold out.'

Trevor watched the screen as Jackson explained the exact shots he wanted. After fifteen minutes of shooting, Trevor brought the drone back in while Jackson threw the ropes back out over the cliff before replacing the green cover over the top.

'Thanks, Trev, that's great. We'll be ready to start shooting again when the others come back at eight-thirty. The welder promised he'd have the cradle repaired and returned for nine.'

Trevor started the generator and connected the drone to

the charging cable. 'The forecast for today is fine so there's nothing to stop us getting the filming wrapped up by lunchtime.'

'I don't like statements like that.' Jackson frowned. 'Asking for an easy day is just begging for trouble.'

'OK, I'll shut up.' Trevor spotted Jemma and Ellie walking towards them. 'Here come the stars of the show.'

* * *

The wind had dropped overnight and the sea was like a millpond as Jemma and Ellie approached the production tent on the clifftop. The fluorescent orange of the tent made it stand out like a beacon.

Jemma pointed at it. 'I thought Jackson wanted the dig to be low-key so we weren't bothered by curious bystanders.'

'Oh well, Mum,' Ellie replied, 'it's the last day today and so far we've only had a few coastal walkers stopping to see what's going on.'

Jemma nodded. 'Have you enjoyed the filming this time?'

Her daughter rubbed her upper arms. 'To be honest, not as much. It's hard doing all the digging while hanging on a rope, especially when you've got a tough climb at the end of the session. Yesterday was a bit scary as well.'

Jemma massaged her own neck. 'Tell me about it. You're way younger and fitter than me.'

Just then a quad bike with a trailer came bouncing down the track.

'Here's the patched-up version,' Jackson said.

The bike stopped and a man wearing dark blue overalls jumped off and shook Jackson's hand. Together they lifted the cradle over to the edge of the cliff.

Jemma checked it over. 'That seems OK. You've done a good job. Thanks.'

The man nodded, gave Jackson his invoice and drove away.

As Vincent reattached the cradle ropes, the others put on their harnesses, donned their hard hats and clipped themselves onto their lifelines.

'I'll go first,' Trevor said. 'Jackson wants a shot of the three of you abseiling down at the same time, bouncing in sync like the guys descending the building at the end of The Blues Brothers.'

Ellie frowned. 'You what?'

'Before your time,' Jemma remarked.

Trevor descended and a few minutes later announced he was in place and ready for their action shot.

Jemma waved her arms with a flourish. 'Off we go for the last time.'

The three diggers abseiled together, bouncing down in a perfectly synchronised display.

Jemma cheered when they reached the digging area. 'How's that, Trevor? That was amazing.'

The cameraman was fiddling with his equipment. 'Oh, sorry. I forgot to press record. Can you go back up and do it again?'

Jemma spluttered. 'What?'

'Ha ha!' He grinned 'Just joking.'

Ellie was overcome with giggling and swung out from the cliff holding her sides. 'Nice one, Trev.'

Vincent frowned. 'Can we get on with this and stop messing around, please?'

'Lighten up, Vincent,' Jemma said. 'We don't want any long faces at the end of filming today. I've got a bottle of Prosecco in my bag to celebrate.'

'I won't be drinking, I just want to get finished and go home,' he replied.

'Don't be so grumpy. I thought you'd be enjoying this,' Jemma said.

Vincent reached for his rope. 'Well, you thought wrong.'

What remained of loading up the fossil went well, and the final body and tail section of the ichthyosaur was soon ready to be winched up to the team above. Jemma checked the bones were secure and Vincent shook the cradle.

'It all looks good,' he said.

Jemma held up her thumb. 'OK, start winching it up.'

The sled moved up a couple of metres, but the newly welded top bar protruded slightly and became wedged against a rock.

'Can you give it a shove to free it please, Vincent?' Jemma asked.

He pushed himself away from the cliff and gave the cradle a shove, which freed it from the obstruction, and it continued moving upwards. As he swung back into position there was a loud crack as his rope snapped and he hurtled all the way down to the beach, landing with a sickening thud on the rocks below.

Chapter 21

Ellie screamed and hung next to the cliffs where she stared down at the rocks below.

Jemma shouted into her mouthpiece. 'Emergency! Vincent's fallen. His rope snapped.'

There was a moment's pause before Jackson finally spoke. 'Can you all try sitting on the ledge you've dug out while we check the other ropes?'

Jemma wedged herself on the narrow ledge and heaved her daughter beside her. They were soon joined by Trevor who looked as though all the blood had drained from his face.

'I was filming him when he fell,' he croaked. 'What if one of *our* ropes snaps as well?'

'We're OK sitting here while they check,' Jemma glared at him. 'Let's just all get back up safely. You alright, Els?'

Her daughter was huddled on the shelf, shivering. 'I think so.'

Jemma glanced down to where, at the base of the cliffs, Vincent's body was being buffeted by the waves as it bobbed against the rocks. She looked away quickly. 'Can we have an update please, Jackson? Urgently.'

'Right,' the radio crackled, 'I want you and Ellie to come

straight back, please. Hold tight and the tractor will pull you up. Trevor, stay on the ledge and do not put any weight on your rope. There's some damage to it up here so we'll get the girls to safety while we sort out a new one for you. An ambulance is on its way.'

'Bloody hell,' the cameraman replied. 'Is it as bad as Vincent's?'

'Unknown at the moment, Trev. Try lying along the ledge once Jemma and Ellie have come up.'

Trevor clenched his fist. 'OK.'

'Jemma, Ellie. The rope will start coming up in three, two, one.'

From somewhere just over the lip, the tractor revved and Jemma and Ellie ascended effortlessly. As they reached the top they heard Jackson shout, 'stop! We'll help you over the edge.' Several arms reached out to grab them and they were quickly pulled up to the safety of the meadow where they knelt on the grass and hugged each other.

Jackson was already there. 'Quick Ellie, unbuckle please so we can send your rope back down to Trev.'

Jemma helped her shaking daughter unclip herself and then her rope was lowered back down to the stricken cameraman. Within a few minutes, he'd rejoined the team at the top.

Jemma hugged him. 'That was awful. Are you OK, Trevor?'

'I am now,' he replied, 'but it's a bit late for Vincent.'

'What happened?' Jemma asked.

'Come and look.' Jackson jerked a thumb towards the back of one of the tractors where a green tarpaulin was covering the towing bracket attached to the ropes. He slowly lifted the cover and she gasped.

'The rope's been cut.'

He grimaced. 'Looks like it. The one Trevor was using had been partially cut through as well but that one didn't give way.'

'Who'd do a bloody thing like that?' Jemma asked.

'No idea, but the police are on their way. I told them it appeared deliberate, but they want to check it out for themselves before sending in a forensic team.'

Jemma gazed towards the cliff edge. 'What about Vincent?'

Jackson touched her arm. 'I called the coastguard as well and someone is on their way to retrieve his body.'

'Oh no,' she said, 'I can't believe Vincent was beside me one minute and the next he was down there in the water. This is awful.'

Jackson frowned. 'I can't see the show surviving this. The insurers were nervous enough about working on the cliffs after the explosion in the first programme, and then finding your grandfather's bones on the Isle of Wight.'

'Just when everything was going so well.' Ellie hugged her mother. 'Does Vincent have any family?'

Jemma thought for a moment. 'He has a daughter in London but he didn't mention her very often. Someone will need to contact her.'

'Don't worry, I'm sure the police will sort it out,' Jackson said.

A young, uniformed policeman strode towards them. 'Good day. Is this the scene of the accident?'

'I'm afraid so, Constable. The victim is Vincent Lawrence from Lulcombe.' Jackson flinched. 'His body is at the bottom of the cliffs down there. The coastguards are on their way to retrieve it.'

The PC removed his notepad from his pocket. 'I need all of your names and addresses, please, and I'll take brief statements before the others arrive.'

As they gave the young constable more details an ambulance arrived and two paramedics rushed down towards the group. The police officer updated them and, after they'd been reassured that nobody else had been injured, the ambulance team left.

'Show me the spot where the rope snapped,' the PC said. 'Everybody else stay back. This could be a crime scene.' Using a stick, he lifted the cover and peered at the damaged ropes, one still attached by a few strands. He allowed the cover to fall back. 'Who else has touched these?'

'Well, since the incident, only me,' Jackson replied. 'Beforehand I don't know as Vincent was in charge of all the ropes.'

The constable spoke into his radio. 'PC Andrews to base. Morning, Sarge. We need some detectives and a forensic team to Lulcombe West Cliffs. The turning is half a mile west of the town on Seaton Road. It appears two ropes have been deliberately cut, one of which broke, leading to a Vincent Lawrence falling to his death. The coastguard is on his way to rescue the body as the tide is high and the beach inaccessible. I'll secure the scene and keep everybody away.'

While a scene developed, Jemma sat with Ellie on folding chairs, both in a state of shock. 'I'd better let Brad know.' Jemma fumbled for her mobile. 'I'm glad the high tide meant he wasn't down on the beach today with the kids. They were watching during the first day. Imagine if they'd seen Vincent fall.'

* * *

Detective Sergeant Amrik Hussain was sitting at his desk when the phone rang.

'Hi, Sarge, what's up?' He checked his watch and thought about the massage he had booked for that afternoon. 'I'm due off at two so I hope this isn't anything complicated.'

'Hard luck, mate, you'd better cancel any plans for later. We've had reports of a sixty-four-year-old local man falling to his death after an accident on the cliffs at Lulcombe.'

‘Why do *we* need to attend?’ Amrik replied. ‘Isn’t this a job for the uniforms?’

‘Well, young Darren Andrews is at the scene and he says there’s evidence of foul play. Somebody nobbled the ropes of a filming team on the clifftop.’

Amrik shifted in his seat, making the leather squeak. ‘A filming team? What were they shooting?’

‘Some documentary about finding a fossil in the cliffs.’

‘Let me guess the programme...’ Amrik sighed down the line, ‘it’s *The Rock Detectives*, isn’t it?’

‘You should be a detective...oh, you are. Good guess. Yes, it was the latest episode.’

‘And you know who’s involved with the show, don’t you, Sarge?’

‘Not Jurassic Jemma, by any chance?’

‘Got it in one. Jurassic Jemma Thorne! She’s bloody lethal to be around.’

Chapter 22

Jemma and Ellie were sitting with thermal blankets wrapped around their shoulders, watching as an SUV parked by the road near the entrance to the clifftop site. A man and woman climbed out and set off along the track towards them.

Jemma smiled thinly. 'I recognise one of the police team. Have you seen who it is?'

Ellie jumped up and rushed over to embrace Amrik.

'Hi, Ellie.' His cheeks reddened as the hug stayed in place longer than usual. 'I'm glad you and your mum are OK.'

She let him go. 'It was horrible. One minute he was there, then there was a crack and he disappeared downwards. He didn't even have time to scream.'

He gave Jemma a more subdued hug. 'Hi, Jemma.'

'Hi, Amrik,' she replied.

Amrik had a special relationship with them both. When Jemma had been wrongly accused of the murder of her colleague, Sally O'Keefe, he'd been her staunchest supporter and the only member of the police team who'd believed in her innocence. His help had led to Jemma's release and both she and Ellie were intensely grateful.

He gestured to his colleague. 'This is DC Salmon.'

'Hi, Jemma. Ellie.' Alongside Amrik the young detective appeared very petite with short blond hair in a spiky cut. 'Call me Hannah.'

Amrik asked Jemma and Ellie for their full statements and moved on to Jackson, Trevor and the other members of the film crew. He requested a copy of Trevor's recording before gathering the whole team together. He pulled up a folding chair and sat beside the group. 'Do any of you have any idea who might have had a reason to kill Vincent and Trevor?'

Jemma rubbed her eyes. 'It's illogical. Other than the programme they had no connection.'

Jackson touched his chin. 'What if they weren't the targets? What if somebody wanted to kill Jemma and Ellie?'

Jemma's eyes widened. 'What? Why?'

'When I arrived this morning, I moved all of the ropes so we could get some shots of the cliffs without them hanging in the way,' he said. 'It's possible I could have laid them back out in a different order.'

'Did you leave them out every night?' Amrik asked.

'No,' Jackson replied. 'Vincent suggested we leave them out last night as we had to finish today and it would save some time when we started.'

Jemma shot Amrik a look. 'Why would somebody want to kill us? I thought all that crap had finished with the deaths of Zak and Gary Richards – or Fletcher – or whoever they were.'

Amrik wrote some extra notes on his pad. 'We've already put out an alert with the ports and airports in case Helen tries to return to the UK. She was the person behind what happened last year with her sons so maybe she used one of her criminal contacts to cut the ropes.'

'Oh, great,' Jemma groaned into her hands.

Ellie frowned. 'But how would anybody know they were being left in place overnight? Every night so far they've been packed away and taken home by Vincent. It was only a last-minute decision when we finished yesterday to leave them all out and connected to the tractors.'

Amrik glanced at Jemma. 'Do you trust Vincent?'

Jemma went pale. 'Well, I suppose you did find those messages from him on Reggie Fletcher's phone after he and his brother tried to kill me.'

'Yes,' Amrik replied, 'but he explained they'd contacted him in connection with their offer to buy the museum site.'

'But what if he was still involved with the family somehow?'

Amrik pursed his lips. 'You mean working for Helen? It seems unlikely but we'll do some delving into Vincent's background to see why anybody might want to kill him, or for that matter you and Ellie.'

'I wonder if he knew the ropes had been nobbled and didn't realise they'd been swapped around,' Jemma said.

Ellie touched her arm. 'But you've known Vincent for such a long time.'

'You never know, Ellie. You just never know.'

* * *

The heat had started subsiding after a magnificent sunset over the mountains to the west, and now Helen and Malek were sitting on the terrace of her villa drinking beer. Despite the darkness, the cicadas continued their incessant rhythm and several fireflies zipped around the garden like miniature fireworks. The smell of the pine forest that had filled the air all day had been replaced by the sickly-sweet fragrance of a night flowering jasmine.

'What time is your cousin due?' Helen asked.

Malek checked his watch. 'He said he'd be here by eight and it's five minutes past now.'

As he spoke, a decrepit white van pulled onto the drive and a short dark-haired man with a moustache stepped out. Malek strolled over to him and they embraced.

'Merhaba, Malek,' Ozlem said.

'Merhaba, Ozlem.' Malek replied. 'In English, please, for Helen.'

'Oh, hello, Helen. Are you well?'

'Yes, thank you. Would you like a glass of wine?'

'Yes, please,' the man replied, 'but only a small one. Police!' He spat.

Helen smirked at Malek. 'The usual for me please, darling.'

Malek disappeared into the villa and returned a few moments later with a glass of red wine for Ozlem and a G and T for Helen. He handed them around and they sat either side of Helen.

She sipped her drink and smiled at the boat captain. 'I hope you have some good news for me.'

'Oh, yes, Mrs Helen.' He wrung his hands. 'I can supply what you need.'

'Just Helen, please. Mrs Helen makes me sound old. OK, tell me your plans.'

He plucked a piece of paper from his shirt pocket, unfolded it and used his hand to smooth it out on the patio table. 'My boat is called the *Goke*. It is named after an Ottoman galleon of the fifteenth century.'

She yawned and checked her mobile.

Ozlem frowned. 'It is eighteen metres with two cabins and basic quarters for twelve. It is three thousand, two hundred nautical miles to the south of England. If we cruise at eight to nine knots, we will arrive in around nineteen days.'

Helen typed into her phone, her long red nails tapping against the screen. 'Let's go for the quickest way of getting there.'

'We need to stop at Cartagena in Spain to refuel, take on

fresh water and supplies, and for the crew to have some time ashore.'

She peered at a map on her phone. 'Will we be able to go ashore?'

'Malek will as a registered crew member, but not you. He said you have a...dodgy passport. Safer not to enter EU.'

'Right.' Her finger hovered over the screen. 'What is your price?'

'The total cost including wages, fuel and food will be ninety-five thousand euros and I get to keep any fish we catch.'

She sipped her gin and tonic. 'Won't it slow us down if you have your fishing nets out?'

'Yes, we can only do four knots whilst using them or else the mouth of the net will close.'

She stared at him. 'In that case, no fishing on the way. How much extra?'

'That would make the price one hundred and twenty five thousand.'

'That's fine.' Helen flapped a hand. 'You can also add ten thousand euros for each day you take off your estimate.'

'OK. Fast it is.' Ozlem wiped sweat from his forehead. 'The price includes up to two weeks of waiting time and a crew of four. That number keeps the cost down and helps with the...how do you say in English...secret keeping.'

'Discretion is very important,' Helen said. 'Do you trust your men?'

'Yes,' he replied. 'The four I've chosen are old friends.' He grinned. 'With such a small team, I may have to call upon Malek for help at times.'

Malek straightened in his chair. 'But my hands have gone soft. I don't want blisters.'

She glared at him. 'I'm sure he'll be happy to do whatever is needed to help with my project. Blisters or no blisters.'

Ozlem glanced at Malek and smiled. 'So, Helen, we have a deal?' He held out his hand and she shook it.

'We have a deal.'

'I'll need fifty thousand euros in advance and the balance when we return, whether we have acquired your...' he chuckled, 'cargo or not.'

She stared at him. 'Oh, don't worry. I'll acquire my cargo. Now, when do we leave?'

Chapter 23

Interview room one had not improved since Jemma had last been there the previous year.

This time, though, she was giving a formal statement as a witness rather than a murder suspect. It was a grey room without a window and had an annoying neon light fitting that flickered noisily. The wall had a mirror that Jemma suspected was two-way, so that other detectives could observe interviews. In front of it sat a rectangular wooden table with two chairs on one side and one on the other, all in seventies orange.

Jemma shivered as she remembered the ordeal of being framed by Gary and Zak Fletcher. It didn't help that one of the people involved in framing her was a serving police officer connected with the investigation and questioning. Gary did his best to discredit everything she'd said and emphasised the importance of her being found covered in Sally's blood after discovering the body and checking for a pulse.

As she attempted to recall the details leading up to Vincent's fall, a tear formed in her eye. She rubbed it away and continued to answer Amrik's questions. After half an hour he closed his file and stopped the recording.

'Thanks for that, Jemma,' he said. 'It must have been difficult after what you went through last year. Would you like to sit in reception and have a coffee while I take Ellie's statement?'

'I think I'll go outside and get some fresh air. This room has memories as bad as the smells.'

Amrik grimaced. 'I'm sure these rooms are designed to be deliberately grotty to make suspects feel uncomfortable. We need to sort out a better room for witnesses to give their statements.' He led Jemma out to reception where Ellie was flicking through a magazine.

She glanced up at her mother. 'Ordeal over?'

'Yeah. It wasn't too bad. It's just that I had flashbacks to being arrested and questioned by that bastard Gary.'

'Oh, right. It's my turn now, is it? Wish me luck.'

Ellie stood and followed Amrik back into the corridor where they disappeared. Finding herself alone, Jemma stepped outside before wandering across the carpark and perching on a wall in the shade of a huge oak tree. It seemed out of place amongst the concrete buildings and carparks of the industrial estate that housed the Police HQ.

After a while, she gazed up into the branches. 'You did well to survive the planning process, didn't you? Oh my God, I'm chatting to a tree now.'

Luckily there was nobody around to witness her descent into madness other than a lone buzzard circling high in the sky, its plaintive call piercing the background traffic noise.

She stared skywards. 'I wish I was up there flying with you.'

'It must have been pretty bad if you're talking to the birds?' A voice from behind startled her.

Jemma jumped down from the wall. 'If you'd have come out a few minutes earlier I was having a one-sided conversation with this lovely old tree.' She smiled at Ellie. 'You were quick in there.'

'Amrik had already got what he needed so he just wanted

to make sure my version of events agreed with yours. At least we both have an alibi for the couple of hours before we started filming.'

Jemma took out her car keys. 'Come on then, let's get home and have showers. I just want to forget what happened this morning.'

'Good luck with that. Brad will want the whole story.'

'Amrik was hopeful they might be able to locate some CCTV or doorcam footage from one of the houses opposite the track down to the cliffs.'

'I hope he does. By the way, why didn't Vincent join the film crew for breakfast this morning?'

Jemma thought for a moment. 'He said he had to take Monty out for a walk and a meeting for breakfast at six was too early for him. He said he'd come down at eight instead.'

Ellie's eyes widened. 'Oh, no. Monty. He'll have been locked inside Vincent's bungalow all day. Do we need to let him out?'

'Don't worry. I told Amrik and he was going to ask one of the uniforms to pop over with Vincent's keys, which they found in his rucksack. They'll pass him over to the animal welfare folks. They're going to send in a forensic team to search for clues about who might have wanted to kill him.'

Ellie touched her arm. 'Or why somebody might want to kill us.'

Jemma swallowed. 'I don't know what to think, Ellie. I trusted Vincent, but maybe he was in Helen's pocket and needed some extra money.'

Ellie hugged her. 'It seems so unreal. You've known him for years.'

'Try not to worry, Els,' Jemma said, 'the police will get to the bottom of it and find out what's going on.'

'I'm starting to worry again, Mum. What with the Zak thing, I haven't been sleeping well for a while, and now Vincent's accident... I know Kira wakes me up most nights but then I just lie there with horrible thoughts running through my head.'

'Do you need something from the doctor?' Jemma asked. 'To help you sleep a bit. We could look after Kira for a few nights.'

'No,' Ellie replied. 'I don't want to go down that road. I need to be able to wake up for her. I just want to stop seeing Vincent down there on the rocks.'

'It'll fade with time, Els. These things do, eventually.'

* * *

Fifteen hundred miles away in the harbour at Kyrenia, Northern Cyprus, a fishing trawler was gently rocking at its moorings when a black Land Cruiser pulled up alongside the narrow aluminium gangplank that sloped down towards the quayside.

Helen Fletcher stepped out of the vehicle and opened the tailgate. She scanned her surroundings before removing two suitcases and a child's car seat. Malek joined her and she pointed at the boat. 'You get these loaded and I'll park the car.'

The harbour was undergoing a massive restoration project, and towers of stone and red bricks were piled around the edge. Some roads were closed and the general mayhem of construction had kept many tourists as well as the nicer yachts away.

Helen left the car in a long stay carpark and paid for a six week stay. She grabbed her carry-on case and a large floppy white hat before crossing the road to where the *Goke* was moored.

Malek was standing at the top of the gangplank. 'Quickly. The fewer people who see you leave the better.'

She stamped on the solid ground for the last time and strode up the plank with the aluminium ringing to the sound of the heels of her dark blue court shoes.

Ozlem walked up behind Malek. 'Welcome to my boat. The only rule I have is that if I ask you to return to your cabin and stay off the deck, you do so, please, for your own safety. This will be your home for the next few weeks so make yourself as comfortable as you can.'

She glanced around and sneered. 'I'm not sure about *comfortable* but it'll have to do.'

Ozlem shrugged. 'She may not be luxury but she can cope with anything thrown at us by the Bay of Biscay.'

Malek frowned. 'That sounds worrying.'

'Oh, yes, I remember when you worked for me.' Ozlem sniggered. 'I have some seasickness tablets if it gets too rough. If you want to get to the destination quickly then we have to steer straight through any bad weather rather than go around.'

Helen narrowed her eyes. 'I just want to get there as quickly as possible, whatever the weather.'

Ozlem pointed up the stairs. 'Come with me to the bridge and I show you the course we take.'

They followed him up the steps and into the control room. As Helen squinted against the sun streaming in through the large panoramic windows, there seemed to be a bewildering array of electronic displays and controls.

Helen peered into a green screen. 'What is that?'

Ozlem zoomed in on the display. 'This is depth. Very important when fishing, but not when cruising at full speed away from the coast.' He went on to show them the radar, GPS, course setting display and a range of other gauges he felt were relevant.

She turned to a chart fixed to the wall behind them. 'Which way do we go?'

He pointed to the north-western tip of Cyprus. 'We depart Kyrenia tonight at nine, pass south of Crete and head towards Italy. Then we sail south west and go past Sicily and Sardinia on our way to Cartagena. After we leave the port, we pass Strait of Gibraltar, head up the coast of Portugal and

Spain before crossing Bay of Biscay. We then steer around Brittany and up English Channel to Brixham.'

'That sounds good. What about the weather, will it slow us down at all?'

Ozlem shrugged. 'It will be fine for a fishing trawler but not for a pleasure cruise. This is an old boat without stabilisers so it will rock and roll, but it's very safe.'

Heavy footsteps echoed up the gangplank, prompting Ozlem to check his watch. 'That is the crew. I allowed them one last meal in restaurant before we start eating food cooked by Tengiz.' He stepped through the bridge door. 'Let me introduce them to you.'

A tall, skinny man with a full moustache came forward. He embraced Malek and shook hands with Helen. 'I am Burak. Nice to meet you and help you with your search.'

She glanced at Ozlem and scowled. 'They know?'

He stared back at her. 'This is a small boat. They have to know about your rescue plans, and family is everything to these men.' He pointed to another man. 'This is Emree. The three of us will be sharing the navigation and sailing.'

Emree was a shorter man who wore a black baseball cap with the word *Galatasary SK* emblazoned on the front. His smile was warm as he greeted Malek.

The final man was large with a bald head and the underarms of his white t-shirt were stained yellow from sweat. He stumbled as he approached them, prompting Ozlem to fire off a stream of Turkish as he thrashed his arms about his head. The man stared down into the planks.

Ozlem caught Helen's eye. 'This is cook, Tengiz. We have to watch him. He likes the drink too much. He is good cook though.'

Tengiz sidled up to Helen and, as she extended her hand, he pulled it to his lips and kissed the back. He smiled with a sneer. 'Good to meet beautiful lady.'

She yanked her hand back, wiped it on her trousers and glared at the man. 'Helen will do.'

The cook bowed and turned back down the steps. Ozlem stared after him. 'Don't mind him. He has some...faults but he makes a good kofte.' He jerked his head towards Malek and laughed. 'And, of course, you already know the final member of our crew. Don't worry, I'll work him hard.'

She patted Malek's shorts-clad rear. 'Don't tire him out too much, will you? He does things for me, too.'

Ozlem grinned and made a rude gesture, gripping his upper arm and lifting his clenched fist. 'Just don't break my bunk, will you?' He checked his watch. 'The tide is good in half an hour so we go then.'

She held Malek's hand. 'OK, let's go.'

Chapter 24

A few days later, Jemma finished packing her case for the upcoming trip to meet her in-laws.

Ellie shouted up the stairs. 'How many bikinis are you taking Mum?'

Jemma leant out of the room. 'Just a couple and one swimsuit. I've got plenty of suncream as well.'

The cottage bedroom was small and on one side the beams were so low that Brad had to be careful when he opened the wardrobe. The tiny window only let in a small amount of daylight so Jemma had painted the walls light blue to help brighten it.

Ellie came upstairs. 'Are you looking forward to meeting Brad's parents?'

She bit her lip. 'Yes, I think so. I was a bit annoyed they wouldn't fly over for the wedding or to meet their grandchildren but they've paid for our flights so it means we can all go.'

Ellie sat on the bed next to the case. 'Brad never seems to talk about them much, does he?'

Jemma sat beside her. 'No, I suppose not. I get the feeling he's never been that close to them.'

'It must be nice to earn your own money but still have

family wealth behind you. He's been really generous with me, helping out financially so I don't have to work and can spend time with Kira. It's so lovely to be with her as she develops day to day. It would be devastating if I had to spend any precious time away from her.'

'Sure is. When I was your age I had two jobs and relied on Mum and Dad to look after you. It wasn't as easy when they moved out to Spain but at least you were older by then.'

'That seems a long time ago.'

Jemma gazed down at the t-shirt she was holding and folded it absent-mindedly. 'It certainly does.'

Ellie started trying on the bikinis she planned taking and twirled around in a red set that was more string than bikini. 'Is this too revealing?'

Jemma feigned shock. 'I wondered where all the dental floss had gone.'

Ellie raised her eyebrows. 'Too much?'

Jemma shook her head. 'No, it suits you. I'm only jealous of how soon you got your figure back after having Kira. I never got mine back after I had you all those years ago.'

'You can't blame me for that.'

'I suppose not.' She closed the suitcase lid. 'At least this shuts.'

'I hope you're leaving lots of space in case we go shopping in Miami.'

'You'll be lucky. I bet it's two hours up to Miami and I'm guessing there aren't many shops in Marathon.'

'Don't worry, Mum, I'll find some.'

* * *

An hour later, Jackson Carter rang Jemma's mobile.

'Hi, Jemma. You OK?' He sighed. 'I come bearing bad news.'

'Oh,' she replied. 'Fire away.'

'I'm afraid the TV company has pulled the plug on *The Rock Detectives*. The insurers won't cover any more filming, so that's it.'

'I'm getting sick of all this. We've had some terrible luck,' she said.

'The combination of an explosion and an injured cameraman in the first series, then discovering your grandfather's skeleton, Vincent's death and a close call with Trevor during this series is all too much.'

Jemma's eyes flicked up. 'Are they going to edit and show the episodes we've just filmed?'

'We're not sure yet. There's probably enough in the can for what we need but we'd have to film a follow-up piece showing what you found. I think they first want to check with Vincent's family to see if they have any objections. Do you know who they are?'

'I know he had a daughter, but I don't think they were close. The last I heard Amrik had contacted her with the bad news.'

'If the family agree then we could add a dedication to Vincent, a quick résumé of his life, that sort of thing,' he added. 'Sorry, Jem, I've never known a TV series to be this jinxed.'

'I'm used to it,' Jemma sighed. 'Everything I touch seems to go wrong.'

* * *

Dusk was falling as the non-descript fishing trawler chugged into the harbour at Cartagena. Helen, wearing a dark blue baseball cap and sunglasses, stood alongside Malek and Ozlem as he steered the vessel past the long concrete embankment that protected the port.

Ozlem pointed to the right. 'That is the Bāleria de San Leandro. How do you say in English...a gun battery?'

'No need for the history lesson,' she snapped. 'Let's get in and out as quickly as we can.'

The captain shrugged. 'I thought after four days of sea you would want to see something interesting.'

She glared at Malek. 'I'm fed up of watching this one kneeling down over the toilet spewing his guts up.'

Malek frowned. 'I ate something bad.'

'OK. We head for the fishing boat section.' Ozlem turned the trawler to starboard before swinging it back around to port. 'Helen, can you stay down while we go past the big cruise ship? Lots of passengers like to video other boats going by.'

The trawler moved past an enormous cruise ship docked at the terminal before heading for the commercial part in the north-western corner. Heaps of damaged fishing nets and rusted equipment gave the place a dismal feel. Many of the moored boats had seen better days and their dilapidated state reflected the tough conditions and meagre returns of modern commercial fishing.

A burst of Spanish came over the radio and Ozlem answered.

Malek grinned. 'I didn't know you spoke Spanish.'

'I know enough to cope in a Spanish port,' Ozlem said.

'What did they want?' Helen demanded.

'They asked if we want fuel, water or ice. I asked for all three. We don't need any ice, but it would be strange to not have any. I also logged that five Turkish crew members would go ashore for four hours.'

She spun around and glared at him. 'Four hours! Can't we leave sooner than that?'

'No. Me and the men need a rest and a meal ashore. We've been on full ten-hour shifts.' He grinned. 'And Tengiz likes to visit the local massage parlour, if you know what I mean.'

'The dirty bleeder,' she mumbled.

'He is a man, and we all hear the noises from *your* cabin. It is better if he spends some time with a lady on shore.'

She shook her head. 'Did you mention a woman going ashore as well?'

Ozlem's eyebrows dipped. 'No, why?'

'Because I want to go as well.'

'Oh no, that is too risky. They check the passports of everybody who enters Spain.'

'But I've got some others with different names.'

'I don't want any of your bad passports linked with the *Goke*. I am captain and you don't go ashore.'

Helen slammed her fist against the edge of the control panel. 'I'm paying your wages and I'm going ashore.'

Malek took Helen's hand. 'Come with me.' They left the bridge and stood on the deck out of sight of land. 'Please listen. If Ozlem tells you to remain on the boat, then it is because he thinks it is not safe for you to go off. I can go and buy anything you want.'

She clenched her fists. 'This is my journey. I'm paying the bills and I won't be dictated to by some bloody Turk!' Her face softened slightly. 'No offence intended.'

He shrugged. 'None taken.'

She took a deep breath and sighed. 'OK. I suppose he knows the workings of a port better than I do. I'll make a list of things I need.'

Malek stepped back onto the bridge followed by the red-faced woman with a scowl on her face. 'Helen is happy to stay on board. I'll get some things for her.'

'That is good,' Ozlem said. 'Would you go below, Helen, while we moor the boat in case they want to board us to check the mesh size of the nets?'

She harrumphed, turned, stamped out of the bridge and down to her cabin.

Thirty minutes later, the crew members and Malek left the *Goke* and were walking along the planks laughing as they headed towards the quayside bars. After giving Malek a list of things to buy, including gin and cigarettes, Helen had returned to the cabin alone to fume.

After two hours sitting in her tiny room scrolling through her phone, she threw it on her bunk, grabbed her cigarettes and stepped out onto the deck. Pulling a baseball cap over her forehead, she strolled around the edge of the ship. The empty gangway leading to the quay looked so tempting that she checked for any locals and stepped up onto the solid ground. Even though the pier was concrete she swayed as she stood surveying her surroundings.

'Bloody boats. Why am I swaying?' She flicked her cigarette over the side. 'I'm off for a walk.'

Before she could take a single step, heavy boots came stamping back along the pier so she turned and rushed back to the ship and hid on the bridge. As she waited in the shadows the thuds persisted until they reached the gangplank then, as she dared not look through the window, they trudged all the way to the ship before stepping on deck.

Reaching down inside her long leather boot, Helen withdrew a nine-inch stiletto blade.

The bridge door rattled as she leant back into the coats hanging on the wall. As the door slowly slid open she silently raised the knife and poised to plunge forwards. The door hit the stop and someone stepped onto the bridge.

Helen could smell whisky on the intruder's breath, making her gag. 'Tengiz. Bloody hell. What are you doing back?'

The slimy cook jumped as if scalded. 'Mrs Helen. I just came to check the weather for later tonight. Ozlem will be back in an hour but I met with a young lady and I am...' he searched for the word, 'very sleepy.' He stepped back through the open door and headed along the deck before turning to glance over his shoulder. ‘If Malek fails to be a man for you, I am here.’ He continued to leer and performed a string of pelvic thrusts as if auditioning for the *Rocky Horror Time Warp*. ‘I have just had some good practice, so I am ready for you if you need me.’

Helen slapped him across the face. ‘If you say anything like that or come anywhere near me again, you are a dead man.’

He stared at her with bulging eyes, rubbed his face and staggered back towards the crew quarters muttering something in Turkish.

Helen smiled and returned the knife to her boot.

Chapter 25

The Heathrow departures hall buzzed with activity as Brad, Jemma, Rocky, Ellie and Kira waited to check in, joining the queue for the kiosks in Zone C. The adults wheeled their cases, while Rocky stared with wide eyes at the hordes of rushing travellers and Kira clung to Ellie amidst the noise of the busy airport.

As they edged forwards, Brad's phone vibrated in his pocket.

'I think you have to turn that off when we go through security,' Jemma said.

He removed the phone and checked the display. 'Oh, it's Pop.' He moved behind a pillar to hear better. 'Hi, Pop. You good?'

'Hello, Brad, I'm fine, but I have some bad news, I'm afraid.'

'What's up?'

'You'll have to abort your trip. Your mom's been rushed into hospital.'

Brad gasped. 'Oh, crap. Is she OK?'

'I think so. They suspect it's appendicitis. She's being

operated on as we speak. The doctor said it's lucky she got in so quickly.'

'Shall we come over and help?'

'No. Can you postpone it for a while? She'd hate to miss seeing the kids. You can rearrange in a couple of months when she's feeling better. Don't worry about the flights. I'll pay for some fresh ones.'

'Right, Pop, whatever you say. We'd better not check in then. Give Mom my love and let me know how she gets on, please.'

'Will do, Brad. See ya.'

The call ended and Brad returned to the queue. 'Bad news, guys. The trip's off.'

* * *

At Swanbourne Police Station, Amrik was attempting to collate the information he'd retrieved from Vincent's phone.

DC Hannah Salmon had set up a large, white murder board on the wall and had added pictures of Vincent, Jemma, Ellie, Jackson Carter and Trevor the Cameraman, all linked with pins, string and copious yellow Post-its.

Amrik approached the board to appraise Hannah's work.

'Any joy with the mobile and email records?' she asked.

'Oh, yes. Once the tech guys had cracked the password, evidently "Monty" followed by "two zero one five," it was a goldmine of evidence.'

'Anything I need to add on here?'

'Well, we have a new suspect called Helen Fletcher, AKA Helen Barnes.'

She squinted. 'Who's she?'

Amrik turned away from the board. 'She's the psychopathic sister of the Fletcher Brothers and the mother of Zak and Gary Richards. Let's just say that Jemma isn't her favourite person. She's an old school gangster. A nasty piece of work.'

Hannah reached for her pile of cards. 'Did she cut the rope?'

'No, but she blackmailed Vincent into cutting the ropes that were due to be used by Jemma and Ellie Thorne.'

Her eyebrows lifted. 'So Vincent sabotaged it himself?'

'That's what I think happened.'

'What did she have on him to get him to cut the rope?' she asked.

'It's a bit unsavoury, I'm afraid,' he replied. 'I found a video she sent to Vincent of him in a hotel room with a young lady who appeared to be underage. They were at it like rabbits. The problem for Vincent was that it was being recorded for blackmail purposes.'

'The dirty paedo got what was coming to him then, didn't he?'

'I suppose so, but I don't think she was underage. I contacted the Cliff Hotel where I thought it might have been filmed.'

Hannah laughed. 'Good spotting.'

Amrik grimaced. 'I took a girlfriend there for a stay myself once. Cost me a fortune and she'd never take my calls afterwards. I remember the old-fashioned flock wallpaper. Anyway, the barman remembered the young lady in question as he'd delivered a bottle of champagne to the room. Before handing it over, he'd asked to see her ID, which showed she was twenty-one. So, as long as it was genuine, Vincent might have been blackmailed over nothing.'

Hannah ran a hand through her hair. 'But who paid for the hotel room?'

'No joy there. It was booked online in the name of Vincent Lawrence but paid for in cash when the girl arrived.'

Hannah gazed at the whiteboard and frowned. 'So you

think Vincent cut through the rope that he then used himself before falling to his death. Is that murder or suicide?'

Amrik rubbed his chin. 'I'm not totally sure. I don't think you can murder yourself so it could be death by misadventure but I need to chat it through with DI Day. She might have an answer.'

'So, Vincent intended to kill Jemma and Ellie after being blackmailed by Helen Fletcher.' She took a blank card and wrote *Helen Fletcher (Barnes)* on it before attaching it to Vincent's picture with a length of string. 'Have you told Jemma and Ellie Thorne?'

Amrik frowned. 'Not yet. They're in Florida and I don't want to ruin their holiday. Hopefully, they'll be safe there.'

'Is there enough evidence to arrest Helen Fletcher?'

'Ah, we have a slight problem there, Hannah.' He sat down. 'Let me explain to you about the Turkish Republic of Northern Cyprus.'

Chapter 26

The airport hotel's reception was quieter now the early morning mass exodus of holidaymakers had been replaced by a trickle of business people checking out. Jemma shuffled forwards until it was her turn.

A receptionist wearing a smart blue suit smiled. 'Good morning, madam. How can I help you? Wait a moment, you checked out earlier. Have you forgotten something?'

Jemma took out her credit card. 'No, but our holiday has been cancelled.'

'Oh, that's a shame,' the receptionist replied. 'I hope you're all OK?'

Jemma nodded. 'Yes, we're all fine. It was a medical emergency at the other end.'

'Nothing too serious, hopefully,' the woman said.

'No, I don't think so.' Jemma slid her card across the desk. 'Can we have two family rooms for three nights, please?'

The girl tapped her screen. 'Ah, Mrs Jones, normally you wouldn't be able to check in until two pm but if you're happy to return to the rooms you left this morning then you can go straight up. They haven't been cleaned yet though.'

'Oh, that's fine, thanks,' Jemma replied. 'The youngsters are shattered after their early start.'

'There you are, Mrs Jones. Two key cards for your rooms on the third floor. There's a tube station in Terminal Five that will take you straight into central London whenever you're ready to explore. Have a lovely stay, again.'

Jemma took the two cards. 'Thank you. We will.' She returned to her entourage lounging on the lobby sofas. 'Right, guys. Plan B.'

* * *

In the Bay of Biscay, the *Goke* ploughed its way through the heavy seas. The boat was both rising and dropping with every wave, but was also rolling from side to side, and all day Malek had been curled on his bunk feeling seasick. Even the super-strength anti-sickness tablets Ozlem had provided had so far failed to be effective.

Helen spent part of the day doing circuits of the ship. The skies were blue and the temperature reasonably warm, so she was happy to brave the wind and stay outside, and even the smell of fishing nets piled on the deck was preferable to the stench in their cabin while Malek searched for any food left in his stomach to regurgitate.

As darkness fell, she stood beside the guard rail and watched the lights of nearby boats as they lifted and dropped like toys in the massive swell. She had found her sea legs within a day of leaving Kyrenia and could walk around the heaving decks in a straight line. Ozlem had offered her a lifejacket and cable to attach to the rail but she'd refused. A voice from alongside made her jump.

'Hello, Mrs Malek.'

'Oh, Tengiz, it's you.' She touched her chest. 'You startled me. And it's Mrs Fletcher, not Mrs Malek.'

The perspiring cook frowned. 'But you are Malek's woman.'

'No, I am not.' She turned away. 'Now leave me alone.'

His whisky-soaked breath was overwhelming as he leaned closer. 'Your guy is not here, and I am a big man.' He pointed to his crotch before glancing over both shoulders. 'We do it now, quickly.' He put his sweaty palms on her shoulders.

She tried to shrug him away. 'Get off me!'

He spun her around so she was facing away from him towards the sea. She shot him a wide-eyed glare and tried to push him off but even in his drunken state, he was too strong. He pulled down his trousers, bent her over the rail and lifted up her skirt.

She had to clutch hard to the rail to prevent herself from going overboard. 'Wait,' she shouted. 'I'll help. We can do it here.'

His lips puckered and he leant away to allow Helen to unfasten her blouse buttons, revealing a lacy bra. He licked his lips and touched the top of her breast.

She gently removed his hand, bent down to unzip her long leather boots, carefully removed the thin stiletto knife and grasped it behind her back. 'Now, come to me, big man, let's see how big you are.'

With a leer, he put his arms around her neck and moved in for a kiss. There was a flash of silver as she expertly slid the knife in between his ribs and straight into his heart. A look of surprise crossed his face and, as his knees collapsed, she stepped aside to avoid the spurt of arterial blood that shot out over the side of the boat. Helen stood back, waited for him to stop twitching and wiped the blade on his shirt before returning it to her boot.

It took several minutes to manoeuvre his body under the bottom bar of the railing. With a final effort, she shoved him over the side with her foot and heard the splash as he hit the water.

She watched the body disappear into the darkness and spat over the side of the boat. 'Good riddance.'

A yellow hosepipe lay coiled like a sleeping snake on the deck and with careful movements, Helen washed the blood from the varnished wooden boards. When she'd finished, she rewound the hose and, after checking she hadn't been observed, wandered back down the swaying staircase towards her cabin with the buzz of a killing coursing through her veins.

Malek lifted his head as she walked in.

'Any better?' she asked.

'A bit. I took extra tablets and I'm feeling hungry. I might check if Tengiz has any food.'

She touched his arm. 'I feel hungry myself...but not for food. I feel rather aroused all of a sudden. Are you up to it?'

He grinned as she removed her blouse. 'I'll do my best.'

Chapter 27

In Swanbourne, Amrik and Hannah were holding a meeting at the Police HQ with Jackson Carter and Trevor Kennedy to go through the recordings from the fateful morning of Vincent's death. The room was full of computers, keyboards and monitors and a bank of large screens faced a line of chairs on wheels. Amrik had spent many hours in this room staring at CCTV footage but he still didn't know how most of the equipment worked.

In the technical suite, Trevor had attached his laptop to the computer and scrolled through the various clips he'd recorded. He pointed to the screen. 'This is the first section of drone footage I took at ten past seven. I sent it up to test the wind because I had to be careful of gusts coming up from the cliffs. These drones cost around five grand each, so I didn't want to smash one on the rocks.'

Amrik peered at the screen. 'Jackson, is that you pulling the ropes up?'

'Yes, it is,' Jackson replied. 'Can you slow it down please, Trev?'

Trevor slowed the speed of the clip. 'There. You're coiling the rope on the left. That was Jemma's position.' He sped on to the next section. 'Here you are moving the second rope which he puts on top of the first one.' He fast-forwarded again. 'Here is the third rope coiled on top of the first two ... and the fourth one went on top.'

Amrik made some notes. 'Were you still filming when the ropes were returned?'

Trevor moved the footage on by half an hour and they watched as Jackson approached the top coil of rope and unfurled it out over the edge at the left-hand point.

Amrik looked at Hannah. 'So the rope that had been in Trevor's number four spot went back into the number one spot that Jemma used and the rope that had been Vincent's in the number three spot went back down in the number two spot where Ellie would use it.'

She sipped her coffee. 'So that means the cut ropes were meant for Jemma and Ellie. Instead, it was Vincent himself who ended up with the damaged one.'

Trevor gulped. 'And me.'

Amrik frowned. 'I don't understand why the ropes didn't tangle at the top after they were swapped.'

'That's easy to explain,' Jackson said. 'We used two long pieces of wood containing notches along the cliff edge. They ensured the ropes stayed the same distance apart and stopped the abseilers from crashing into each other. When I put the ropes back down, each one returned to a slot two metres from the next. I didn't notice I'd swapped them around.'

Amrik grimaced. 'But you saved Jemma and Ellie's lives.'

Chapter 28

DC Hannah Salmon worked through a batch of CCTV and door cam clips taken from the vicinity of the road leading to the entrance of the dig site. She ran her hand through her hair as she concentrated on the screen.

Amrik was sitting alongside her and swore at the mouse as he tried to move the cursor around. 'Why won't this bloody thing work?'

She leant over and lifted his hand before turning the wireless mouse around one hundred and eighty degrees. 'It helps if you're holding it the right way up, sir.'

'Ah, I suppose you're right. Thank you, DC Salmon.'

'You're welcome, sir. These new mice are a bit confusing.'

He grinned. 'No need for sarcasm. How are you getting on?'

'Nothing yet but I'm hopeful of this one.' She pointed to the screen. 'It's door cam footage from the farmhouse opposite the track that leads down to the clifftop site. It's new and the owners hadn't set it up properly, so it triggers every time something goes past on the road. Hundreds of short videos. I'm through to five am.'

Amrik stared at her monitor as she played the fifteen-second clips.

'Luckily, there weren't too many cars passing in the early hours,' she said, 'but it's getting busier now.' She worked through some more recordings and then sat upright in her chair. 'Got you! Look. This clip shows a dark-coloured estate car pulling onto the track and immediately turning off its lights. Someone gets out but that's when it stops.'

He checked his notepad. 'Vincent drove a dark blue VW Passat. It's got to be him. Can you focus in on the reg number?'

She paused the clip and zoomed in. 'I can but it's not very clear so I'll email this section to the tech guys. Let me move on a bit and see if it comes back out.'

After trying the next few clips, she pointed at the screen. 'This is the clip just before it leaves. Another vehicle drives past and its headlights illuminate the rear of the car about to back out. If I freeze it here and zoom in...look.' She peered closely at the monitor. 'Does Vincent, by any chance, drive a car with the plate VIN 60?'

'Bingo!' he shouted.

She grinned. 'No. Vingo.'

* * *

Several hundred miles south of Lulcombe, Ozlem steered his boat through the busy shipping lanes of the English Channel, past Portland Bill, and called the Brixham Harbour Office on his radio.

'Brixham Harbour, this is trawler *Goke,* trawler *Goke,* trawler *Goke.* Come in. Over.'

There was a few seconds of crackling static before a reply returned. 'Trawler *Goke,* Brixham Harbour Office. Over.'

'Brixham Harbour, mooring needed for seven days. I'm

waiting for a replacement winch motor, but it may take a while.' Ozlem replied. 'Over.'

'What is your LOA? Over.'

'I am eighteen metres long. Over.'

'OK. That is just below our maximum size. The cost per day is one hundred and thirty-two pounds, payable by credit card. We're not busy so you can stay until you're fixed. Over.'

'Thanks. Over.'

'How many of the crew will want to come ashore? Over.'

'Four. Over.'

'Right. Just register the passports of anybody who wants to temporarily enter the UK. Where are you from? Over.'

'We're out of Kyrenia in Cyprus via Cartagena. Over.'

'That's all logged. What is your ETA? Over.'

'Tomorrow at eleven am. Over.'

'Mooring booked. Call in again before you dock and I'll confirm the berth number. See you then. Out.'

Ozlem knocked on the window and beckoned Helen from the deck.

She turned from the railing and entered the bridge. 'What?' she said.

'I've booked a place in Brixham harbour for eleven tomorrow morning.'

She punched the air. 'Yes! I'm ready to step back on dry land for a bit. You've made good time. I won't forget your bonus. No news about Tengiz?'

Ozlem shook his head and frowned. 'I still don't know what happened. I found an open bottle of whisky in his cabin so he must have been drunk and fallen overboard. It's a shame as I've known him a long time. Apart from his problems, he was a good man and I will miss him. It also means we're a man down for the rest of the trip and I have to choose the food for the rest of the journey.'

'Oh, well, I'm happy to help with some of the cooking. I'll

buy some provisions as well once I know when we're coming back.'

'Thanks,' he replied.

* * *

Helen returned to her cabin, pulled her suitcase from under the bunk and scanned the small room. Despite its compact size, there was a place for everything they had brought. Her belongings and clothes were soon packed and she returned the case beneath the bed.

Malek stirred. 'Are we there yet?'

She powered up her mobile. 'One more day then we can get off the boat.'

'Good. I'm fed up of rocking and rolling.'

She waved her finger. 'Shush while I call Harry.' Her nails clipped against the screen as she selected a number from her contacts. She pressed the speaker button and it rang out.

'Hello. Harry Collins.'

'Hi, Harry, it's Helen.'

'Oh.'

'Don't sound so enthusiastic,' she said.

A pause. 'Sorry, but you worry me, Helen, I never know what you're going to ask me to do next.'

'Don't be such a wuss. We will be docking in Brixham at eleven am tomorrow so can you make sure the Range Rover is parked up by midday? If it's busy we may stay on the boat until it's dark, but I'll decide then.'

There was another pause. 'Right. It's all arranged so I'd better drive it down today and catch a train back to London.'

'Thanks. Will you send a text message with the reg number in case there's more than one Range Rover about? I don't want anyone calling the police if we try opening the wrong one.'

‘OK. It will be there and the house is ready with some basic food in the fridge.’

‘That’s great, Harry, I owe you.’

‘You certainly do, Helen, you most certainly do.’

Chapter 29

At Swanbourne Police HQ, Amrik rubbed his eyes and checked his phone. *7 pm.* His shift had finished an hour ago but he'd continued putting the file together regardless. Hannah had left thirty minutes earlier for a date. *Lucky girl.* He'd never had much luck with girlfriends, especially those his parents had tried setting him up with.

He'd thought he was alone on the detective's floor so when the door opened behind him, he jumped.

DI Day came over. 'Burning the midnight oil?'

'Evening, Laura. I'm tidying up a few loose ends on the cliff fall case.'

'Are you sure it's murder and not just an accident?'

He explained how the evidence pointed towards Vincent being a victim of blackmail and cutting the ropes himself but, in a twist of fate, had lost his life when the ropes were swapped.

'Mmm. Interesting. So, you've sort of wrapped up the investigation but we've got to leave Helen Fletcher's intentions unprosecuted?'

Amrik frowned. 'Yeah. That's so frustrating.'

She rubbed her chin. 'Do you think Jemma's in danger?'

He nodded. 'I'm afraid so but we don't know if Helen Fletcher will try paying somebody to kill her or even attempt to return herself. I've never met her but I get the feeling she's a vindictive person who'll never give up.'

'She's used multiple passports before so she could have a go, I suppose.'

'I'm sure she won't be that stupid, but you never know.'

There was a sudden burst of the "Dambusters" theme and a phone that was charging on the shelf beside Amrik danced around the desk as it vibrated.

He picked up the mobile. 'Oh, my God. Helen's ringing Vincent's phone. What do I do?'

'Put it on speaker and mumble something. Let me set voice memo recording on my phone.'

'Ready, Laura?' Amrik asked.

She held up her thumb. 'Ready. Go!'

He pressed answer and waited. 'He...lo, He...n,' he said quietly in a posh BBC announcer's voice.

'Oh, Vincent. It's about time you answered. Is it done?'

Amrik swallowed. 'Yes.'

'Good. We're moving on to phase two. I'll be in touch. Bye.'

'Bye.'

The call ended and Laura burst into laughter. 'Your mother would have kittens if she could hear her son putting on a distinguished British gentleman's accent.'

'I'll have you know I *am* a distinguished British gentleman.'

She frowned. 'Seriously, though, what the hell is phase two?'

He shrugged. 'I've no idea.'

'Is there any chance of tracing the call?' she asked.

'I've requested a warrant for the phone company to try to get the location of the cell towers, though nothing's come back yet.'

'Can you keep it charged in case she rings again? Better still, connect it to the system and try calling her tomorrow. I'm prepared to allocate some resources to keep tabs on her.'

* * *

The *Goke* chugged slowly into Brixham Harbour. The Victoria Breakwater with its white lighthouse protected the main harbour from the open water swell coming in from the east. The journey up the English Channel had been rough so Helen and Malek had spent the night strapped into their bunks. As they passed the lighthouse, the harbour master called the ship on VHF channel fourteen and advised them to moor on their port side at berth eight.

Ozlem manoeuvred the boat up to the moorings and a port worker sauntered closer to grab the rope thrown across by Emree. It was hitched to a cleat and then the action was repeated at the stern.

Ozlem stood next to Malek on the bridge. 'I'd wait until this evening before you both leave the boat,' the captain said. 'Can you come with the three of us to register our passports at Border Force Devon? They might think it strange if a trawler of this size was operating with a crew of three.'

'OK,' Malek replied. 'I'll go and tell Helen. She won't like waiting. She's desperate to get off the boat and start searching.' He strolled down into the hold and opened a storage compartment. 'You can come out now, Helen. It doesn't look like anybody is going to check us out.'

She crawled out and dusted herself down. 'Thank God. The stench in there is awful.'

He laughed. 'Ozlem said the last time he used it to hide some passengers it had five occupants.'

Her eyes widened. 'Five! It was awful in there with just me. Anyway, when can we get off the boat?'

He checked his watch. 'He says we should leave once it

gets dark so that will be around…' he made a mental calculation, 'nine o'clock in the UK.'

She looked at her phone. 'At least this has reset to British time. Have you seen the Range Rover?'

Malek nodded. 'I think so. I can see a dark one in the corner of the carpark, but I can't read the number plate. I'll take a look when we go to register our passports and bring the keys back.'

'Will you take the suitcases over so we're ready to go? Harry said it will be an hour's drive to the house he's rented.' She sighed. 'Oh, it will be lovely to spend some time on solid land. I bet it will take days for the rolling sensation to go.'

Malek frowned. 'At least you weren't seasick.'

'I thought you'd helped Ozlem on his boat before,' she said.

'I did…for a few weeks, but I kept being sick whenever the sea was rough or the deck smelled of fish, which was every day.'

A couple of hours later Ozlem, Malek, Burak and Emree went to the harbour master's office to complete the immigration forms and register their passports with Border Force Devon. As they stood in the booths completing the paperwork, the harbour master turned to Ozlem.

'How long will you be here?'

The trawler owner shrugged. 'It could be one week, it could be two. It depends when the motor arrives.'

'If you need any help with the replacement, or even getting the motor, we have some excellent marine engineers in town.'

'That's good of you,' Ozlem replied, 'but we have two experienced engineers and it won't be a big job once we get the part.'

The harbour master gazed out at the boat. 'Do you want to offload any fish?'

Ozlem shook his head. 'We're OK, thanks. We'd arranged to unload at Cartagena and then the winch for the net died so we're empty. We'll just take some fuel and water, and we'll stock up on food at your supermarket.'

The official took their immigration forms and checked them over. 'Oh, you're from Northern Cyprus. We don't get many Turkish fishermen here.'

Ozlem smiled. 'It was best to come here to have the motor replaced. Thanks, we must go now. I can smell a pint of your English beer.'

The harbour master filed the completed papers in the drawer. 'Don't overdo it with the booze. Some of the real ales and local ciders are very strong. The police around here are used to drunken tourists and they often end up in the cells overnight.'

As they strolled back to the ship, Malek wandered nonchalantly around the waterfront as if surveying the other boats. He passed the dark Range Rover and dropped his hat on the floor. As he knelt down to pick it up, he reached around behind the nearside front wheel and retrieved a plastic bag. He pocketed it, stood and replaced his cap before heading back to the boat, whistling a Turkish folk song as he sauntered. As soon as he arrived back at the cabin, Helen yanked open the door.

'Have you got them?'

He held up the bag.

She snatched it off him, ripped it open and took out the keys. 'I'm fed up of waiting, I'm going now.'

He touched her arm. 'Ozlem said it's best to wait.'

'I don't care what he says. Come on, let's go.'

Malek shrugged and manhandled a suitcase from under the tiny bunk.

She led the way and was about to walk down the gangplank when she saw a policeman peering in through the window of the Range Rover before removing a radio from his pocket and speaking into it.

'Shit,' she said, 'it's the fuzz.'

Chapter 30

Amrik stared at the photograph of Helen Fletcher on the murder board where several lengths of string connected her image with those of Vincent, Jemma and Ellie. The grainy image had been taken at an immigration point when she'd previously flown into the UK under the name of Helen Barnes seeking revenge for the deaths of her brothers.

'Where are you, you psychopath?' he asked.

'I'm here, DS Hussain.' A voice came from behind him.

He spun around and his mouth fell open when he saw his superior, DI Laura Day.

'Sorry, I didn't mean you, ma'am,' he stammered.

She grinned. 'I know, Amrik, I'm winding you up.'

He breathed out. 'Phew, you had me there.'

'Well, any ideas about our most wanted woman?'

'I'm afraid not. We keep trying to track the number's location, but my guess is it's turned off when she's not making a call.'

'Did you up the alert level at all airports and ports?'

'Yep. Everywhere's on red alert and we've distributed this picture and an older one from her passport application.'

'Any joy with Cyprus?' she asked.

'We put in a formal request for information about her through the British Embassy in Larnaca, but we've had no response. It doesn't help that there are no embassy or consular officials in Northern Cyprus.'

She rested her hand on the board. 'It's a strange situation, isn't it? A country no one recognises except Turkey.'

'Why does Turkey recognise them?' he asked.

She stared at the map. 'Because they're the country that invaded Cyprus and established the north.'

He rubbed his chin. 'Then we need to give them a good reason to send Helen back. Maybe she has assets there they could seize.'

Laura smiled. 'It might be worth hinting that to them, but I bet they won't care.' She checked her watch. 'I'd better go. I've got a meeting to review next year's budgets.'

He nodded. 'The joys of being a DI.'

She frowned back at him. 'I much prefer doing this detective stuff.'

'Best bit of the job, ma'am.'

* * *

Helen and Malek peered through the salt-stained window of their cabin towards the policeman standing beside the Range Rover speaking into his radio. Five minutes later a car drew up alongside him and a second uniformed man stepped out.

'That's not a copper,' she whispered. 'Different uniform.'

'Is it an immigration man?' he asked.

Helen looked through a pair of binoculars. 'I don't know.'

They watched as the lights illuminated the carpark and the other man shook hands with the constable before taking a large pack from his satchel.

Helen barked. 'It's a bloody traffic warden. He's giving us a parking ticket.'

Malek frowned. 'Is that bad?'

'It shouldn't be a problem as long as they don't clamp it.'

The warden finished writing the ticket, sealed it inside a small plastic envelope and stuck it to the windscreen. He then patted the policeman on the shoulder and drove away.

'They're hunting in packs now, the bastards,' Helen said.

'Packs?' Malek asked.

'Yes, like wolves.'

The policeman removed his helmet, used a handkerchief to wipe his forehead, replaced the helmet and started walking in the direction of the town.

'Come on.' Helen jumped up. 'Let's grab our stuff and go.'

'Is it dark enough?' Malek asked.

'I don't give a toss,' she said. 'I'm off. Bring the stuff.'

She strolled up the gangplank straight towards the Range Rover before pressing the remote key. The hazards flashed and she opened the door before climbing in. Malek put their luggage in the boot, removed the parking ticket, sat in the front seat and produced a scrap of paper. 'This is the address, no?'

She snatched it from him, turned on the ignition and entered the postcode into the satnav. 'Ninety minutes. Let's go.' She put the car into drive and carefully pulled away.

The journey was uneventful and, as it was a warm evening, they drove with the windows open until reaching the A38 where they could speed up.

'Oh, it's good to be off that sodding boat at last. Two weeks at sea is way too long unless it's on a luxury cruise ship.'

He grimaced. 'The *Goke* is not luxury.'

Just over an hour later they arrived at a remote address five miles north of Swanbourne. It was a detached house with four windows and a front door arranged in the same two-up two-down pattern used by nearly every child who is asked to draw a house. Ivy grew on both sides of the entrance and Helen had to move some aside to read the house's name plate.

'*Heath Cottage*. This is it. The key's in the glove box. Bring the stuff but we don't unpack anything. Whenever we go out we take the bags with us in case we have to make a quick exit.'

'Not too quickly, I hope. I'm not ready to go back on the boat yet.'

She narrowed her eyes. 'We go when we have the baby, OK?'

'Of course.'

She unlocked the door and stepped inside. The living area was spacious and the kitchen worktop had two carrier bags filled with food. Helen opened the fridge, which contained milk, butter, cheese, beer and two bottles of white wine. She grabbed two glasses.

'I fancy a bath so bring the bottle.'

Chapter 31

Jemma repacked her suitcase and gazed at the magnolia-coloured walls of their anonymous hotel room.

Brad was sitting on the floor with Rocky, colouring in a book of dinosaur pictures with some multi-coloured crayons, his tongue peeping out from between his lips as he concentrated on a triceratops.

Jemma grinned. 'What time tomorrow will the car be delivered?'

'Eleven,' Brad replied. 'It took some retrieving once it had gone off to the long-term storage place the hotel uses.' He stood and stretched. 'You OK, Jem?'

'Yeah, I'm alright,' she said. 'I'm just disappointed we had to cancel but these couple of days in London have been different. I'm not sure about the London Eye though.'

He nodded. 'I thought you were OK with heights now.'

'I am normally but that was very high.'

He slipped his arms around her. 'Don't worry. We'll get our vacation in the sun in a couple of months.'

She squeezed him. 'I know. It's just that we all needed a break after what happened with Vincent.'

Her mobile rang and Amrik's name appeared on the screen. She pressed to accept. 'Hello, Amrik. You OK?'

'Hi, Jemma. I'm fine, thanks. Sorry to call while you're in America but I thought you ought to know something.'

'We're not in America, we're in London, but that's another story. What's up?'

'I'm afraid that, from the evidence we've gathered, it looks like Helen Fletcher was blackmailing Vincent into attempting to kill you and Ellie.'

'What?' A terrible pain shot straight to her heart. 'How was she blackmailing him?'

'It appears that she obtained a video of him with a young escort and then told him the girl was underage.'

'That doesn't sound like him.'

'It was a honey trap set up but he definitely fell for it. I know, I had to sit through the matinee.'

'Yuk. Is she still in Cyprus?'

'As far as we know. She'd find it difficult entering the UK as we've put out a red alert for her at ferry ports and airports.'

Her hands were shaking. 'That's reassuring, at least. Should I be worried?'

'We're not sure. We want you to just keep an eye out for anything unusual.'

'OK, but you're not putting a watch on me again, are you?'

There was a pause. 'No, not at the moment.'

'Good, because I don't want a police car outside my house again. The last time was horrible, like someone was spying on me.'

'It was for your own protection.'

'Oh, I know. I just didn't like it.'

'Sorry to worry you,' he said, 'but I felt I ought to tell you.'

'Thanks for that. Will you let me know if the situation changes?'

'Will do. Bye, Jemma. Oh, when are you back?'

'We should be back in Lulcombe tomorrow night. We're going to Chessington to see the animals on the way back. Rocky was disappointed about not going on the plane so we're trying some distraction therapy. Can we talk again once we're back?'

'Yes, OK,' Amrik replied, 'but in the meantime, be careful, won't you. Bye.'

'Bye, Amrik.' She ended the call and turned to Brad. 'Did you follow all of that?'

He reached for her hand. 'Just about. Have we got to start watching out for strange people?'

She shrugged. 'Possibly. If she tried to blackmail Vincent into killing me then she might try again by paying someone else.' She picked at her fingernail. 'I still can't believe that Vincent betrayed me like that and tried to kill us.'

He lowered himself into a comfy chair. 'I bet you wish you'd never found the fossil that set this all in motion.'

'Don't blame Plessie. If I hadn't discovered her, I'd have probably still clashed with the Fletcher brothers over the museum sale.'

'It's a shame I can't carry a gun in England.'

Jemma frowned. 'You didn't carry one when you were in the States, did you?'

'Nah, I never could be bothered with the paperwork.'

Jemma stared at her son lying on the floor. 'I'm worried, Brad. Not for myself but for Rocky and Kira. It's hard to protect them if you don't know what's coming. I don't want to spend my entire life on edge in case somebody turns up who might harm them. My family's so important to me. What with Dad being ill and now your Mum as well, our time together is so precious. What can we do, Brad?'

He shrugged. 'I don't know but if the police think you need protection then I'd accept it until they get this sorted out.'

She leant down and stroked Rocky's hair. 'But will they, Brad, will they get it sorted out?'

* * *

One hundred and fifty miles away in Lulcombe a black Range Rover drove along Seaton Road and parked down the street from Jemma's house.

Helen checked her phone. 'I think there's a footpath that cuts through the houses and goes around the back of Jemma's place.' She and Malek stepped out from the car and walked down the path. She reached out. 'Here, hold my hand like we're a couple.'

He did as she said. 'But we *are* a couple, aren't we?'

She rolled her eyes. 'If you say so.'

They strolled between the houses without meeting anybody and when they reached the field she pointed. 'The footpath cuts across there so that one must be Jemma's house.' She sauntered up to the gate and peered around the garden. 'Doesn't look very lived-in. I need someone to ask. Where's Vincent when you need him?'

'Where does he live?'

She patted Malek on the back. 'Now, that's a good idea. Let's pay him a visit. It'll be such a pleasant surprise when we turn up.'

After she took a few photos of the back of the cottage, they returned to the car and entered another address into the satnav.

'It's only five minutes away,' Helen said. 'Let's go.'

They drove to the bungalow with the amazing sea views and pulled up outside. Helen reached for the door handle but Malek thrust out an arm, stopping her.

'Why is there yellow stuff across the door?'

'Oh, my God, that's police crime scene tape. Let's get out of here.'

She drove back into Lulcombe and parked in the industrial estate. 'Search on the internet for Vincent Lawrence, will you?'

He tapped his phone screen. 'Bok! It says here that Vincent Lawrence, sixty-four from Lulcombe was today named as the abseiler who fell to his death while filming an episode of *The Rock Detectives* with fossil hunters Jemma and Ellie Thorne. A police spokesman said they were treating the death as misadventure while their investigations continue. The article is dated two weeks ago.'

'What? Two weeks ago! Then who answered Vincent's phone the other night?' she demanded.

He stared at her. 'Maybe it was a policeman. If they were investigating his death then they may have kept his phone.'

Helen shuffled inside her bag for her mobile, ripped out the battery and sim card, leant out of the car door and ground them under her boot on the pavement.

'Bloody hell. That might have let them know I'm in the country. We need to grab the kid and disappear. Pronto.'

Chapter 32

Amrik pulled up outside Jemma's house in his silver Ford Focus and waited for a young couple to pass his door before stepping out. He watched as they strolled along hand in hand, laughing as they talked.

It's alright for some people who can lead normal lives. I've got no chance being a copper.

He ran a hand through his hair and walked down the drive. There was no sign of life at the cottage, and he couldn't see anything unusual in the road or around the back of the property so he called into the station to report all was quiet. DI Day had agreed to some regular checks of Jemma's house unless any intelligence came in to justify more intensive protection.

Dusk was falling as he moved his car further down the street and settled in to watch for a while. Unwrapping a foil package, the smell of one of his mum's samosas filled the vehicle.

I could always go to Mum and Dad's for a drink. Better than an empty apartment.

A bat started circling under the light down the street and he checked the time.

Nine o'clock. I'll give it another half an hour then go home.

* * *

Ten minutes after Amrik left, a black Range Rover slid into a space between two parked cars and switched off its lights.

Helen sighed. 'Where are they all? That's two days and we've seen nothing.'

Malek grinned. 'Maybe they're on holiday. Perhaps they've gone to Cyprus.'

'That's not funny.' She peered at the dashboard clock. 'Another hour and we'll give up.'

* * *

Twenty-five minutes later, Jemma pulled onto her drive and hugged Brad. 'That's been a tiring day.' She twisted around to check the backseat. 'Arrrh. Sleeping babies.'

Ellie slowly opened her eyes. 'Are we there yet?' She rubbed her face and checked the child seats either side of her. 'Now to try and get them both to bed without them waking up.'

Brad climbed out and stepped towards the back. 'I think they enjoyed today. Rocky loved the rhinos.'

Jemma joined him at the car boot. 'He told me they looked like dinosaurs.'

Ellie knelt on the back seat and peered over as they unloaded the luggage. 'Any chance of letting me out? The child locks are on.'

Brad laughed and walked around to open the door. 'You could have stayed in there all night; I'd have brought you in for breakfast.'

'Thanks,' Ellie replied as Kira started crying. Ellie shook her head. 'Goody. Missie's awake now.'

Brad wheeled the two cases up the path. 'What's happening with Dino?'

'He's OK.' Jemma replied. 'I told Mum I'd fetch him in the morning.'

Ellie grinned. 'I bet he'll go mad when you pick him up.'

* * *

Further down the street, in the shadows of an overhanging tree, Malek opened his eyes and stretched. 'Helen. Look. Lights are on in Jemma's cottage and there's a car on the drive. They're back.'

She jerked awake and took a moment to realise where she was. 'Oh, my God. They're here. Thunderbirds are go.'

He frowned. 'What?'

'Never mind.' She shook her head. 'Let's go and start a family.'

Chapter 33

The following morning, Kira gurgled with laughter as Ellie lay on the bed and balanced her on extended arms.

'I can't do this for long.' Ellie panted. 'My poor muscles feel like I've done arm day at the gym.' She glanced from side to side. 'Not that I go to the gym, but don't tell anybody.'

Her daughter continued bouncing and held out her hands as if to say *again*.

'OK, miss. One more time but that's it.'

Ellie's mobile buzzed from the nightstand. She answered. 'Hi, Dan.'

'Hi, Ellie. You OK?'

'Yes. I'm good thanks. You?'

'Great. Sorry to hear about the holiday.'

'It doesn't matter. Brad's mum has had her op and she's doing well. We're going to try again in a couple of months when she can cope with two energetic youngsters.'

'That's good. Do you fancy meeting tomorrow at the beach café for something to eat?'

She paused. 'Oh, I can't do then. It's Vincent's inquest in the morning.'

'Would you like any moral support or a babysitter?'

‘That’s sweet but Mum’s already asked Gran so she’s having both Kira and Rocky. I could do the day after though.’

‘Cool. How about half ten down there?’

‘OK. Thanks, Dan. I’ll see you then.’

‘Bye.’

She ended the call and started bouncing her daughter on her chest. ‘I do believe I have an admirer.’

* * *

Jemma’s doorbell rang and Dino barked. Through the glass, she recognised Amrik and unlocked the door.

‘Hi Jemma,’ he stepped inside and they hugged. ‘You remember DC Salmon?’

Jemma reached out and shook hands with the young detective. ‘Of course. Hannah, isn’t it?’

‘Yes, that’s right. Good to meet you. Shame about the holiday.’

‘Oh, well. Just one of those things. We can go when Brad’s mum recovers. Have a seat. Tea, coffee?’

Amrik slid into one of the chairs by the table and Hannah followed suit. ‘Tea, please,’ he said.

Jemma turned on the kettle. ‘Milk and one sugar?’

He nodded. ‘That’s right. You’ve got a good memory.’

‘I’ll have a black coffee, please, no sugar,’ Hannah added.

Jemma made the drinks and sat with them. ‘Right, what’s the latest before the inquest?’

Amrik took some notes from his briefcase and spread them over the old, scarred oak table. Ellie always complained it resembled an axe-throwing target and they needed a new one, but Jemma loved its character and it had been with her ever since she’d first moved in.

Amrik gestured to his notes. ‘We believe that Helen Fletcher blackmailed Vincent Lawrence into trying to kill you both. He drove to the dig site at five-thirty. We have doorcam footage of his car driving onto the track. We think he partially cut through two of the ropes lined up for you and Ellie. Jackson then temporarily removed the ropes to take some continuity shots of the cliffs but put them back in a different order. The filming commenced and Vincent fell to his death. Trevor was lucky his rope didn't snap as well.'

Jemma frowned. 'Will that satisfy the inquest?'

'Hard to say,' he replied. 'We traced a deposit of twenty-five thousand pounds in Vincent's bank account back to a company in the Turkish Republic of Northern Cyprus. The company was the same one that purchased the museum site and the credit was marked property consultancy.'

'Any news of Helen Fletcher?' Jemma asked. 'I dreamt about her last night and I've never even met her. I thought she was standing over the bed watching me.'

Hannah cleared her throat. 'She made a call to Vincent's phone, which Amrik answered. She asked if "it was done" but rang off when Amrik tried to impersonate Vincent.'

Jemma giggled. 'I'd like to have heard that.'

Amrik frowned.

Jemma's smile faded. 'Sorry, Hannah, please continue.'

'Helen had previously sent several messages asking Vincent to call her urgently. We don't think she knew he was dead at that point.'

'Were you able to trace the call?' Jemma asked.

Hannah shook her head. 'By the time we sent a warrant to the phone company the mobile had been turned off and we haven't had any pings since. It didn't connect to a UK cell tower so they're still trying to track it.'

'Maybe my English ex-military voice wasn't convincing enough for Helen and she shut down the phone,' Amrik said.

Jemma took a gulp of tea and ran a hand over her brow. 'Could she be in the country?'

'We don't think so,' Hannah replied. 'We've got extensive resources at airports and ferry ports, including some super-recognisers checking video footage of arrivals from Turkey and Cyprus.'

'What's a super-recogniser?' Jemma asked.

'Someone who's skilled at spotting people on a TV screen.'

Jemma's eyebrows lifted. 'You learn something new every day. No sightings yet, though?'

'No,' Hannah replied.

'Jemma,' Amrik hesitated, 'we'd like you to consider police protection for you and your family.'

She banged down her mug, making everybody jump. 'No. I don't want that again. It was awful last time. It felt like such an intrusion to see the police car on the road outside. '

Amrik rubbed his forehead. 'It was for your protection at a dangerous time.'

'I know that,' Jemma said, 'but I didn't like being watched all the time.'

'That's your decision, Jemma, but we may need to ask again if there's any sign of Helen.'

'We'll see,' Jemma replied. 'How do you think the inquest will go tomorrow?'

Amrik shrugged. 'I'm not sure. It will be difficult to prove beyond reasonable doubt that Vincent cut his own rope, so what they'll make of that is anybody's guess. Are you and Ellie OK about giving evidence?'

'Oh, yes. I felt guilty about Vincent's death to start with as I'd organised the whole thing.'

'You can't blame yourself,' Hannah said.

'I'm not anymore,' Jemma replied. 'Now I just feel sorry that another life has been wasted because of that bitch. Is that everything?'

Amrik collected his notes together and stood. 'Yes, thanks. See you in court.'

* * *

Helen and Malek were sitting with ice creams in the black Range Rover parked in the beach carpark in Lulcombe. It was a beautiful, sunny day and the town thronged with tourists. They had tried sitting on the sea wall to eat their ice creams but the seagulls kept swooping down, threatening a fly-by mugging. Instead, they sat in the car with the engine running and the air con turned up, which drew a few disapproving stares from passers-by.

'Ice cream good?' Helen asked.

'It's OK. Not as nice as Turkish,' Malek replied. 'Is it time for another drive-by?'

She looked at the time on her phone. 'Give it another ten minutes and we'll check if the visitors have gone. The man who went in looked like Plod to me.'

'Plod?'

'PC Plod. A copper, policeman.'

'Oh. Got you.'

'We must be careful, but we have to take *some* risks as we've been here two days and Ozlem is pressing me for a departure day. He says the harbour master now seems a bit suspicious and has told him they'll need the mooring in four days.'

'What will you do if you don't have your granddaughter by then?'

'I'm not sure yet. The ship could move to a dry berth, but you can only get out if the tide is right.'

Malek chewed on his bottom lip. 'The girl is bound to leave the house with her baby soon.'

'That's true, Malek, and when she does I'll be waiting.'

Chapter 34

The Grade II listed building of Bournemouth Civic Centre, formerly the town hall, stood in an elevated position within the town. The multi-windowed Purbeck stone building with its tower and Union Jack made an impressive sight as Jemma and Ellie pulled up. A large board in front of the building showed a plan of the various departments and facilities. On the other side of the entrance, a modern purple sign looked out of place beside the older stone of the facade.

Jemma smiled. 'That sign makes me hungry.'

'What?' Ellie replied.

'It's Cadbury purple and now I fancy some chocolate.'

'I know, Mum. I'll buy you a cup of tea and a block of Dairy Milk afterwards. Or even better, a piece of cake. Aren't you nervous?'

Jemma thought for a moment. 'No. I should be sad, but Vincent got what he deserved for getting into bed with the Fletcher family and trying to kill us.'

Ellie frowned. 'Too bloody right.'

They entered the coroner's court where a clerk took their details and, after they'd passed through security, they were shown to their seats.

Ellie leant towards her mother. 'I didn't realise there would be so many people.'

'I bet half of them are press,' Jemma replied.

'Who else is here?' Ellie asked.

Jemma glanced around the chamber. 'The coroner will sit on the raised platform.' She pointed to a spot just in front of it. 'The clerk will sit there. Our row is for the witnesses, the public will be in those chairs and the seats with tables attached will be for the press.'

Ellie's eyes widened. 'Wow. How many of these have you been to?'

'Well, I was a witness when Anna was murdered and then again when I sort of killed Keith and Reggie Fletcher. My third appearance was when Zak and Gary drowned in the mudflow on the beach.'

More people entered and Jemma waved as Amrik, Jackson and Trevor arrived and sat on the witnesses' bench.

Amrik shook their hands. 'You both good?'

'Yes, we're fine,' Jemma said. 'We just want to get this over.'

There was a rush of people into the public seats and more journalists joined their colleagues at the press tables. The unlucky ones grumbled as they realised they'd have to stand for the proceedings. A woman and man sat on their own in the row in front of the coroner's desk.

'Who's that?' Ellie whispered.

'I don't know,' Jemma replied. 'It might be Vincent's daughter and her husband.'

The clerk stood and banged a gavel against her desk. 'Please be upstanding for His Majesty's Coroner.'

There was a hubbub of chatter as everyone stood and faced the wall behind the raised section. A tall man with grey hair and a brown suit stepped through the door and stood behind his desk.

'Please be seated,' he said, and everybody took their seats.

He sipped from a glass of water. 'Good morning, ladies and gentlemen. Welcome to Dorset Coroner's Court. We are here today to consider the death of Vincent Charles Lawrence. My commiserations to his family.' He nodded to the lady seated at the front.

'My task here today is to consider the following questions: who was the deceased and when, where and how did the death occur? We are not here to decide any criminal or civil liability. I'll call a number of witnesses to give evidence and statements.'

He checked his notes. 'The first witness I would like to call is Detective Sergeant Amrik Hussain of Swanbourne Constabulary who is heading the investigation into the events of the third of May.'

Amrik picked up his file and strode towards the witness box. He gave his name and rank before swearing on oath that his evidence would be truthful. He then went through a summary of the events leading up to Vincent's fall.

Jemma listened attentively and made a few notes in her notepad. Amrik finished giving his evidence and then she was called to give her version of what happened. Her testimony was noted and the coroner had no questions. Ellie, Jackson the director and Trevor the cameraman all followed in due course and after just over an hour the coroner asked if the family had any questions or comments.

The lady on the front row answered in the affirmative before standing. 'I'm Debbie, Vincent's daughter. On behalf of the Lawrence family, I would like to apologise to everybody affected by his foolish actions.' She sat and wiped her eyes.

The coroner stood again. 'The facts of this case are very unusual as it appears that Vincent unintentionally fell to his death due to the fact the ropes he'd intentionally damaged had been swapped around. I was tempted to offer a conclusion of misadventure or unlawful killing but neither of these fits the circumstances. Instead, I'll issue a narrative conclusion factually describing the circumstances of Vincent's death. This will enable a certificate to be issued and the funeral to be arranged.'

He took a sip of water. 'My conclusion is, therefore, that Vincent Charles Lawrence was unintentionally killed due to his own actions in cutting through the ropes being used in the recovery of a fossil from Lulcombe Cliffs. I'm satisfied the TV company and the director of the television programme acted properly and could not have anticipated the deliberate sabotage of the climbing equipment by the experienced rope safety expert they'd engaged.' Finally, he declared the inquest closed and left the courtroom.

Jemma sighed and touched Ellie's shoulder. 'I'm glad that's over.'

Ellie hugged her. 'You did really well, Mum.'

Jemma smiled thinly. 'And you did too, Els.'

They shuffled out into the hazy sunshine of a warm Dorset day where Vincent's daughter, Debbie, approached before offering Jemma a stiff hand.

'That must have been difficult for you,' Jemma said.

'It was.' Debbie replied. 'It's a relief now as we can finally arrange the funeral, although I'm not sure if anyone will want to go after what Dad did.'

Jemma smiled. 'Oh, I'm sure they will. He knew quite a few people and had done a lot for the town. It's only been the last few years that he got caught in the talons of the Fletcher family.'

Debbie frowned. 'Have any of them been arrested?'

'No,' Jemma replied. 'Four of them are dead and the only one still alive is in Cyprus.'

'That's Helen, isn't it?' Debbie asked. 'She sounds like a nasty piece of work.'

'She is that,' Jemma confirmed, 'but luckily she's a long way away.'

* * *

On the opposite side of the carpark, a dark Range Rover was parked in the shadow of an oak tree while the occupants observed the group outside the building.

Helen pushed up her sunglasses, grasped Malek's hand and squeezed. 'It won't be long now. You don't know what's going to hit you, Jemma Thorne,' she said.

Chapter 35

Brad and Jemma were lounging in bed each reading a newspaper covering the events at the previous day's inquest. The curtains were fully open and the sun streamed into the bedroom dominated by their king-size bed.

Jemma folded her paper and dropped it on the floor. 'Hopefully, now we can draw a line under what happened that day and move on with our lives.'

Brad put his paper down and stretched his arm around her. 'I'll second that. How about a life without drama for a while?'

She snuggled up to him. 'That would be perfect. It's a shame we didn't get our holiday.'

'We'll rebook it,' he said, 'as soon as Mom is better.'

She closed her eyes, snuggling closer, and as she did the front of her robe fell open.

He grinned and gently cupped her exposed breast. 'How long will Ellie keep Rocky playing with Kira?'

She opened her eyes and shook her head. 'Don't get any ideas, Romeo, he'll come running back just as soon as he gets bored of playing games with a one-year-old.'

'Shucks.' He checked the clock. 'I suppose I ought to do

some work. I've got a number of fossil dealers to contact about the list of pieces my clients want.'

She turned and looked into his eyes. 'We could get hunting and find you some new ones.'

'I'm not sure about that. Fossil hunting with you is dangerous.'

* * *

At the end of Jemma's road, a black Range Rover with tinted screens was parked beneath a large sycamore tree that covered part of the street.

Using Malek's phone, Helen scoured the internet. 'Any sign of life yet?'

'No.' Malek placed his binoculars on the dashboard. 'Do you want to do some looking? My eyes are tired.'

'I'm busy,' she snapped. 'I'm searching for an alternative mooring for a fishing trawler. Loads of things keep popping up in Turkish. It's a right pain.'

'Well, it is my phone,' he said.

'I'm getting fed up of all this waiting.' She put the mobile back on charge. 'Why doesn't the girl ever leave the house alone with the baby?'

Malek picked up the binoculars again and recommenced watching Jemma's house. 'She will soon. I'm sure.'

'Are you happy with what we're going to do?' she asked.

'No problem. I'll drive alongside her, jump out, grab her and push her onto the back seat where you'll be ready with your smelly cloth ...what is it?'

'Chloroform.'

'That's it. You will use that to put her to sleep.'

'Back in my day, they used to call me the Chloroform Queen. We'd catch rivals to our crime empire and take them to a deserted swimming pool for some fun. A bit of torture and drop the body into some foundations my brothers were building.' She went glassy-eyed. 'Oh, they were happy days. Anyway, back to what you're doing...'

Malek frowned and shook his head imperceptibly. 'You're evil, Helen. Pure evil.'

She grinned. 'That's the best bit.'

He shivered. 'Anyway, once you have the girl, I'll pass the baby to you, dump the buggy and drive off. Fast but within the speed limit.'

'That's the plan.'

* * *

At quarter past ten, Ellie dressed Kira and put her coat in the pocket of her buggy. 'Anything you want from town, Mum?'

'Don't think so,' Jemma replied. 'Are you going shopping?'

'No, I'm meeting Dan at the beach carpark and we're going for a walk along the cliffs. Do you want me to take Rocky and Dino as well?'

Jemma laughed. 'I'd say Dan needs to get used to the idea of Kira being around before you start taking Rocky and Dino as well. You don't want to scare him off.'

Ellie slipped on a pale blue denim jacket. 'He seems to like kids. Comes from a big family with lots of nieces and nephews.'

She loaded her daughter into the pushchair, gave her mum and Rocky a hug and headed for the door. Dino rushed over and nuzzled up to Kira, determined not to miss out on the cuddles.

'See you later, Mum.'

'Bye, Els.'

Ellie stepped outside to the pavement while she sent a text message to Dan. *Just leaving at ten-twenty. See you in fifteen minutes.*

A reply came straight back. *OK. X*

Ellie grinned and showed the screen to Kira. 'He keeps using a kiss now on every message.'

Kira reached for the phone but Ellie snatched it away before it became covered in the teething infant's slobber.

She returned the phone to her pocket. 'Let's go.'

* * *

'She's there!' Malek shouted. 'And she's with the baby.'

Helen jumped up, almost banging her head against the roof. 'Let's do this.'

He waited until Ellie had turned the corner and started down towards the town centre before driving along the road and pulling over thirty metres past her. He jumped out, removed a suitcase from the boot, placed it on the pavement and opened the near-side rear door as if he was about to transfer the case to the car. As he was effectively blocking the walkway, he held a hand up to the approaching girl. 'Sorry, I won't be a moment.'

'No problem.' Ellie took out her phone and began checking for messages before dropping it in the buggy's pocket and leaning over to talk to Kira.

Malek scanned the street, seized Ellie and shoved her into the back seat where she struggled to free herself, but Malek held her tightly while Helen thrust the chloroform-soaked cloth over the girl's mouth before she had chance to react.

He threw the suitcase back into the boot, handed the child to Helen, folded the buggy and threw it over a garden hedge. He slammed the boot, ran around to the driver's side, jumped in and immediately drove away.

'Go. Go. Go,' Helen shouted.

Chapter 36

Dan perched on the sea wall, staring at the white-sailed yachts out in Lyme Bay. At that distance, they hardly seemed to be moving. *Are they small or far away?* He chuckled at the memory of the scene from *Father Ted*, his dad's favourite comedy TV show.

The number on his watch face was on a go-slow. *Ten-forty-five. Where are they? I bet Ellie's doing some shopping on the way.*

He tried ringing her but the call went to voicemail. Fifteen minutes later, before he started counting seagulls, he jumped off the wall to head back through the town with the intention of meeting Ellie on her way down.

* * *

Malek pulled into the Swanbourne industrial estate, parking behind an empty unit. 'I'll change the plates here and then again before we get back to the boat. Harry left some other sets in the back.' He nodded at the unconscious girl. 'Is she alright?'

After finishing strapping Kira into the car seat, Helen

spared a glance for Ellie. 'Yeah, she's fine,' she flapped a hand, 'as long as she doesn't swallow her tongue or choke on her own vomit.'

He frowned. 'Watch her. I don't want to be part of a murder.'

'Just swap the bloody things so we can piss off,' she snapped.

He moved around to the front of the vehicle and knelt with a screwdriver, deftly removing the plate before doing the same with the one at the rear. He attached the new ones, dropped the plates he'd removed into an overflowing skip outside a neighbouring unit, jumped back inside the vehicle and slammed the door.

'OK to go?' he asked.

'OK to go,' she replied. 'Don't forget. Fast but legal.'

'That can be my nickname,' he laughed, '*Fast but Legal.*'

* * *

Dan arrived at Jemma's house just after five past eleven. As he stood on the drive, panting and dripping with sweat, he wished he hadn't decided to run up the hill. After catching his breath, he knocked on the door.

Jemma opened it as Rocky rushed up behind her.

'Hi, Dan,' he shouted through Jemma's legs.

'Hi, Rocky.' Dan glanced back up to Jemma. 'I'm worried about Ellie.'

Jemma's hand flew to her mouth. 'What's happened?'

He checked the time. 'She sent me a message at twenty past ten saying she'd see me in fifteen minutes, which meant she should have reached me at ten thirty-five. It's now ten past eleven and there's no sign of her. She's not answering her phone. It's just ringing out.'

'She's probably just distracted by something in a shop,' Jemma tried to reassure him.

'I don't think so, she'd have rung to let me know she'd be late. I suppose I could go back down and check in all the shops on the way.'

'Tell you what, you go back down the road, I'll set off across the fields and ask Brad to drive down with Rocky and meet us there in a bit.'

Jemma sat down with her walking boots and started lacing them up. 'Brad,' she shouted.

Brad rushed downstairs. 'I don't like that tone of voice. Oh, hello Dan. What's up?'

Dan repeated what he had told Jemma.

'OK,' Brad replied. 'I'll stick Rocky in the car and have a drive around. If we don't find her by half past we can meet up somewhere else.'

'The beach carpark,' Jemma said.

Brad put Rocky's shoes and hat on, grabbed his keys and headed out to his truck. 'Come on, buddy, let's find your sis and Kira.'

His son's eyes lit up. He loved being taken for a ride in his dad's SUV.

Dan set off down the road and Jemma rushed across the field with Dino to join up with the South West Coast Path.

* * *

On the town's outskirts, Helen spotted the sign for Swanbourne Heath Nature Reserve. 'In here. This will do nicely. Drive in slowly and, if there's nobody about, go around the back.'

'What are we doing?' Malek asked.

'Dumping the girl,' Helen replied.

He carefully manoeuvred around the large potholes and up towards the carpark's second level, out of sight of the entrance and road beyond.

Helen exited. 'This is it. Give me a hand to lift her out.'

He jumped out and rushed around to the side where together they manhandled Ellie's inert form into a patch of bracken.

'For such a skinny bint she's bloody heavy,' Helen's knees almost buckled, 'but it'll be a while before anybody finds her here.'

'Isn't it dangerous leaving her here before we've made it back to the boat?'

'No, she'll be out for ages, unless you want me to kill her so she can't talk when she comes back to her senses.'

He stared at the unconscious girl. 'No. I'm not getting involved in a murder. I'm already worried enough about what you're making me do.'

She smirked. 'Oh, you're such a girlie. Toughen up a bit.'

'Can we just go,' he said. 'I don't want to get caught.'

She burst out laughing. 'Oh, that's so neat.'

He turned to face her. 'What?'

'I think this might just be the exact same spot Zak dropped Ellie after she took a drug overdose.'

He frowned. 'Did he try to kill her?'

'Yes, but I don't want to do that anymore. I want her and Jemma to both suffer the pain of losing a child.'

'You're sick at times.' He stepped back inside the vehicle. 'You're certain she's still breathing?'

'She's fine.' Helen fastened her seatbelt under the intense scrutiny of the one-year-old in the child seat. 'When she wakes, she'll just have a headache that will last for a few hours and a nasty taste in her mouth that might last for the rest of her life.'

Chapter 37

After meeting back up, Jemma and Dan rushed back through Lulcombe, checking every shop and café they passed. Brad followed in his truck, driving up and down every side street. Mr Khan in the newsagent's wanted to chat but after Jemma explained about Ellie and Kira, he promised to keep an eye open for them. Dan tried Ellie's phone again but it was still ringing out without being answered.

Jemma bit her lip as they left the last shop before the hill up towards her cottage. 'I'm worried, Dan. I think I'd better call the police. I'm aware it's been less than an hour, but something doesn't feel right.'

As they walked up the hill, Dino suddenly barked and lurched at a gate to their left.

Jemma pulled back on his lead. 'Stop it, Dino. You're not chasing cats now... Wait a minute. Dan, ring Ellie's number again.'

He did as she said then snapped. 'Shush a moment. I can hear ringing.'

They rushed through the gate and into the garden of a small cottage.

Jemma pointed. 'Oh, my God. That's Kira's buggy. Ellie's

phone must be in the net.' She ran up the path and hammered on the door. After what seemed an age, she spotted movement through the glass door followed by the sound of bolts and locks being unlatched. The door creaked partially open and an elderly lady peeped out through a security chain.

'Is Ellie with you?' Jemma demanded.

'Hello, dearie. Who's Ellie?' the lady replied.

'Do you have a young girl and a baby with you?'

'No. I'm on my own. Have been for seventeen years, since my Bert passed on. Do you want to come in for tea?'

'No, thank you. I'm looking for my daughter and granddaughter.'

'Oh dear. I hope you find them. Goodbye.' The door slowly closed and the bolts were slid back into place.

Jemma turned to Dan. 'I'm ringing the police. Can you flag down Brad when he drives past?' She flicked to Amrik's name and jabbed the screen.

He answered immediately. 'Hi, Jemma. How are things?'

Jemma gabbled, 'Ellie's gone, Amrik. They've taken her and Kira.'

'What? Calm down and tell me what's happened.'

Jemma told Amrik everything she knew about the morning's events.

'So, she's been missing for an hour?' Amrik queried.

'Yes, but with your warnings, I think something's happened.'

'We have protocols for these situations with regards putting out alerts but with the abandoned buggy and the heightened concern about your family, I'll launch a full missing person and child investigation right now. Stay where you are, a car will be with you in ten minutes. I'll call when I'm on my way.'

The call ended as Brad came running up the path holding Rocky. Dan was alongside him.

Jemma hugged Brad and burst into tears. 'They've taken them both. They've got Ellie and Kira.'

* * *

At Swanbourne Police HQ, Amrik had called an emergency meeting of all detectives and dispatched two uniformed PCs that were nearby to the address Jemma had given. He explained the position to DI Day and she agreed to co-ordinate from headquarters while he and DC Salmon headed to the scene.

He grabbed his radio and a map and rushed out to the carpark with Hannah Salmon. Reaching his car, he threw her the keys. 'Here, you drive. I'll check the map and call Laura.'

She caught the keys and her eyes widened. 'What? Drive your Focus ST? You sure?'

'Just get on with it. I'll shove a blue light on the roof.' He opened the glove box, removed a light, switched it on and stuck it on the roof. 'You've done your emergency driving course?'

'I took it last year and passed with flying colours.'

'In that case, put your foot down.'

She spun the wheels as she exited the car park.

He grimaced. 'Oy, mind my tyres.'

'Yes, sir.' The car hurtled down the road.

Amrik unfolded the map and called back into the station. 'Laura, if you check the map on the wall, there are some good spots where we could set up roadblocks.'

'Do we know what vehicle we're on the lookout for?'

He thought for a moment. 'No idea yet but they can check for a girl and a child.'

'We can't set up a roadblock in search of something so vague. There'll be massive queues before we know it. I'll send a patrol car with a watching brief to each of the main junctions heading on to the A30, A35, A38 and M5. I'll start with Dorchester and Honiton.'

'OK, Laura. I'll get some door-to-door checks going to try to find some car details. Can you get somebody on to the traffic cameras?'

'Can do but it's better if they know what to look for.'

'We'll try finding some eyewitnesses. Can you alert neighbouring forces in Hampshire, Devon and Somerset?'

'Will do. Can you try to locate some pictures of Ellie and Kira?'

'There's already one of Ellie on the system after the episode with Zak Richards. I'll ask Jemma as well.'

'I bet she'll have some,' Laura said. 'If she's a typical grandmother, she'll have hundreds.'

'Thanks.' He ended the call and looked up from the map. 'Ooh, I feel a bit queasy. I never could read while in a car, especially one that's being flung around the bends like this.'

Hannah grinned. 'I've never driven one of these before. Goes like shit off a shovel.'

He rubbed his stomach. 'You might need to ease off the pedal a bit. I don't want to puke on my own car mats.'

She checked the satnav. 'We're here anyway. Look, there they are.'

They pulled up behind Brad's SUV, where another police car with blue lights flashing was already parked. Hannah turned the hazards on.

Amrik jumped out and ran over to Jemma. 'Any news?'

'No,' she replied. 'Your colleagues here asked a few neighbours but nobody saw anything. An abduction in broad daylight and nobody saw a bloody thing.'

* * *

Malek drove along the A380 at a steady pace past Newton

Abbot. On the left, the shimmering blue expanse of Torbay looked beautiful in the late morning sun.

Helen checked the satnav. 'Right, we'll be there in half an hour. I'll warn Ozlem.' She rang a number on Malek's phone, and a male voice answered.

'Hi, Malek. You've got a departure time?'

'Ozlem, it's me, Helen. Malek's driving. We'll be with you in thirty minutes so we can go as soon as you're ready.'

There was a pause. 'We must depart by ten after twelve as after then we'll miss the tide and won't be able to leave for another six hours.'

She checked her watch. 'That's fine. We'll be with you by eleven fifty-five so we can leave at twelve. We only need to unload the merchandise and get a ticket for the car.'

Ozlem laughed. 'The only problem is, Emree is having a drink in the town somewhere.'

She pursed her lips. 'Well ring him and tell him that if he's not back by midday, we leave him behind.'

'But I can't do without another crew member.'

'We leave at twelve.' Helen ended the call.

Arriving in Brixham, Malek drove into the rear carpark of a boarded-up pub, manoeuvred around a discarded shopping trolley and some fluorescent orange traffic cones, and changed the number plates for the second time. He placed the old ones by the suitcases in the back of the car, wiped his hands and drove away.

The car was suddenly filled with a wailing sound and an awful smell as Kira decided it was time to fill her nappy and complain about the lack of milk or food.

'Aman Tanrim! Korcunc koku,' Malek shouted.

Helen laughed. 'I can guess what that means. It is a bit ripe, isn't it? We'll have to wait until we're back on the ship before we change her now. I'm not doing it in the car.'

He opened his window and breathed deeply.

'Shut that,' she said. 'That's why it has tinted glass, so nobody can see us. Just man up and get us to the marina.'

He screwed up his face and dry retched. 'I think I'll swim back instead.'

She narrowed her eyes. 'That can be arranged, if you want...just like Teng... Oh, nothing.'

He stared at her wide-eyed. 'Did you kill Tengiz?'

She flapped a carefree hand. 'He tried to rape me when he was drunk, so he went over the side instead.'

'Then he's a bastard, but you shouldn't have killed him.'

She glared at him. 'It was self-defence. I wish I hadn't said anything. It was nothing.'

He turned away and stared out of the window.

At eleven fifty-five they drove past the replica of *The Golden Hind,* arriving at Brixham Marina where tourists mingled with boat users, and numerous couples and families strolled along the quayside admiring the more glamorous yachts. There was nowhere to park so Malek circled around until an elderly couple returned to their Volvo.

Helen checked her watch while the couple stepped inside before proceeding to mess about with their bags. 'Come on, come on. We've got a boat to catch.'

The ancient gold Volvo backed out of the space and Malek swooped in before any other motorist tried outflanking him. He grabbed a handful of pound coins, donned his sunglasses and strolled towards the ticket machine. Halfway through the purchase he twisted around and walked back in the direction of the car to read the registration number before hurrying back and entering it in the machine, taking the ticket and rushing back to the car.

He opened the door and stuck the ticket onto the inside of the windscreen. 'All done.'

'You took your time. Right, you go first with the cases and, if the coast is clear, put your hand up and I'll bring the child seat.'

Malek got out, lifted the tailgate and pulled out the two cases. He thrust the old number plates inside a carrier bag, closed the door and headed for the Fish Dock. On the way, he dropped the bag into a litter bin and stepped onto the gangplank of the *Goke*.

Ozlem rushed down towards him and took the suitcases. 'Quick, Emree is on his way back.'

Malek twisted around to wave at Helen before walking back with the keys.

She opened her door and walked around to the side of the car where she reached inside and unbuckled the child seat. Removing it out through the gap, along with a crying infant, was a tight squeeze.

Malek watched while she strolled across the carpark before he locked the Range Rover and placed the keys behind the front wheel. He then followed her back to the boat.

'You ready to go?' Helen asked Ozlem as he came down the gangplank.

He glanced towards the town. 'Nearly, Emree is almost here.'

She scowled at her watch. 'We go in five minutes, whether he's here or not.'

Chapter 38

Brad pulled up outside Jemma's cottage and Jemma, Dan, Rocky and Dino exited the car. They rushed inside the house and Dino ran around with such excitement that he knocked over a bucket of fossils Jemma had left by the door.

Jemma fussed her dog and ignored the mess. 'Where can they be?' She spread an Ordnance Survey map of Western Dorset over the kitchen table along with a motoring atlas that covered south west England.

Brad leant over the maps. 'Amrik said they were watching airports and ferry ports in case Helen is involved. They've got no evidence yet, but he's sure she's involved somehow.'

She dragged a hand through her hair. 'He said they were watching ones with direct flights to Cyprus or Turkey, and also major ports. They could always be flying somewhere else first or using a minor ferry port.'

Dan wrung his hands. 'I feel so helpless, like I should be doing something but I don't know what. It's all my fault. It was *me* who asked her to come down to the café.'

Brad put his hand on Dan's shoulder. 'It's not your fault. I bet they'd have grabbed her some other time anyway.'

Dan shrugged. 'Maybe.'

* * *

At Swanbourne Police HQ, Amrik and Hannah were standing by the incident board pondering the information.

'Any news?' Laura asked as she came up behind them.

'No,' Amrik confirmed. 'It's like looking for a needle in a haystack. We don't even know what vehicle they're in.' He checked his watch. 'They could be in London by now.'

Laura peered at the map. 'Nothing has come in from the observation patrols at Honiton or Dorchester, but they don't really know what they're looking for.'

'I've been checking the traffic cam footage from the road between Lulcombe and Swanbourne. I got to two hundred registration numbers in an hour so someone else has taken over while I check through the owners of those cars. We need a sighting,' Hannah said.

'Did you check the airports and ferry ports?' Laura asked Amrik.

'Yep,' he replied. 'Nothing from the facial recognition software or super-recognisers. We've alerted the authorities in France, and the Greek part of Cyprus, though we could do with a more up-to-date picture of Helen Fletcher. Other than the grainy immigration shot, the only one we have is from an arrest twenty years ago.'

'What was she arrested for?' Hannah asked.

Amrik checked the board. 'Actual Bodily Harm was all they could ever pin on her. She managed to get away with a suspended sentence.'

'Don't forget,' Laura added, 'it could be somebody else she's paying but we've no idea who.'

* * *

Helen was standing on the bridge of the *Goke* watching the second hands move around on the clock. Ozlem paced up and down and rang Emree again. He received no reply and continued pacing.

She called Harry Collins who answered immediately.

'Helen.'

'The Range Rover is ready to collect. We've reattached the spare plates and paid for a twenty-four-hour ticket.'

'OK,' he replied. 'I'll book a train and come fetch it.'

She grinned. 'By the way, you've got a parking fine on its way for the day you left it as you didn't stick long enough on the ticket.'

'I'll sort it. I hope you had a good trip.'

'A very good trip and I got a lovely souvenir.'

* * *

Lying in the bracken, Ellie opened her eyes. Her head was spinning and, as she tried to sit up, she was overwhelmed with nausea. She twisted to the side to be sick, spat into the grass and wiped her mouth with a sleeve. Her eyes burnt so she shaded them from the sun overhead. As consciousness gradually came back to her, she pushed herself onto her hands and knees and twisted her body until she sat upright. Taking in her surroundings, she was overcome with a terrible feeling of déjà vu.

'Oh no,' she groaned. 'Not here again.'

She slowly stood upright and surveyed the reserve before once again feeling dizzy and falling back to her knees. She tried to clear her mind, to think why she was back here. Slowly focusing on her surroundings, she realised something was missing, and in an instant knew what it was. 'Kira!'

Chapter 39

Malek called across the bridge to Ozlem. 'We go now.'

The captain glanced at his phone. 'He'll be here in a minute. We're already a man down with the skeleton crew we have.'

'Can we go to Cartagena and pick up somebody else there?' Helen asked.

Ozlem frowned. 'We can't go without him.'

She stared at him. 'We go at ten-past-twelve. If he's not here, he flies back.'

Ozlem's hands shook as he started the engine and shouted at Burak to untie the mooring ropes.

* * *

A lone buzzard cried in the sky as Ellie stumbled across the nature reserve towards the top carpark while her eyes darted around looking for cars or somebody out walking. The movement made her retch again and she fell to her knees. Once the sick feeling passed, she returned to her feet and staggered across the gravel.

Reaching the carpark and finding nobody around, she was unable to stop the tears from running down her cheeks. Each step was an effort and she needed several minutes to shuffle further as she gazed into the distance. 'Where's my baby?' Another wave of nausea hit her and she bent over to be sick. As she wiped her mouth she sobbed. 'Somebody help me, please.'

Just when she decided to try the main road, a white Vauxhall estate swung into the carpark and stopped. The driver's door opened and a middle-aged lady in a dark green cardigan and black trousers got out. She lifted the tailgate and a golden retriever jumped down before noticing Ellie and dashing straight towards her. It pushed its nose against her hand and she stumbled again, dropping to her knees.

'Bella. Come back here,' the woman shouted.

Ellie put her hands on the dog's back to steady herself and its tail wagged faster.

The lady rushed over. 'I'm so sorry, she's normally so well-behaved.'

Ellie lifted her head and tried to talk but only a whisper came out.

The woman's eyes opened wide. 'Oh, my goodness. Are you alright? You look terrible. You're not drunk or on drugs, are you?'

Ellie shook her head but it made her feel worse. 'I've been attacked. My baby's been kidnapped.'

The lady's eyes bulged before she ran back to her car and returned with a coat that she draped around Ellie's shoulders. 'I'll call the police. What's your name?'

'Ellie,' she croaked. 'Ellie Thorne.'

'I'm Tina. Come and sit in the car while I ring them.' She slipped her arm around Ellie and led her towards the car before helping her into the passenger seat. She took out her mobile and called the emergency services.

* * *

Amrik was sitting in the major incident room with a map of Southern England spread before him on the desk. He drew an arc through Exeter and wrote *one hour* by it. He added a larger circle centred on Lulcombe that passed through Southampton and wrote *two hours* on it.

He tutted. 'Such a massive area. Where are they going?' He grabbed his mobile and called Jemma.

The call was answered instantly. 'Amrik, what is it? Have you found her?' a frantic voice asked.

'Sorry, Jemma. Nothing yet. A question for you. Does Kira have a passport?'

Jemma hesitated. 'Yes. Both Kira and Ellie's passports are in the kitchen drawer at home.'

'Thanks. I wondered if whoever took Kira would be able to fly out of the country.'

'Oh. Right.' Jemma's voice trailed off.

'I'll let you know when we hear anything.' He ended the call and put down his mobile before adding *No Passport* to the space underneath the photo of Kira on the incident white-board. The phone on his desk chirped and he answered it. 'DS Hussain.'

'Amrik, it's Sarge. I've had a call from the emergency controller. A lady has rung in claiming to have found Ellie Thorne in a confused state at Swanbourne Scenic Viewpoint. They dispatched a car first and then called us.'

Amrik grabbed his radio. 'Thanks, Sarge, I'm on my way.' He dropped the receiver onto its base. 'Laura, Ellie's been found alive. Hannah, come with me.' He grabbed his car keys and ran for the stairs with DS Salmon panting behind him.

Laura called after him. 'Update me on the way.'

* * *

Jemma and Brad were on their laptops scribbling down the details of any flights to Northern Cyprus.

'Are you finding many scheduled flights?' Jemma asked.

Brad shook his head. 'No, they're mainly charter ones linked to holiday companies. I've listed them all anyway and emailed the list to Amrik. I've also suggested they check any private planes as Helen's got loads of money after the hotel site sale.'

Jemma's mobile rang and she answered immediately. 'Hi, Amrik.'

'Jemma, Ellie's OK. She was found in the Swanbourne Scenic Viewpoint carpark.'

She started sobbing. 'And Kira?'

'No sign, I'm afraid. I'm on my way to the carpark now.'

'We'll see you there in a few minutes.'

Brad hugged her. 'I'll just get Rocky and then we can go.'

She grabbed her coat and phone. Dino stuck his head up out of his basket. 'Sorry, Dino, I'll take you out later.'

They rushed out of the door and headed to Swanbourne.

* * *

As Burak coiled up the ropes and removed the gangplank, Ozlem confirmed to the harbour master that they were leaving and thanked him for the berth. He pushed the throttle forward and the ship moved away from the quay.

'Wait,' Malek shouted, 'here he is.'

A figure was sprinting across the carpark and, as Ozlem reversed the boat slightly, Emree jumped from the quay and landed in a sprawled heap on the deck. He stood with a grin and dusted himself down. 'That was close.'

* * *

Malek strolled up onto the deck away from the noise in the cab where Helen was busy trying to placate the screaming infant. He leant on the rail and stared as Torbay disappeared behind the chugging trawler. *Is this all worth it? What have I got myself into?*

Chapter 40

Brad raced along the road from Lulcombe to Swanbourne. Traffic was light and he'd already overtaken two campervans and a tractor.

An unknown number flashed up on Jemma's screen. She took a breath and answered. 'Hello.'

A croaky voice spoke. 'Mum, it's me.'

'Ellie! Are you OK?'

'I'm fine but somebody's got Kira.'

'I know, Els, Amrik told me. We're a few minutes away from the viewpoint carpark. See you in a bit.' Jemma ended the call. 'Quick, Brad. It's just over the next hill.'

* * *

Helen stood outside the bridge holding a cigarette. She took a deep drag and then threw the butt over the side of the ship before sliding open the door and entering.

Ozlem nodded. 'Morning. I didn't know you smoked.'

'I don't...normally, but our cabin guest is being a little difficult.'

'So, Malek is in charge now?'

'Yes. We've tried a bottle of milk to see if that does the trick.' She peered at the instruments. 'Can't this crate go any faster?'

'No, the engines are running at eighty per cent. I can't push them any more with twenty-four-hour operation and only three people sharing the bridge.'

'How long will it take to get back?' she asked.

'Eighteen days with an overnight stop in Cartagena to refuel and take on water and supplies.'

She shook her head. 'Can't we keep moving through the night? I'll pay extra.'

'Sorry. We only have a crew of three, which is half what we need. We should also do some fishing at some point. If we arrive back in Kyrenia without a catch the harbour authorities may be suspicious.'

'I don't care about sodding fish. If you can get us back quicker than eighteen days, I'll pay you ten thousand euros for every day you save. Use some of the money to bribe the port people to ignore the lack of fish.'

Ozlem rubbed his eyes. 'OK, I'll try.'

She turned and stepped off the bridge. 'Just do it.' The door banged shut as she headed back to the cabin.

* * *

Brad swung his truck into the viewpoint carpark and skidded to a halt on the rough gravel.

'You go,' he said. 'I'll bring Rocky.'

Jemma jumped out leaving her door wide open and ran across to where some people were huddled around a police patrol car with flashing blue lights.

She pushed through the small group. 'Excuse me...Ellie?'

Her daughter wrapped her arms around her. 'Oh, Mum. It was awful.' She burst into tears. 'I don't know where my baby is.'

One of the constables touched Ellie's arm. 'Can I finish taking your statement, please, Miss Thorne?'

Ellie pulled herself free from her mother's embrace. 'OK. I won't be long.'

The policeman continued asking Ellie questions and writing the answers on his tablet.

Brad joined Jemma and Rocky ran over to his sister.

'Hey, matey. How you doing?' Ellie asked.

Rocky looked around. 'Where's Kira? I want her.'

Ellie wiped away her tears and hugged her little brother. 'She's playing hide and seek, but we'll find her soon.' Her voice cracked so she took a swig of water from the bottle she was holding.

Another vehicle swung into the carpark and Jemma recognised Amrik at the wheel of the orange sports car with a stick-on blue light flashing on its roof. He rushed straight over, closely followed by DC Salmon. One of the uniformed officers met him first.

'Afternoon, Sir, I've emailed you a copy of the basic statement Miss Thorne has just made.'

'Good work, PC...' Amrik's voice rose towards the final word.

'Daly, sir.'

'Good work, PC Daly. Important points?'

'Miss Thorne seems OK but has refused a hospital check. Her daughter is still missing and she hasn't seen her since the abduction. All she can remember is that the pavement was blocked by the door of a large dark vehicle, black or blue, and a suitcase. A man stood in the way, so she waited. He grabbed her and pushed her into the back of the car where an older woman covered her nose and mouth with an evil-smelling cloth before she blacked out. Next thing she knew, she woke up in the bracken at the back of the carpark.'

Amrik smiled at Ellie. 'That's great for now. We'll need a

fuller statement back at the station, but time is critical. Any ideas about the make of vehicle?'

Ellie rubbed her eyes and paused. 'It was big. One of the four by fours.'

Hannah tapped her phone and held up the screen with some vehicle pictures. 'Any of these look familiar?'

Sunlight reflected off the mobile display so Ellie shielded it with her hand and scrolled down the page. 'No. No. No. Wait, this one. That's it, a Range Rover.'

Amrik took out his radio and called into Police HQ. 'Vehicle involved in the child abduction in Lulcombe is believed to be a dark Range Rover, most likely black or dark blue. Please circulate the details, and I want a list of the plates of any vehicles matching that description that passed any traffic cameras within two hours of Lulcombe.'

A silver van pulled up and four people wearing white Tyvek suits climbed out of the back. One of them led the way towards the detectives while the others followed carrying plastic cantilever boxes.

'DS Hussain?' the woman asked.

Amrik smiled. 'How did you guess?'

'Er...you looked the most senior, sir,' she replied. 'Where do you want us?'

He pointed. 'The kidnapping victim was left in that area by a vehicle we believe to have been a dark-coloured Range Rover or similar. I'd like a search for any very fresh tyre tracks or footprints, although quite a few people have been traipsing around.'

'Right, sir, we're on to it,' the woman said.

The team dispersed around the area Ellie had been dumped and started searching.

Amrik turned to Ellie. 'We need to get you checked over. Sounds like they used chloroform on you and that's pretty nasty stuff.'

She took another long swig of water, rinsing her mouth

and spitting into the grass. 'Tell me about it. I'm not bothered about hospital, I just want to start looking for Kira.'

The scene's gathering was swollen by the arrival of a white and orange ambulance. It stopped close to Jemma and two green-uniformed paramedics rushed out.

Amrik pointed to Ellie. 'Check her over, please. She'll say no.' He grinned. 'But ignore her. She's been abducted and unconscious for around fifteen minutes to half an hour. It's possible they used chloroform to knock her out.'

One of the medical team took Ellie's arm, led her towards the ambulance and sat her on the bed.

Amrik pressed some buttons on his radio. 'Laura, does the name *The Chloroform Queen* mean anything to you?' He waited a few moments.

'Oh,' he replied. 'Can you check on the system, please?'

He lowered his radio and spoke to Jemma. 'I'm sure I've read something recently about that name.'

He listened again. 'Yes, Laura. Bloody hell, thought as much. The bitch got through somehow. I'll be back soon with Ellie and Jemma.'

He turned to them. 'I think Helen Fletcher was involved in the abduction. Her nickname twenty years ago throughout London crime circles was *The Chloroform Queen*.'

Jemma gulped and the colour drained from her face. 'Do we want to know why?'

Amrik shook his head. 'Let's just say she used it to make some of her rivals more compliant before she did bad things to them.'

'But why should she want Kira?' Brad queried.

Ellie's eyes widened. 'Oh, my God,' she gasped. 'She wanted her grandchild. Kira is Zak's child and she's the fucking evil gran.'

Chapter 41

A bleary-eyed Ellie sat at Jemma's old kitchen table with her laptop resting on its scarred wooden surface. Jemma perched on the edge of a chair with an atlas on her lap while Brad flicked through his iPad. Dino lay curled in his basket with Rocky on the floor beside him stroking his back. The only sound in the room, apart from fingers tapping computer keys, was the rhythmical ticking of the sideboard clock.

It was seven am and nobody had slept much the previous night. After the paramedics pronounced Ellie was OK, she just wanted to go home.

'Brad,' Jemma said, 'can you make a list of European capitals that fly to Istanbul, please?'

'Can do,' he replied. 'What are you thinking?'

'I reckon she'll avoid the main channel ports, which are bound to be watched, but she could be trying to get to the continent somehow before flying back that way.'

Ellie thumped the table. 'I feel so bloody helpless. What more can I do?'

'Try to stay calm, Els. Amrik is going to call at eight with an update.' Jemma checked her watch. 'That's in fifty minutes. Anybody want tea or coffee?' She put the kettle on and returned to Western Europe.

* * *

At the police HQ in Swanbourne, Amrik was standing next to DI Day in front of the assembled group of detectives.

Laura tapped the desk. 'Thanks for coming in early. Sorry to have cancelled your time off but the first forty-eight hours in a disappearance is crucial. We've already got some extra team members from Devon and Hampshire.' She nodded in the direction of four officers sitting together. 'Thanks and welcome. Right, I'll hand you over to DS Amrik Hussain who'll be leading the investigation and allocating tasks. Amrik.'

'Thanks, Laura.' He checked his notes. 'First, a recap.' He pointed to a red cross on the whiteboard map. 'Just here, on Hill Street in Lulcombe at approximately ten-thirty am yesterday, Ellie Thorne, a twenty-one-year-old single mother, and her twelve-month-old daughter, Kira Thorne, were abducted by two people. It was broad daylight, but no witnesses have yet come forward. Sometime between ten forty-five and eleven am, Ellie, who had been rendered unconscious with chloroform, was dumped in the carpark at Swanbourne Scenic Viewpoint.' He pointed again at the map. 'Here.'

One of the visiting officers raised a hand. 'How long a drive is that?'

'Depending on traffic,' Amrik answered, 'around twenty minutes. Any other questions so far? No? OK, Ellie was shaken and queasy but otherwise unharmed. There was no sign of the youngster. In her statement, she described the vehicle, which we think is a dark Range Rover, and the abductors. One is a young male in his thirties with a Mediterranean appearance. The other is an older white woman who we think might be Helen Fletcher, AKA Helen

Barnes. She was the mastermind of a nasty plot to avenge the deaths of her brothers by killing Jemma Thorne, Ellie's mother. The attempt ended in failure and also caused the deaths of Helen's two sons in a mudslide on Lulcombe Beach.'

Another hand was raised. 'What's the connection between Jemma and the Fletchers?'

Amrik grimaced at Laura. 'I'll update the newcomers on the full story later. I could fill a whole hour with *that* history. Suffice it to say we believe Helen Fletcher is Kira Thorne's grandmother and has deliberately abducted the child. She lives in the Turkish Republic of Northern Cyprus, which does not have an extradition treaty with the UK, so we do not anticipate any help from the authorities there. If she manages to get the child to her home, there may be nothing anyone can do to rescue her. The next few hours are crucial.'

He continued to explain how he thought Helen might try to get home, as well as the checks they'd already put in place. 'Any final questions?'

'Are you naming Helen Fletcher as the suspect?'

Amrik rubbed his chin. 'Possibly, but we may just say she's a person of interest as we don't yet have any proof. We've recovered some fingerprints from the child's buggy, which was thrown into a garden, but they're not on the system. I've made a list of tasks with names, so if you could please get stuck in... Laura and I will contact the family to arrange a press conference and appeal for later this morning. Laura?'

Laura stood. 'Thanks, Amrik. I'm continuing to chase any spare staff, even if they're not spare. Let's get Kira back.'

* * *

Jemma drove Ellie to Swanbourne leaving Brad to look after Rocky and take Dino for a walk. With all the strange happenings occurring, the poor dog seemed to be feeling left out.

Amrik had called, asking them to come into the HQ for a televised appeal and press conference at ten am.

'Oh, God, this brings back all the memories from when Rocky was taken,' Jemma gripped the steering wheel. 'I know what you're going through, Els.'

Ellie frowned. 'I hope we get Kira back as quickly as we did Rocky. At the time I didn't fuliy understand how hard it was for you. I realise now what you went through. It's like a part of me is missing.'

Jemma took her hand from the wheel and stroked Ellie's arm. Rocky had been kidnapped by Zak Fletcher but luckily somebody had heard Rocky crying in an empty apartment and he'd been rescued unharmed.

They arrived at the police headquarters and Amrik showed them up to the press room where a number of television crews and journalists had already assembled. Amrik took them into a side room and told them what would happen, explaining to Ellie what she should say and not say. Ten minutes later, they stepped back into the press room and Ellie took a seat on the podium alongside Amrik and DI Laura Day.

A large photograph of Kira was displayed on the projector screen behind Ellie. She turned to stare at it and had to fight back the tears.

Laura grasped her hand. 'You OK to start?'

Ellie turned back to face the front. 'Yes, I think so.'

She scanned the large room. A number of desks and chairs were lined up in front, all full of press people holding microphones and laptops. At the back of the room several larger TV cameras on tripods all pointed in her direction. She sipped water from her glass and cleared her throat.

Laura called for silence. 'Good morning. We are here to help find Kira Thorne, the one-year-old daughter of Ellie Thorne, who is here on my right.' She turned to the wide-eyed girl. 'Ellie.'

Ellie took a breath. 'Thank you, DI Day. I'm Ellie Thorne

and my daughter, Kira, has been kidnapped. I don't know where she is but I'm desperate to have her back.'

Laura took over. 'We have descriptions of the kidnappers, which we will circulate. The kidnapping took place on Hill Street in Lulcombe at around ten-thirty am yesterday. Both Ellie and her daughter were snatched by a couple in a large dark vehicle. Ellie was attacked by an older woman with a chloroform-impregnated cloth and was later dumped at a nature reserve in Swanbourne. There was no sign of Kira. If anybody saw anything on Hill Street or in the vicinity of Swanbourne Nature Reserve at around eleven am, then please get in touch at the number on the bottom of the screen. That's the end of our statement. Any questions?'

A number of hands were raised and for fifteen minutes Laura answered questions without giving much more information. Finally, the questions dried up and she turned to Ellie. 'A final word please, Ellie.'

'Please help me get my daughter back.' She broke down and Amrik helped her off the podium and out of the room.

* * *

After leaving the English Channel, the *Goke* passed west of the French port of Brest and headed for the unpredictable waters of the Bay of Biscay.

The rolling of the boat, which was not designed for passenger comfort, did not pacify Kira. Her screams exacerbated, prompting Malek to sit for long periods wearing his headphones.

After attempting to feed the youngster a bottle of powdered milk, Helen returned her to the cot. 'That's enough now, you little bitch, just be quiet.'

Malek removed his headphones. 'Perhaps you should take her back or drop her off somewhere, like over the side.'

She clenched her fists. ‘Don’t be so stupid. I’ve invested too much money in this project to give up now.’

She handed him the milk. ‘Here, you have a go, I need some fresh air.’

He stared down at the screaming child, who let out a noisy wet trump, followed by a barrage of nappy-filling gurgles.

Helen grinned. ‘You’d better change her first.’

He grimaced. ‘I’m not changing a nappy.’

‘Just get on with it,’ she tapped his chest with a finger, ‘or you can say goodbye to your new Porsche.’

Chapter 42

Harry Collins paid the taxi driver, donned his sunglasses and rucksack and headed for Brixham Harbour, having decided to wear shorts and sandals to blend in as just another Devon holidaymaker. There were some strange glances on the Paddington platform at six am but once he left Paignton station he felt less conspicuous.

Even at ten-thirty in the morning, crowds had gathered around the Fish Dock quayside waiting for the boats to unload their morning's catch to a barrage of seagull calls. He skirted the small crowd of shoppers and wandered into the carpark where the dark Range Rover was parked under a tree on the far edge. He strolled over, dumped his rucksack by the front wheel and, with a quick glance at his surroundings, knelt to sort through the bag's contents whilst smoothly reaching behind the tyre to retrieve the small plastic bag containing the keys.

He climbed inside, adjusted the seat and mirror before driving from the carpark and heading out of town. After a couple of miles, he spotted the deserted pub and pulled around the back, out of view of the road. He removed the old plates, opened his rucksack and pulled out a pair of new ones. Peeling off the adhesive pads, he stuck them onto the car.

'Back to my own plates. That'll confuse them.' He chuckled to himself and headed towards the M5 to start the long drive back to London.

* * *

Helen stepped onto the bridge. 'Is it going to be as rough as it was on the way here?'

'Oh no,' Ozlem replied.

'Thank Christ for that.' She sighed.

He glanced at her. 'Let me finish, please... It's going to be a lot worse. A low-pressure system is building out in the Atlantic and it will hit us soon.'

'Oh, shut up,' she growled. 'That'll cheer up Malek.'

He reached for a couple of bright orange lifejackets and handed them to her. 'You must wear them for the next few days whenever you are on deck. And these two cables are to clip yourself to the safety rail as well.'

'That's bloody wonderful.'

'Don't worry. The *Goke* is designed for seas much rougher than we'll see down here. It's just that there will be plenty of side waves and a five-metre swell. You can fasten yourselves in your bunks if you're struggling and I've got more straps for your...cargo.'

'Thanks,' she muttered. 'How long will it last?'

Ozlem paused. 'Depends on how deep the system gets. We're due to go through the Strait of Gibraltar on day six so it could be a bit rough for three or four days. We can always call in at A Caruna or Lisbon if it gets too much for you.'

She narrowed her eyes. 'We're not stopping any extra nights.'

'OK,' he replied. 'Two-two-five degrees it is and heads down.'

She held up the life jackets. 'I'll give Malek his present and the good news about the weather.'

* * *

Following the press conference, Jemma and Ellie drove back to Swanbourne Police HQ for an update. Amrik met them in reception before taking them up to the major incident room.

'We don't normally allow civilians up here, but you've been to the station so many times it's easier to go through stuff here.'

The large room had windows all along one wall with a bank of computer monitors on desks at the other side. A long table with twelve chairs dominated the centre, and was covered with maps and printouts.

'Thanks,' Jemma acknowledged. 'Any joy?'

He nodded. 'We took a lot of calls after the appeal and we have a team going through all the responses. I'm afraid these things drag all the creeps and attention seekers out from the woodwork. Nothing useful so far though. We've been doing house-to-house enquiries all along Hill Street and I've got teams going through traffic cam footage from Swanbourne, Honiton, Dorchester, the M5 at Exeter, the M3 at Southampton and the M4 near Bristol Airport.'

Ellie rubbed her eyes. 'They've got to show up somewhere. What about airports?'

He shook his head. 'With the surveillance we've got in place and the fact they don't have a passport for Kira, I'm sure we'd know if they tried to fly out.'

Jemma stared at a wall map. 'Could they be hiding out nearby, waiting for the search to tail off?'

He stood next to her. 'Possibly, but, if it is Helen, she'll probably want to be back in Cyprus as quickly as she can.'

'No response from the TRNC?' Ellie asked.

He shook his head. 'Nah, they don't acknowledge

anything we send. I keep ringing but I never get through to anyone who's willing to do anything.'

Ellie frowned. 'What about the carpark where they dumped me?'

'Forensics have been all over it. All they found were some tyre tracks, which they've identified as Pirelli Scorpion Zeros. They're pretty common on over a dozen makes of SUV, including Range Rovers, so we're sure that's what they used.' His head tilted. 'Have the press been chasing you?'

'A bit,' she replied. 'I've done some telephone interviews and went out to talk to a couple of journalists hanging around the front gate.'

'Just watch them,' Amrik said. 'In cases like this, they often twist the things you say and accuse the parents.'

A thin smile crossed her face. 'They seemed nice enough and they're happy to share Kira's photo in their articles. I haven't mentioned Helen's name yet, as you said.'

He shrugged. 'That still seems right as we don't have any evidence to prove she's taken Kira or even been in the country.'

'Oh, she's been here,' Jemma said quietly. 'I can feel her malignant presence.'

Chapter 43

The rest of the week flew by in a whirl of meetings, interviews and telephone calls. However, as the days passed the media interest in Kira's kidnapping diminished as other headline-grabbing stories took precedence. By Thursday, the reporters who'd camped outside Jemma and Ellie's house had drifted away one by one, drawn to a warehouse fire in Bristol and the Minister for Health's extra-marital affair. Only the local paper still ran daily updates, buried now on page six.

Ellie watched the latest news on South-West TV and sobbed. 'There's been no mention of Kira again, Mum. They've forgotten about her already.'

'Don't worry, Els, there's a lot going on behind the scenes,' Jemma replied. 'Amrik's got fifteen people on his team, all looking for her.'

Ellie wiped her face with a sleeve. 'I know but so far they've found nothing, nada, zilch, sod all.'

'They will, though, somebody's got to have spotted something.'

'I feel so helpless,' Ellie said. 'I need to do something, but I haven't a clue what to do. My gut feeling is she's not in the country anymore. I should be going to Cyprus and searching there.'

Brad reached over for her hand. 'If that's what it takes, we'll do it. Let's all keep our bags packed in case there's any news so we can leave at a moment's notice.'

Ellie stared at him through her tears. 'You'd do that?'

'Of course, I would. We'll tear the place apart to find her if we have to.'

* * *

Amrik and Laura were sitting with mugs of tea at the front of the briefing meeting in the Major Incident Room at Swanbourne Police HQ. The equipment had been beefed up and there were now twelve computer monitors on desks along one wall. Half were linked to telephones but only one was currently in use logging any calls still coming in after the TV appeal. The initial surge had dwindled to just a few per hour.

'Morning team,' Laura Day said. 'Can we have the latest update please, Amrik?'

Amrik stood. 'Certainly, DI Day. We now know seven dark Range Rovers passed Swanbourne traffic cameras in the two hours following Kira and Ellie's abduction. We have managed to track down the owners of six but the final one was using false plates.'

He pointed a remote control and a grainy image of a car appeared on the white wall behind the bank of computers. 'This is an enhanced version of the image. You can just about make out the faces of a man and a woman, though it's not clear enough for an accurate ID. We've searched for those numbers on all SUVs within eight hours of the abduction time with no success.'

He pressed the clicker again and another close-up picture of a car windscreen appeared. 'We checked the motorway cameras for any other dark Range Rovers within the eight hour period and got over one hundred and eighty hits. We're following up on every registration but haven't found that number again. They may have changed plates.'

A hand raised. 'Could they have flown from Exeter Airport?'

'Good question,' Amrik replied. 'We've checked every flight out during the following forty-eight hours and every child under the age of four has been identified and accounted for. We have to face the fact they might have gone to ground or possibly taken a boat of some kind from one of the Marinas at Torquay, Paignton, Brixham, Dartmouth or Plymouth.' He sipped his water. 'We're currently checking the immigration records for all of those but many are voluntary and rely on passengers to sign in and out themselves.'

Laura gestured to a larger map of Europe. 'So, they could be somewhere on a vessel back to Cyprus?'

'Yes,' Amrik conceded. 'The problem is there are thousands of boats out at sea between here and the Med. Without any idea of the boat involved, it's very difficult.'

* * *

Brad and Jemma were in the workshop gazing at the ichthyosaur bones laid out on the workbench.

She stroked the skull. 'You know, sometimes I forget I'm a fossil hunter. I've had so much shit going on in my life since I found Plessie, I never seem to have time to do what I really love: find and prepare fossils.'

He came up behind and slipped his arms around her. 'It has been a wild time since I came back to England.'

'I bet you wish you'd never seen my face again,' she said.

He kissed her gently on the back of the neck, making her tingle. 'What, and not had my time with you and Ellie...and Rocky...and Kira...and Dino. I wouldn't have missed a minute of it. We'll be a full family again soon, I'm sure of it.'

Jemma turned and rested her head on his chest. 'I just want some normality without child kidnappings, murders, thefts and general madness. I want us all to be happy but it's not happening.' She started sobbing. 'Why can't we be a normal family?'

'I don't know, Jem. You're a bloody hard worker and you deserve some peace in your life.'

'One day, Brad, one day.'

* * *

Thirteen hundred miles south of Lulcombe in southern Spain, the fishing trawler *Goke* made its way past an enormous cruise ship into Cartagena Harbour and moved alongside the fuel dispensers.

Ozlem stepped off the bridge and spoke to one of the dock staff. 'Llenarla por favor, fill her up.'

The dock worker rubbed his hands on his stained blue overalls and put his thumb up.

'Ningun problema,' he shouted back and handed the end of the pipe to Emree.

After taking on fuel and fresh water Ozlem paid for those and the mooring fees and pulled up next to a large berth.

He went down and knocked on Helen's cabin door.

She opened it a crack and peered out. 'What?' she snapped.

'Can't we stay overnight? We're all exhausted and need a night in a proper bed.'

'No. Remember your bonus. I want to leave as soon as possible.'

'We can't spend a bonus if we sink because of a mistake due to tiredness,' he snapped.

'Look,' Helen said, 'I'm the one paying for everything on this trip, and I say what we do.'

Ozlem pointed his finger a few inches from her face. 'And

I'm the captain of the *Goke* and I'm the one responsible for the safety of the crew and passengers.'

She smacked his hand away. 'Well, you did a great job with Tengiz, didn't you?'

He clenched his fists. 'That was not my fault. He drank too much.'

'Don't be so melodramatic.' She sneered. 'Malek needs to buy some nappies and three hours is all we need.' She glanced behind her. 'Our cargo is a shitting machine.'

'If we sink, it's your fault.' He threw up an arm. 'Tell Malek we go ashore in ten minutes...without you.'

'I'll wake him up,' Helen said.

Two and a half hours later Ozlem, Malek, Emree and Burak were in the queue at the immigration and customs desk. They each presented their passports to the uniformed officer who copied them, stamped them with a flourish and noted their details on his computer.

He glanced up. 'Anything to declare? Alcohol, drugs, large amounts of currency?'

'Nothing much.' Ozlem pointed at their carrier bags. 'A few bottles of whisky and my friend here has bought lots of nappies to take home to his wife.' He laughed. 'They're cheaper here.'

'Back home to noisy babies then. Sounds like he'll be glad to be back at sea.' The customs officer grinned. 'OK, all is good, off you go.'

They left the office and headed back towards the boat with Emree and Burak chatting in Turkish.

Ozlem nodded at Malek. 'She's mad you know, your woman.'

Malek shook his head. 'There are times when I wish I'd never met her. She's going to be the death of me.'

Chapter 44

Friday was Kira's first birthday and the family had gathered at Jemma's cottage for a subdued celebration where Ellie had bought a pink cake covered in animal characters. Jemma's father, Bernard, was doing well after coming out of his coma but wasn't ready to leave the care facility yet. Her mum, Carol, had come, but was finding it difficult to stop crying.

Jemma opened a bottle of Prosecco and Ellie cut the cake while sniffing back tears. They raised their glasses to the framed photo and pile of wrapped presents on the sideboard.

With a shaking hand, Ellie picked up a piece of cake and stared at it before bursting into tears and throwing it into the sink. She ran through the door into her cottage and stomped upstairs.

Rocky stared at the adults. 'Is Ellie OK?'

Jemma ran her hand through his hair. 'She's just missing Kira. She'll be better once she's home.'

'When is Kira coming home, Mummy?' he asked.

'Soon, Rocky. Soon.'

Brad stood. 'Shall I go and check on her?'

Jemma shook her head. 'I'd leave her for a while to have a good cry. I'll go up a bit later.'

* * *

DC Hannah Salmon spent a frustrating morning on the phone with Interpol trying to speak to an officer who might be able to help. Using a map of Europe while assuming an average yacht speed of five to ten knots per hour, she'd been able to plot a range of possible ports where a boat might call on the journey from the southwest of England to Northern Cyprus. DI Day had allocated a small budget for interpreters to help with calls to ports in France, Portugal, Spain, Sicily and Crete. While her interpreter, Isabella, rattled away to an official at the Spanish National Police, Hannah measured and added the next two days to the chart.

'Gracias. Adios.' Isabella finished the call and turned to Hannah. 'They will speak to the Policia Municipal and immigration and customs in Cartagena and will call back if they have any information.'

Hannah clenched her fists. 'I feel so helpless just sitting here by the phone. I should be out there searching with the others.'

* * *

Helen leant on the guard rail of the *Goke* watching the lights of Crete to the north.

Malek stood beside her with his arm around her waist. Kira had finally fallen asleep in the travel cot they'd strapped to the bunk in their cabin.

'Some peace at last,' she murmured.

Malek sighed. 'It helped when she ate some baby food instead of powdered milk all the time.'

'I'm still rocking in my head, even though the sea's much calmer now,' she said.

The Bay of Biscay had lived up to its fearsome reputation with two days of atrocious weather. They'd both been seasick, even after taking the tablets Ozlem had given them. As soon as they'd passed through the Straits of Gibraltar the waves had calmed and the last day had offered clear skies and an azure blue sea.

Helen hugged Malek. 'I could almost get used to life on board a ship. It breaks down into eating, sleeping and looking after the baby.'

Malek shook his head. 'No way, I can't wait to be back on solid land.'

She grinned. 'How did you manage when you worked on the boat with Ozlem?'

'It was awful,' he replied. 'I only lasted a month and the rest of the crew laughed at me.'

Her arms tightened around him. 'How do you feel about your new family?'

He thought for a moment. 'I haven't really thought it through yet. It won't sink in until we are back safely at the villa with her.'

'I feel complete now. She's all I've got left of my family, Zak's final gift to me.'

He slipped his hand inside her shirt. 'Do you think Kira will still be asleep?'

She put her hand over his and moved it down under the top of her skirt. 'You must be feeling better. Come with me. I found a quiet spot near the back of the ship where nobody can see us.'

She led him off by the belt and he followed with a huge grin.

* * *

Hannah took the return call from Spanish immigration at Cartagena. Luckily the officer who returned the enquiry spoke excellent English, so she thanked Isabella and told her she could go home.

'No British women or children under the age of three have come ashore during the last week but two days ago four nationals from the Turkish Republic of Northern Cyprus came through.'

Hannah paused. 'Do you see many yachts from the TRNC in Cartagena?'

'Not many,' he replied. 'But it wasn't a yacht, it was a fishing trawler. They are even less common unless they're trying to sell fish here.'

'Did they offload any fish while they were in port?'

'No, and I don't think they had any in the hold as the boat was sitting quite high in the water. That means it was probably empty. The captain said they had problems with their net winch motor so were heading back for repairs.'

Hannah made some notes. 'What was the boat called?'

'The *Goke*.'

'And who came ashore?'

He gave her the names of the four crew members who had checked in. 'I noticed one strange thing, though.'

'What?' she asked.

'One of the crew came through customs carrying some large packs of nappies and lots of baby food. The captain said they were for the man's wife in Cyprus as they were cheaper in Spain. That stuck in my mind as I thought things were cheap in Cyprus. The trawler left three hours after it docked.'

Hannah's heart beat faster as she scrawled down these details. 'Do you have any photographs of the crew?'

'I can send you a copy of their passport photo pages.'

'That's very helpful. Thanks.' She gave him her email address and cut the call before ringing Amrik.

'Hi, Hannah.'

'I may have found where they've been, sir. Can you pop up to the Incident Room?'

* * *

Helen and Malek snuck back to the cabin to find Kira standing in her cot with yet another smelly nappy.

'Oh, Malek, can you change this one? I need to borrow your phone to ring Turkcell and order a mobile with a new number. We should be within range now we're approaching Turkish-controlled waters.'

He pouted. 'I'm not your servant, you know.'

She stroked his arm. 'I know you're not but think of your lovely Porsche.'

* * *

The next morning, Amrik called Jemma and told her they'd discovered something interesting before suggesting she and Ellie drove to Swanbourne to see some photographs.

Brad volunteered to take Rocky and Dino for a walk along the clifftop path, so Jemma headed out of Lulcombe with an excited daughter.

'What do you think it is, Mum?' she asked.

'He did say not to get your hopes up, but they had some more information,' Jemma replied.

They arrived at the police headquarters twenty minutes later and were shown up to the Major Incident Room.

Amrik welcomed them. 'I'm surprised you haven't got a seat here with your name on, Jemma.'

She frowned. 'Not funny. What've you found?'

He beckoned Hannah over. 'Well, Hannah has been phoning loads of foreign ports and has got something back from Cartagena in south-eastern Spain. Will you tell them please, Hannah?'

The young DC told them about the *Goke*, the crew who went ashore and the nappies. She showed them the photos and had put one of them, a Malek Aydin, alongside the traffic cam picture on the incident board.

Ellie shouted. 'That's him. That's the man who blocked the pavement. Can't the navy or the coastguard stop them?'

Amrik sighed. 'There's a slight problem with that. They stopped at Cartagena three days ago so might not still be in Spanish waters. The Spanish Navy are looking out for the *Goke* as are a couple of British naval vessels based in Gibraltar. Our guess is they'll head for Turkish waters as they get nearer to home. Unfortunately, the Greek and British navies are not allowed to enter Turkish waters or go anywhere near the coast of Northern Cyprus.'

Jemma pointed at the north coast of Cyprus. 'So, if they reach here there's nothing any of us can do?'

He shook his head. 'I'm afraid not, but at least we know where Kira might be now.'

Jemma pursed her lips. 'I'm going to kill that bitch.'

* * *

Ozlem checked his radar and glanced at Helen. 'We're about five kilometres from Turkish waters but there is a Greek naval destroyer fifteen kilometres behind us going at nearly twenty-six knots. They're heading straight for us on an interception course. I think they're looking for your cargo. It will be very close.'

'Can't we go any faster?' she snapped.

He checked the throttle. 'We're already doing ten knots. It would be dangerous to go any faster than that.'

She reached beyond him and pushed the throttle forward so hard that the entire boat started vibrating.

'Shit, Helen, you'll blow the engines.'

'Leave it. Call the Turkish Navy and tell them you're being attacked by a Greek naval ship and need help.'

'I can't do that. It could lead to an international incident.'

She watched the green blips on the radar, one of them gradually gaining on the other.

'Fucking do it.'

Chapter 45

Amrik slammed down the phone and shouted. 'Bugger and damn it.'

Hannah shot him a glance. 'What's up?'

'The British High Commission in Nicosia won't do anything else about the *Goke*. They say they've asked the Greek and British Navies to keep a look out but have had no response from the TRNC or Ministry of the Interior in North Nicosia.'

She frowned. 'What do we do next?'

He turned to a fresh sheet of his A4 pad. 'We go through everything again. The authorities said to come back once we have definite proof of who is involved in the abduction.'

She turned away. 'Let's get some proof then.'

* * *

The trawler juddered as it raced along at eleven knots. On their stern, Helen could make out a sleek grey destroyer, with waves surging under its bow, slowly closing the gap. Her heart beat faster as she watched. 'No, not when we're so close.'

Ozlem looked repeatedly over his shoulder whilst scanning

the radar screen. 'I can't believe how fast they're going. They might catch us.'

She peered at the green screen. The white spot to their west seemed alarmingly close. 'What did the Turks say?'

He pointed. 'There's the patrol boat on its way. It's a lot faster than a destroyer but with much lighter guns. The nearest large vessel is two hours away.'

A smaller blip approached them from the north.

She wrung her hands and hissed, 'what will they do if they catch us?'

He shrugged. 'They may try to block us off or send an inflatable boat with some men to board us.'

'Have you got any weapons on board to fight them off if they do?'

'I'm not taking on the navy for anybody.'

She stared at him with narrowed eyes. 'Let's hope they don't catch us then.'

For the next fifteen minutes, she was unable to look away from the radar screen and the way the white shapes moved closer to each other like a deadly cat and mouse chase in a slow-motion eighties video game.

Ozlem again stared at the screen as he pushed the throttle forward as far as it would go. The engine screamed and the whole boat juddered as it reached twelve knots. The two dots were now so close that he had to zoom in on the display to put some space between them.

'When do we hit Turkish waters?' Helen asked.

'We're six kilometres from the coast, so very soon,' he replied.

She looked behind again. 'Bloody hell, I can see the crew out on the deck and they're uncovering a boat. Oh, my God. They can't catch us now after everything we've been through.'

* * *

Jemma stared at the small suitcase on the kitchen table. 'That's some stuff packed in case we need to dash off at a moment's notice. Can you think of anything else we need to pack for Kira, Els?'

Her daughter checked her phone. 'I've packed clothes, shoes, passport, formula milk, bottles and some baby food. I can't think of anything I've missed.'

Jemma nodded. 'If we have a couple of rucksacks between the three of us, we can travel light with just hand luggage and one suitcase.'

Brad dropped his papers by the case. 'Have you got your driving licence, Jem?'

'Yep. It's in the rucksack.'

Ellie clenched her fists. 'That's it. We're ready to go whenever we need. Will Gran be OK to have Rocky and Dino for however long it takes?'

Jemma nodded. 'So she says. There's no chance of them sending Dad home for at least a month so she can take Rocky with her when she visits him.'

'Oh, Mum.' Ellie held back the tears. 'I just want my baby back.'

* * *

Ozlem wiped the drops of sweat from his forehead and pointed over the bow. 'There's the Turkish patrol boat. Where's the Greek boat?'

Helen peered through the window at the rear of the bridge. 'It's getting nearer. I can see the crew's faces. Some of them have machine guns.'

'We're about to enter Turkish waters,' Ozlem shouted.

Thirty seconds later, the Turkish patrol boat bounced past them before making an abrupt ninety-degree turn to come to a slow cruise behind them. The Greek inflatable boat suddenly lurched in the water, turned around and headed back towards the destroyer, their crew making obscene hand gestures towards their Turkish counterparts.

Ozlem pulled back the throttle to a more restrained speed and slumped back in his seat. 'I'm going to stick to fishing in future. No more people smuggling.'

A stream of Turkish came over the radio. Ozlem answered and there were several further exchanges before the Turkish patrol boat passed them with a wave and sped away.

'What did they say?' Helen asked.

'They asked why the Greeks were after us. I told them they thought we were fishing in their waters, but I explained our winch is broken so we had no nets out. It was just a misunderstanding.'

She patted him on the back. 'Very good. You've earned an extra bonus when we're back.'

He again wiped his forehead and stared after the rapidly disappearing patrol boat. 'Course eighty degrees. Kyrenia here we come.'

Late that afternoon, the *Goke* arrived at Kyrenia Harbour and Helen and Malek left Kira sleeping in her cot to join Ozlem on the bridge. The captain called the harbour authorities on VHF channel fourteen and was given permission to dock at berth twenty-four. The harbour master sounded surprised when Ozlem told him they wouldn't need any facilities for unloading fish due to damaged equipment, though he explained they had already sold some fish in southern Spain before the winch motor failed.

Helen rubbed her hands. 'When can we get off this heap of shit?'

Ozlem patted the wheel. 'You mean, this heap of shit that got you to England and back while outrunning the Greek Navy?'

She gave him an awkward hug. 'Thank you.'

He checked his watch. 'You must go down below until it's

dark. Send Malek up to help out. You can disembark after nine-thirty and unload your cargo.'

They tied the *Goke* to the mooring and Emree and Burak shook hands with Malek before disappearing down the gangplank with their duffle bags slung over their shoulders.

Through the cabin window, Helen could see the castle standing guard over the harbour, just as it had done for the last four hundred and fifty years. Its Venetian tower caught the late afternoon sun beneath skies that were still blue. She smiled at the child on her lap and gave her a hug. Kira responded with a chuckle.

'We're home, little one. We've only gone and done it. I hope you're ready for your new life away from that bitch and her daughter.'

* * *

They were moored away from the tourist part of the marina with its sleek yachts so their section was quiet. They were also undergoing extensive renovations so the waterfront restaurants were all empty.

At nine-thirty, Malek took their cases and left to fetch Helen's Land Cruiser from the long-term car park. He loaded the luggage, drove back to the harbour and parked right beside the *Goke*. He strode up the gangplank and returned two minutes later with a folded travel cot hanging from his shoulder. Helen followed wearing a baseball cap and with Kira held close to her chest. They all entered and Malek drove away at a sedate speed.

Helen touched his shoulder. 'Thank heavens we're back. I've now got a granddaughter and nobody is going to take her away from me. Ever.'

* * *

Jemma, Ellie and Brad were sitting at the kitchen table with a map of Northern Cyprus open on a laptop.

Ellie's shoulders slumped. 'Where do we start?'

Jemma chewed on her lip. 'We need to find Helen's address.'

'How do we do that?' Brad asked.

Jemma sipped her tea. 'I don't know but I might know a man who does.'

Chapter 46

At six am, the sound of crying woke Helen and she was forced to open her eyes. Light streamed in through the thin curtains as Malek lay beside her, breathing heavily. She stretched, reached for her robe and padded through to the adjoining room where the teary-eyed youngster was standing with her hands on the edge of the travel cot.

'Mamma,' Kira said.

Helen reached for her. 'Say Granny.'

'Mamma,' came the reply.

'No. Granny.' She lifted the child and carried her to the king-sized bed in her own room. She climbed back under the sheets and tapped Malek on the shoulder. 'Put some clothes on. You'll scare the poor little thing.'

He grumbled in Turkish and walked over to the wardrobe.

Helen leered at the view from behind. 'Although that is a mighty fine ass.'

He pulled on a pair of shorts and a T-shirt and returned to bed where together they played with Kira, who gradually stopped crying.

'The name *Kira Thorne* will be on international news.'

Helen ran her hand through the child's hair. 'She needs a new name.'

Malek held the youngster above his head while she gurgled with delight. 'She seems very happy with her new family but she should have a Turkish name and passport. I know a man who will help, for a thousand euros.'

Helen stroked his neck. 'OK. Anything in mind for a name?'

He hummed for a moment. 'My grandmother was called Ada. That is a proper Turkish name.'

Helen tickled Kira under the chin. 'How about Ada? Do you like that? Ada. That sounds nice.'

'Mamma,' Kira gurgled.

'Don't start that again.' Helen rubbed Malek's chest. 'Will you do me a favour and pop to the garage, please? There is an old wooden cot in the rafters. Bring it in, will you?'

He frowned. 'What? Now?'

'Yes, please. I want to put her in something she can't escape from,' she replied.

He tutted, slipped on his flip-flops and left to do as she said.

* * *

Jemma scrolled through her contacts until she reached Dave's details. She hadn't spoken to her ex for over a year, but she often thought about him. He'd moved out when he overheard her talking to Ellie about her affair with Brad, which had led to Rocky's conception. Dave had transferred away from Swanbourne Police and now worked in Southampton. He had a useful contact in Special Branch who seemed to have access to information that even the police couldn't find.

The line rang several times before he answered. 'Morning, Jemma.'

'Hi, Dave. How are you doing?'

'I'm good thanks. You?'

'I'm OK but we've got a problem.'

'So Amrik told me. I'm sorry but what do you want?'

'I'm trying to find an address for Helen Fletcher who lives in Northern Cyprus.'

'I don't think I can help,' he said curtly.

'I wondered if your old friend in Special Branch might be able to come up with something.'

He sighed. 'I haven't spoken to Max in ages. I don't know if he still works there.'

'Would you mind having a go? Please. I thought he might have a few contacts at the army base in Cyprus.'

'I can ask, I suppose. What do you want it for?'

'Oh. I'm trying to find it for Amrik. They might have more success with the Turkish authorities if they have some more details.'

'OK,' he said. 'I'll try to get it on one condition.'

'What's that?' she replied.

'You have to promise you won't do anything stupid.'

'Who, me?' Jemma replied.

* * *

DC Hannah Salmon pinned a long list of names and addresses to the whiteboard in the Major Incident Room at Swanbourne Police HQ.

Amrik wandered over and started to read it. 'Who are these people?'

'These are the registered keepers of dark blue or black Range Rovers captured by traffic cams on the M3, M4 or M5 within forty-eight hours after the abduction. I've got to break it down into areas covered by different forces and ask them to pay the owners a visit to make sure they're not false addresses.'

He pointed to a name. 'That's interesting.'

Hannah peered at the list. 'Who's Harry Collins?'

‘He’s the slimeball of a solicitor who acted for the Fletcher family when they were buying the hotel site.’

She raised her eyebrows. ‘You think he could be connected?’

‘I think I’d like to have a little chat with him.’ He checked his watch. ‘It’s five past nine. We could be in Slough by midday. If he’s in, we’ll have a word. If not, we grab some lunch and wait for him to come home. Might be a long day but worth a punt.’

‘Sounds good,’ she replied. ‘Do you need to discuss it with DI Day?’

‘I’ll call her on the way and ask her to OK it with the local police up there. It’s courtesy when we’re on their patch.’

Three hours later, Amrik pulled his Ford Focus ST onto the drive of a large detached house on the outskirts of Slough. As he parked, he spotted a black Range Rover through the open door of a double garage.

‘Looks like we might be lucky.’ Hannah took her notepad out from her bag.

He locked the car and they strolled up to the palatial front door of the mock Tudor red-brick house. ‘Soliciting must be paying well,’ he said under his breath.

‘What?’ she replied. ‘Oh, yes of course he’s a solicitor. I thought you meant…’ She stopped talking as the door swung open and a middle-aged man wearing a pale blue sports jacket and beige trousers appeared with a quizzical frown.

He sneered. ‘Whatever it is, I don’t want one and I don’t need converting to be a Jehovah’s Witness, Mormon or whatever you are.’

Amrik grinned at Hannah. ‘Oh, no, Mr Collins, you’ve got us all wrong.’ He held up his warrant card as Hannah did the same. ‘DS Hussain and DC Salmon from Dorset Police.’

His quizzical frown only increased as he looked down his nose at them. ‘Dorset Police. You’re a bit off your patch, aren’t you?’

'We fancied a scenic drive up from the coast and your name appeared on one of our lists.'

Another flicker of concern. 'Lists? What lists?'

'We're investigating the abduction of a young mother and her baby from Lulcombe and are checking all owners of dark Range Rovers that passed traffic cameras on certain roads in the days following the incident.'

Harry folded his arms. 'And?'

Amrik checked his notepad. 'A black Range Rover,' he pointed towards the garage, 'with those plates passed a camera on the M3 near Winchester at eleven-fifteen am on the twenty-fifth of May.'

Harry sneered. 'I'd been to a client meeting in Southampton and was on my way back to the office here in Slough.'

Amrik coughed. 'And can your client verify the details of that meeting?'

'I'm afraid our confidentiality rules prohibit me from revealing their name.'

'I'm sure you're aware,' Amrik replied, 'that the rules of client/lawyer confidentiality do not apply where actions have been taken in furtherance of a crime.'

'Strangely, officer, I am aware of that.' He checked the time. 'I'm afraid I'll have to end our little chat. I have work to do and I'm going out at six.'

'Would you mind if we took a quick look inside your vehicle, Mr Collins?'

'I do mind but if it means you leave more quickly, you can have a few minutes.' He grabbed a set of keys from a side table in his hall and walked towards the garage before pressing a button that made the vehicle's lights flash. Amrik and Hannah each opened a door and leaned inside the vehicle.

Amrik sniffed. 'Wow, that's a strong smell of air freshener. Has it been valeted recently?'

'Oh, yes. When one spends over a hundred thousand on a car, one likes to keep it in good condition.'

They spent ten minutes checking the car under the watchful eye of the solicitor but found nothing of interest. Amrik glanced at Hannah, who shook her head.

'OK, Mr Collins. You've been very helpful and I think we're about done here.'

'That's good.' Harry headed back towards the house. 'I'm sure you can see yourself out.'

Amrik started to walk away but twisted back, calling after Harry. 'Oh, and how's Helen Fletcher?'

Harry turned around slowly. 'I never discuss my clients so I'm afraid I can't help you. Look, if it's that important...' he removed a card from his wallet and handed it to Hannah, 'this is my secretary's number. Give her a call and she'll confirm I was in Southampton on the twenty-fifth and was nowhere near Dorset the previous day.' He entered the house. 'I bid you both good day. Safe journey home.'

Amrik and Hannah walked back to their car. 'Quick, pass me that card, please.' He took it and dialled the number. 'What a surprise. It's engaged. I wonder who she's talking to.' He ended the call and they drove out from the driveway. 'Well, what do you think?'

'Guilty as hell but it will be difficult proving anything. One thing he said was interesting, though.'

'What's that?' he asked.

She grinned. 'He said he hadn't been anywhere near Dorset the day before he was on the M3...Neither of us told him that was the day of the abduction.'

* * *

After Harry had finished speaking to his secretary, Naomi, he cut the call and sent a text to Helen Fletcher. *Be careful. The police came calling today asking questions about the Range Rover.*

A few seconds later, a red exclamation mark appeared beside the text together with the words, *Message not delivered.*

* * *

Malek snatched up his mobile and stamped across the drive, almost tripping in his flip-flops. He pressed the door clicker and waited while the mechanism engaged and the door started rolling up. Whilst waiting, he checked his emails and sent a quick reply to Ozlem. He turned to enter the garage, and his eyes widened as he found his way blocked by a sparkling silver Porsche 911 Carrera 2S Cabriolet. He stepped forward and touched the bonnet. A voice made him jump.

'Do you like it then?' Helen was standing behind him with Kira on her hip.

He ran to kiss her on the lips. 'It's beautiful. Nought to a hundred in just over four seconds. Top speed two hundred and eighty-nine kilometres per hour. Oh, Helen, this is amazing. Thank you so much.'

She beamed. 'Thank you for helping me rescue my granddaughter. Now we can all be a big happy family.'

'Oh, Helen,' he said, 'I love you.'

Chapter 47

The sun shone from a pale blue sky as Jemma walked with Dino along Lulcombe Beach. It was a beautiful day on the south coast with a calm sea and waves that whispered rather than crashed. As it was seven am there weren't many tourists about, only a few fossil hunters stooping their way along the shingle, eagle-eyed for their next find.

Jemma's pocket vibrated so she took out her mobile and answered. 'Hello, Dave.'

'Morning, Jem. Sorry it's so early but I'll forget if I get stuck in to work.'

'That's fine. I'm taking Dino for a walk.'

There was a pause. 'Rub his neck from me.'

Jemma swallowed. 'Will do.'

'Anyway, I've got an address for you. I'll text it through in a minute.'

'Wow. That's brilliant,' she replied.

'It's near a village called Lapta in the Kyrenia Mountains in Northern Cyprus.'

'How did Max find it?' she asked.

'Some of his mates in the SAS are doing exercises at the

British Army base in the south of the island. They've got a few contacts in the north. Don't tell anybody where you got the info and, once again, please don't do anything stupid.'

'Thanks, Dave. I really appreciate this.' She cut the call. *I'm happy but there are times when I miss you, Dave.*

Two minutes later a message pinged through. *HF, Gizli Gorusler, Lapta, Kyrenia, 99742 TRNC 35.334733/33.157456.*

She smiled. *Dave, you're a star.*

* * *

Amrik was sitting in Laura's office with a mug of coffee. Somehow it always tasted so much nicer when it came from her machine; one of the benefits of being a DI with their own office.

Laura looked up from her files. 'Any updates, Amrik?'

He handed her a sheet of paper with an address written on it.

'What's this?'

'Jemma has managed to get hold of an address in Northern Cyprus for Helen Fletcher.'

Her eyes narrowed. 'She's not planning a commando raid or something, is she?'

He shook his head. 'I wouldn't put it past her, but she thought we could use it to lean on the authorities.'

'And have you used it?'

'I've passed it to the British High Commission in Nicosia, but they won't approach the authorities in the North without photographic proof or documentary evidence.'

She frowned. 'Did you give them the traffic cam images of Malek Aydin and the links to Harry Collins?'

'Yeah,' he replied, 'but they say the images could be anybody, as they're not very clear. All circumstantial stuff. We need someone over there to get a picture of Helen with Kira. Can we afford a plane ticket?'

She stood and walked to the window. 'Firstly, the budget won't stretch to any international flights and accommodation. Secondly, if it was Greek Cyprus they'd be helpful, but the TRNC is different. They won't cooperate at all. They're unhappy that nobody, other than Turkey, will recognise them as a legitimate country.' She returned to her desk and slumped back down in her seat. 'Can't we lean on Harry Collins a bit more? Bring him in for questioning or something?'

He shrugged. 'He knows the score. We rang him again and he said, "don't come back here again without a warrant, and if you want to drag me in for a grilling you'll have to arrest me." Smarmy git!'

She frowned. 'It's so annoying now we've hit a brick wall. What do we do if Helen manages to get the child to Cyprus?'

Amrik sighed. 'I don't know, Laura, I really don't know.'

* * *

Two thousand miles away in the Turkish Republic of Northern Cyprus, Helen Fletcher was lying on a sunbed with a gin and tonic in her hand and a smile on her face. The ice clinked as she took a sip and licked her lips. After a session in the pool, Kira was now asleep in her cot having screamed with delight when Helen threw her in the air and caught her as she splash-landed. Malek had gone out for a drive in his shiny Porsche, happy like a child with a new toy. It had taken a lot of organisation to source the car and have it delivered to the villa so she could surprise him after they returned from their fishing trip, though it had certainly been worth the effort. The previous night, Malek had been extra energetic, and now she was exhausted.

The memory prompted a fresh wave of tingles. 'Hurry home, Malek, I fancy an encore.'

The landline rang from the kitchen and she shuffled inside to answer it. 'Hello.'

'Morning, Helen. It's Horace from the British High Commission in Nicosia.'

'Hello, Horace. How are you?'

'I'm good. I've been trying to call you, but couldn't get through.'

'Oh, I had to change my phone and get a new number. I'll text you the new one. How can I help?' she asked.

'We're getting questions about you from the British police and the British Army base in connection with a missing child. I don't know what's going on and I don't want to know but this is just a heads up to stay out of the way.'

'That's very thoughtful of you, Horace. I hope you enjoyed the case of wine?'

'Oh, yes, Helen, it was lovely. We finished the last bottle a week ago.'

She smiled. 'I'll have to see if I can find you something else then. I'm sure there's a case of vintage port down in the cellar somewhere.'

'That sounds delightful, my dear.'

'I'll sort it out and get it delivered. Plain packaging as usual. Thanks for the call.'

'You're welcome, goodbye.'

She ended the call and wandered back outside. As she sipped her drink, the Porsche pulled onto the drive with a roar and a crunch of gravel. Malek climbed from the driver's seat and strutted over puffing out his chest.

'Enjoy it?' she asked.

'It's incredible. So fast. I need to practice driving it as the wheels spin a lot on these roads.'

'You'll have to take me for a drive sometime. Will a child seat fit in the back?'

'It doesn't feel right taking a baby in a car like that,' he said. 'What if it's sick on the leather seats?'

'You'll just have to wipe it off. Get a seat ordered.'

He clenched his fist and turned away.

She stood. 'By the way, I've had a thought. We could do with some more privacy around here. I'm thinking of a two-metre-high wall all around the garden. Do you know any builders who could do that for me?'

He shaded his eyes against the sun. 'That's a long wall. A big job. I have a cousin who's a builder. I'll give him a call.'

She tilted her head. 'How many cousins do you have?'

He shrugged. 'Many.'

* * *

Jemma and Brad were sitting with Ellie at her kitchen table. Ellie had been crying and Jemma had bitten her fingernails until they were sore.

Jemma sipped her tea. 'This is so frustrating. Amrik said that even with the address, the British High Commission in Nicosia won't approach the TRNC authorities without photographic proof.'

Brad exhaled. 'Could we hire a private dick in Cyprus?'

Ellie spat out her tea. 'A what?'

He frowned at her. 'A private dick. Private detective. Oh, dick. I get it. Sorry. Can't we engage the services of a private investigator over there to take some photos?'

Jemma made some notes on her pad. 'Tell you what, I'll ask Amrik if they can find any contacts through the police over there.'

Ellie stared at them. 'We should go over there and get our own photos, pass them to the police and get my daughter back.'

Jemma held her hand. 'Let's bloody do it,' she said. 'What do we need? Flights, accommodation, car hire, supplies. We've got a lot of stuff packed already and Mum's OK to look after Rocky and Dino.'

At the sound of his name, the dog lifted his head from his basket, padded over and rested his head on Jemma's lap.

'Don't worry, Dino, Mum loves looking after you both.'

Brad thought for a moment. 'You'd better add a telescope, camera with a long lens and a book of Cypriot birds. I think I'll be a birdwatcher. That will be a good cover.'

Chapter 48

The back door of Jemma's cottage banged open and Brad shuffled in carrying bags and a full rucksack.

Jemma glanced up from her laptop. 'You've been busy.'

'Sure have. Have you got your list?'

She opened a file on her screen. 'Yep. Fire away.'

'One Opticron birdwatching telescope.'

'Tick.'

'One Cannon R6 camera with five-hundred-millimetre lens.'

'Tick.'

'Two pairs of Viking binoculars and a book on Birds of the Eastern Mediterranean.'

'Tick. Tick.'

'All useful stuff if you're planning a trip to spot a...' he opened the book randomly, 'er, Cyprus Warbler. Remember that one. The guy in the shop was so excited about the amount I spent that he gave me a lesson in cell phone photography and using the telescope.'

'Did you fetch any currency?'

He reached into his rucksack and produced two plastic envelopes. 'Ta-dah. One thousand pounds worth of euros and another thousand in Turkish lira.' He dropped them on the table. 'How ya doing on your assignments?'

Jemma waved a sheet of A4 paper. 'We've got three single flights from Bristol to Larnaca tomorrow at two-thirty, a villa booked in Larnaca for two weeks and another in Kyrenia for the same two weeks. If we need longer, we can always book it while we're there.'

'Car?' he asked.

'Yep. An SUV for three weeks with a special policy to cover both Southern and Northern Cyprus. Ellie's sorted out everything she might need for Kira in case the police storm Helen's house and rescue her.'

'Shall we drive to Bristol or book a taxi?' he asked.

'Dan came around to see Ellie and volunteered to take us. If you can add him to your insurance, he can take us in your truck so there's more room.'

He frowned. 'Drive my truck? But he's so young... Oh, I suppose it would help if he did. What about work?'

'The uni has given me a month's compassionate leave, so I'm good to go,' she said.

* * *

An open-backed pickup reversed into the drive of Helen's villa. The driver's door opened and a tall, dark-haired man with a beard slid down from the seat.

Malek wandered over and they embraced, rattling away in Turkish.

Helen came out from the lounge and joined them.

Malek slipped his arm around her. 'Bayram, this is my... lady, Helen. Helen, this is my cousin, Bayram. He will build the wall for you.'

Bayram looked around the garden. 'Wall where?'

Helen stepped to the side. 'I want a two-metre-high gate

here across the drive and a two-metre-high stone wall around the whole garden.'

His eyebrows rose. 'That is a big job. Very expensive. Why do you need a wall? It is remote here.'

'I want more privacy.' She leant in. 'I like to sunbathe with no clothes on.'

'Not when my workers are about, please. They will stop work.' Bayram swallowed and wiped his forehead. 'I will take a look at the site.' He wandered off around the edge of the plot where a thin, single-strand wire fence already marked the boundary.

Helen held Malek's hand. 'What were you talking about when he arrived?'

He grinned. 'He asked me if I had a nice cruise on Ozlem's boat. Ozlem wouldn't tell him where we went but was happy with what you paid him. I said we had a load to collect from Amsterdam, and he nodded and touched his nose.'

'Good thinking,' she said.

Bayram returned. 'I'll come back with a price for the wall. I'm busy so it will cost more if you want me to start soon. I'll need half before starting so I can buy the stone.'

She frowned. 'Add the extra and start tomorrow.'

* * *

Amrik was sitting with Laura in the Major Incident Room.

'Are you sure we haven't any wiggle room in the budget for a cheap plane ticket and basic room?' he asked.

She shook her head. 'I'm afraid not. The overtime for the abduction is already hitting us hard.'

'How about if I take some holiday?'

'Sorry, Amrik, we're already stretched.'

He put his hand to his forehead and groaned. 'Oh dear, I feel some work-related stress coming on. I might need to visit the doctor.'

She frowned. 'Don't even think about it.'

* * *

The shredder whirred as the papers were dragged down into its ravenous maw. In the unoccupied office, Harry Collins checked his watch to see how much more time he had before the first of the staff arrived for work. An hour and a half. He glanced at the pile of files on the desk. 'Bloody hell. I wish I'd never heard of the Fletcher Family.'

Chapter 49

Tears streamed down Carol's face as she hugged Jemma. 'You will be careful, won't you?'

'Of course I will, Mum!'

'I'd hate for Rocky to lose his mother. Those sound like dangerous people you're going up against.'

Jemma touched her arm. 'We're not going up against anybody dangerous. We're just trying to take some photos we can pass to the police.'

'I suppose. Now, have you left plenty of clothes for him?'

Jemma glanced beyond her mother to where her son was rolling around in the grass with Dino. 'He might need a few bits washing if he keeps on like that but there should be plenty. I've also left Dino enough food for three weeks.'

'When will you know how long you're staying in Cyprus?'

'I don't know, Mum. We've got to wait and see what happens. I've got a month's compassionate leave from uni, but I might be back in a week. I'll be in touch once I know more.'

Her mother gave her one last hug. 'Good luck, Jem. Bring her back.'

Dan drove them to Bristol Airport in Brad's truck and passed the '*Is Brad happy to let him drive his truck?*' test. After dropping them and their luggage off, he headed back to Dorset.

The airport was relatively quiet as they queued at the check-in for the Jet2 flight to Larnaca.

'Glad to be doing something?' Jemma said to Ellie as they waited with their cases.

Ellie nodded. 'I felt so helpless sitting at home just staring at maps. This is much better. All we've got to do now is find her and take her home.'

After dropping off their cases they passed through security and ate lunch before boarding the silver and red Airbus A321.

To try taking her mind off the task ahead, Jemma read an article in the in-flight magazine about the conflict that split Cyprus back in nineteen-seventy-four when Turkey invaded the northern third of the island. The invasion was triggered by the Cypriot coup d'état but, after that, the Turkish forces refused to leave and later declared independence as the Turkish Republic of Northern Cyprus. The island was left as two distinct areas with a UN buffer zone known as the Green Line established to keep the two sides apart.

While Jemma tried distracting herself, Brad slept and Ellie watched some films she'd downloaded to her iPad. The four-and-a-half-hour flight soon passed and, as the sign illuminated for all passengers to fasten their seatbelts, Jemma moved her watch forward by two hours before turning to the map of Cyprus at the back of her book. *Where are you, Kira?*

* * *

DI Day ascended the stairs to the Major Incident Room on the top floor of Swanbourne Police HQ and pushed open the door.

As the investigation had run out of resources the team had dropped to three. DS Hussain and DC Salmon now only had one uniformed PC helping out, manning the ever-quietening phone lines.

'Afternoon, Amrik, Hannah,' Laura said.

'Afternoon, ma'am,' Hannah replied.

Amrik swivelled around in his chair to face Laura. 'Well, any news about a possible trip to Cyprus?'

She shook her head. 'Please stop asking. I've spoken to the Chief Superintendent and we have no budget for any travel. They also don't want you or anybody else running around in the TRNC causing a diplomatic incident with the Turks so don't even think about sneaking off under your own steam. All I've managed to wangle is a budget of five hundred pounds to fund a local private investigator who might be able to take some photos of Helen with Kira that we can send to the British High Commission.'

Amrik sighed. 'Oh, well, it's better than nothing, I suppose.'

'Do you want to find some PIs in the North and get some quotes?'

'It just so happens I already found a chap in Northern Nicosia.' He grinned and peeled a yellow Post-it from his monitor. 'He specialises in marital disputes so hopefully, he'll be discreet.'

'Did he give you a price?' she asked.

'It's on his website. It costs four hundred euros for two surveillance sessions and any photos he manages to take.'

Laura nodded. 'OK, I'll authorise that. It might be a complete waste of money but at least we'll have tried.'

Amrik started typing an email. 'I'm on it.'

* * *

Malek's cousin, Bayram, pulled onto the villa's drive and wandered over to sit in the shade of the poolside terrace.

It was a blisteringly hot early summer's day and eerily

quiet. Even the cicadas had decided it was too hot to vibrate their tymbals.

'Beer or iced lemonade?' Helen asked.

'Lemonade, please,' he replied.

'Malek...'

Malek tutted. 'Don't worry, I'm on my way.'

Bayram laughed. 'Is he your wife?'

'No, he is not my wife.' She frowned. 'He just knows when he's on to a good thing. Anyway, how much for the wall?'

Bayram wiped the sweat from his forehead onto his sleeve which earned him a glare from Helen in a bid to ensure he didn't wipe it on her patio table.

'My basic price to start next week would be eight thousand euros, but I could start tomorrow for nine thousand five hundred. I'd have to pull men from another job and pay extra for somebody else to finish.'

Malek returned with a tray of iced lemonade and placed it on the table.

Helen removed one of the glasses and took a sip. 'Start tomorrow. How long will it take?'

'Nine days,' he replied. 'We will be here at seven, have two hours for lunch and work two until six.'

'OK, we'll see you in the morning,' she said.

Bayram drained his glass, shook her hand, hugged Malek and climbed back inside his truck before driving away.

* * *

The Jet2 plane flew in over the coast of Cyprus and the massive salt lakes. As they landed alongside the sea they saw the welcome sign for Glafcos Cerides - Larnaca Airport.

They strolled up the air bridge tunnel into the arrivals building where the corridors were shiny and clean with pale floor tiles. Large glass windows gave views of the airplanes lined up in neat rows, just like any other airport in the world.

Jemma and Brad stepped on the moving walkways, while Ellie, ever the rebel, walked alongside them, her long legs stretching as she tried to keep up.

At passport control, a uniformed official checked their documents. 'And what is the reason for your trip?'

Jemma gulped and smiled. 'Holiday.'

Brad leaned towards the glass. 'We've come for some bird-watching. I want to see a Cyprus Warbler.'

The man peered over his glasses at Brad and grinned. 'Fingers crossed you find one.'

After clearing immigration, they collected their cases and wheeled them through to the car hire counters. Jemma and Brad presented their licences and were shown to a red Kia Sportage in an underground carpark.

There was plenty of room in the spacious cargo area for their luggage. Brad sat in the driver's seat. 'Ah, looks like you'll be the one driving, Jem, I don't do stick shift.'

She tutted as they swapped seats. 'Bloody Yanks and their automatics.'

The electric seat buzzed forward as she adjusted it and she fed the address of their first villa into the satnav. Adjusting the rearview mirror, she caught Ellie's eye. 'You OK in the back?'

Her daughter nodded. 'I'm just glad to be here and actually doing something to find her.'

'Let's get a move on then.' Jemma donned her sunglasses and cautiously pulled out from the parking garage into the blinding light and scorching heat of a Cypriot afternoon.

Chapter 50

Amrik dialled the number for the private detective in Nicosia and listened to a few seconds of clicks and whirrs as the connections were made. The ringing tones were long and drawn out, a sure-fire way to tell the recipient was overseas.

A deep voice answered. 'Günaydin. Hakan Yilmaz.'

'Hello, Mr Yilmaz, do you speak English?' Amrik asked.

'Oh, yes, I speak Turkish, English, French, German and some Greek. How can I help you?'

'I'm calling from Dorset Police in England. I'm Detective Sergeant Hussain and I'd like to engage your services as a private investigator to take some photographs for us.'

'That sounds interesting. What exactly are you after?'

'We're investigating a missing child and would like you to try taking some photos of the occupant of a villa near Kyrenia, hopefully with a one-year-old youngster. It says on your website that for four hundred euros you will undertake two sessions of surveillance and send any pictures you take.'

'Yes, that price is for normal surveillance only. If it involves photos on private property, the cost is five hundred euros.'

'That's fine,' Amrik replied. 'How do you wish to be paid?'

‘I’ll send you a PayPal request that will state surveillance with photographs. If you let me have the name of the target and the address of the villa, I’ll do some initial research and come back with some pictures within two weeks.’

‘Thank you. I’ll send you my email address. If you can be any quicker that would be helpful. A child’s life is at risk.’

‘I’ll do my best. Good day to you, Detective Sergeant.’

Amrik put down his handset and reached for the mouse on his desk. Ten minutes later an email arrived with the invoice attached so he paid it from his personal PayPal account and made a note to submit an expenses claim for Laura to approve. He smiled as he made notes in the system about what he’d achieved.

* * *

The road from Larnaca Airport to the villa was quiet. Jemma drove along the wide dual carriageway edged with bushes, small trees and the occasional needle-thin cypress tree. The blue sky was unsullied by clouds and they were glad the car had efficient air conditioning.

Jemma followed the satnav’s instructions. ‘I’m glad they drive on the left over here.’

Brad shrugged. ‘Be better if they drove on the right side of the road.’

Jemma smiled. ‘I thought you’d be used to it by now.’

‘I am but it’s still weird,’ he replied.

Ellie pointed at the pavement. ‘It’s also strange seeing lots of British post boxes painted yellow.’

Jemma grinned, excited to share her new-found knowledge. ‘They were repainted after Cyprus gained its independence in nineteen-sixty.’

‘Every day’s a school day,’ Ellie murmured.

As they approached Larnaca City, a row of palm trees marked the central reservation and the traffic increased.

Jemma turned off the main road and onto an older one surfaced with well-worn cobbles. Rows of shops and cafés lined the street.

Jemma pointed. 'We could grab some food here.'

Ellie frowned. 'Can't we go straight to Helen's villa and take some photos? I want to find Kira.'

'You need to eat, Els.' Jemma said. 'You've not had much today and that's not like you.'

Brad checked the time. 'How about we go out for a meal tonight while we can and then try to grab some sleep? That way, we can cross the border early tomorrow and go straight to the next place.'

Ellie pouted. 'I suppose. I just want to start searching as soon as we can.'

Jemma twisted around in her seat. 'Look, there's the sea.'

Ellie peered over the tops of several parked cars. 'This would be a lovely place to come if we were on holiday.'

Jemma drove past a yellow stone church and down a small side street where parked cars and mopeds made it difficult to manoeuvre between the old buildings. Several pedestrians with death wishes stepped out into the road from the safety of the reflective bollards marking the edge of the pavement. After a few minutes of crawling along at walking pace, Jemma pulled up in front of a green gate.

'Is this it?' she asked.

Brad jumped out and tapped a code into the keypad. A motor whirred and the gate rolled sideways to reveal a large parking yard with olive trees in pots in front of a white, two-storey villa. While Jemma parked the car, he approached the door, tapped the code into the key box and entered.

Jemma and Ellie climbed out, removed the cases and rucksacks and basked in the hot air filled with the delicious smells emanating from the bakery next door.

Brad placed the cases by the door. 'I'll leave them here if we're heading straight out tomorrow.'

Ellie peered into the lounge and up the stairs. 'It's cooler in here. I'm going to grab a shower before we go for food.'

'Good idea,' Jemma replied.

* * *

Helen smiled as Malek played in the pool with Kira, or Ada as they had started calling her.

Her mobile rang and she answered the unknown number. 'Hello. Who is this?'

'Good evening, Mrs Fletcher. I am Hakan Yilmaz, a second cousin of Malek.'

She smiled. 'Not another one!'

'Yes, we have a very large family. I'm a private investigator and have been approached by the British Police to carry out some surveillance and take some photographs of you with a young child.'

The phone suddenly became quite clammy in her hand. 'What?'

'They have given me your name and address and have paid for two sessions.'

Her eyes narrowed. 'Why are you telling me this?'

'I wondered if you might like to pay me to not take any photos or, even better, to take some with an older child. That way I can earn some extra money from this small assignment.'

'And where will I find an older child?'

'I had an idea that for seven hundred euros I could lend you my five-year-old niece. Perhaps she could come and play in your pool? I could then take some photos using a long lens and send them to the police.'

'Why should I pay you to do this, Hakan? What is in it for me?'

'Well, the police are very interested in you in connection with a missing child. I thought it might help you, and Malek, if they were distracted. They might then believe they were mistaken and leave you alone.'

'I suppose that's a good idea. I'll pay you two thousand euros to do that but also to keep an eye open over the next couple of weeks for any suspicious behaviour. I am having a wall built around my house, but it won't be finished for a while.'

'Two thousand euros sounds fine, thank you, Helen. Is there anything in particular you would like me to watch out for?'

'Just anybody who looks out of place. Some evil people want to take my granddaughter away from me and I won't let them.'

Chapter 51

The temperature had reached twenty-eight degrees by the time Brad, Jemma and Ellie finished some breakfast pastries and loaded the cases back into the Kia. Brad set the satnav for the Metehan border crossing.

The drive north to the island's centre passed along a well-kept dual-carriageway so it only took an hour to reach Nicosia. They'd driven over a small range of hills with limestone outcrops on either side, but the traffic was light until they arrived at the divided city.

As they followed the blue signs for the TRNC border crossing the road became busier with a mix of cars, vans and lorries queuing to cross. The checkpoint itself was relaxed and they were waved through without any document checks.

Brad grinned and returned the passports to their folder. 'That was easy. I expected a more formal process.'

'Don't get excited,' Jemma replied. 'That was just leaving the Greek part. We're not at the Turkish side yet.'

'Oh,' he said as they joined two queues of vehicles approaching a large covered area with a number of kiosks. Although they were only a few hundred yards from the Greek side, the Turkish buildings appeared a lot less maintained.

After a half-hour wait, they pulled up to a kiosk and handed over their passports. A stern-faced officer with a big moustache peered through the open windows into the car. 'Three people?'

'Yes,' Jemma replied. 'Could you please stamp a piece of paper instead of the passports as we're planning to visit Athens later in the year and I've heard the Greeks don't like it if you've got a Northern Cyprus entry stamp in your passport. They're still touchy about your invasion.'

The immigration official rolled his eyes, stamped three slips of paper and placed them inside the passports. 'You should forget Greece and visit the antiquities in Turkey instead. Much better. What are you coming here for?'

Jemma smiled. 'For a holiday.'

'And some birdwatching!' Brad added from the passenger seat. 'I want to see a Cyprus Warbler in the Kyrenia Mountains.'

'And how long are you staying for?' the man asked.

'Two weeks,' Jemma replied.

The officer handed back the passports. 'You can stay up to ninety days maximum. There is a fine if you overstay.' He pointed down the road. 'There aren't many petrol stations, so I suggest filling up at that garage. It is good fuel; my cousin owns it.'

'OK, thanks, we will.' Jemma started the engine.

'One more thing. As you're driving a hire car, you need to buy a Turkish insurance policy from that building.' He pointed to a ramshackle shed by the road. 'Otherwise, you are not insured. Our police do not recognise policies sold on the Greek side, whatever the car hire people have told you.'

Jemma nodded. 'We'll do that as well.'

They pulled up alongside the hut. 'We're nearly across. Let me guess.' Jemma grinned. 'His cousin owns the insurance kiosk as well?'

* * *

Bayram edged his lorry load of stone up to the gate of Helen's villa while she stood and glared.

'Stop!' she shouted. 'You're about to hit it!'

He climbed out of the cab, followed by his two workers. 'We need to get right in,' he said, 'so we will take down one pillar and rebuild it afterwards.'

'Fine.' She turned back towards the house.

He called after her. 'Is it OK to block the road for a few hours?'

Helen glanced in both directions. 'Yeah, no problem. Nobody ever comes down here anyway.'

He handed two sledgehammers to his men and pointed at the brick pillar.

* * *

After a slow drive from Nicosia to Kyrenia, they pulled up outside their second villa.

'Well, that was different.' Jemma stretched out her limbs. 'It's amazing how everything just changed; the Turkish signs and number plates. Even the driving seemed more manic.'

Ellie yawned. 'Never noticed. I slept all the way.'

Brad found the key box and opened the door. The house was a two-storey white building with a terracotta tiled roof and small pool.

Jemma stepped inside. 'Oh, it's cool in here, heaven!'

'It is a little bit warm out there,' Brad said. 'We'll need plenty of water if we're outside on watch.'

'Are we unpacking here?' Ellie asked.

Jemma shook her head, 'No, let's leave the cases in the car in case we have to depart in a hurry. We can leave the key in the code box when we go out, so we don't have to come back if shit hits the fan.'

They quickly toured the new villa and returned to the Kia. Brad entered Helen's address into the satnav and added the nearest supermarket as a waypoint. Their side road joined the main one by a red octagonal sign with *DUR* on it.

'What's Dur?' Ellie asked in a Bart Simpson voice.

'I think it means *stop* in Turkish,' Jemma replied.

The supermarket was small but they managed to buy plenty of water, some snacks and three SIM cards from a Turkcell machine. Loaded down with their survival rations, they returned to the Kia.

Jemma held their hands. 'Are we ready to go hunting?'

'You bet,' Brad responded and Ellie nodded enthusiastically.

The road snaked along the coastline but eventually cut inland through a greener area. They passed through fields full of olive trees and then reached a stretch where they could smell the deliciously heady scent of citrus that came on the breeze from the orange groves. After passing several small villages with white painted houses the satnav warned them of an approaching right turn leading into the mountains which towered above the coastal plain. The road twisted for several miles before arriving at a single-track section. Jemma moved at a crawling pace whilst trying to avoid the potholes.

'We're very near,' Brad said.

Jemma braked and the car stopped. 'Shit. There's a builder's lorry blocking the road.'

Brad checked on his phone. 'That's it, that's Helen's villa.'

'Looks like he's going to be in the way for a while,' Jemma said.

Ellie checked the map she'd unfurled on the back seat. 'We might be able to go up into the mountains and come back down from behind. There's a Turkish Tank Memorial up in the hills so there must be a road. It will be a long detour but it's better than hanging around here. It might be useful to know a back way into her villa.'

Brad tapped his phone while Jemma reversed carefully back down the track. 'Back towards the main road and take a left in five miles... Or is it kilometres? I'll try sticking *Turk Tanki* in the satnav.'

They headed back along the coast road before turning onto another, smaller road, where they had to repeatedly traverse long stretches riddled with potholes. As they climbed, the scenery changed from olive groves surrounding isolated farmhouses to cypress and pine trees.

After an hour, they reached the summit and passed through a gorge of white limestone that dazzled in the bright sunshine, catching occasional glimpses of the sea and coastal towns below the treeline. Concrete barriers flanked the road, though some gravel stretches had no barrier and frightening drops. At one point, Jemma veered too close to the edge and sprayed stones up the side of the car.

Ellie screamed. 'Careful, Mum. That was close.'

'It's fine.' Jemma kept her eyes fixed on the road ahead. 'But I wouldn't fancy driving this in the dark.'

After the ninety-minute detour, they arrived at a forested section, which both Brad and Ellie thought might give them views of Helen's villa.

'We're only half a kilometre from the house,' Ellie said. 'Pull into those trees and let's check out the view.'

Jemma reversed up a rough track into the forest and applied the handbrake.

Brad took the telescope from a case and attached it to the tripod before handing both Jemma and Ellie a pair of binoculars. 'Right, we're after a Cyprus Warbler and a lesser-spotted British bitch.'

They moved through the trees whilst being careful to make as little noise as possible before arriving at an opening where the light streamed in. Clearing the edge of the forest, they found themselves at the top of a small cliff with clear views across the valley and down towards a grand villa with a large, azure pool.

Jemma punched the air. 'Bingo.'

* * *

At five to twelve, Bayram reversed his lorry through the newly widened entrance and headed back down the hill to the main road at the end. He parked in the first village outside a café where the three workers would enjoy a rejuvenating lunch.

* * *

Brad watched the villa through the telescope as Jemma and Ellie ate a makeshift meal on a picnic blanket, fighting off legions of ants intent on liberating the crumbs from their baguette.

'Anything yet?' Jemma asked.

'The lorry's gone,' he replied. 'I'm not sure what they're doing but they've knocked down a gate post and unloaded a great pile of stones. Looks like the Turks stop for lunch at twelve.'

Ellie stretched out and lay back in the blanket. 'It's a strange country with a dividing line and lots of troops about. Why did the Turkish troops invade Cyprus?'

'Didn't you read the magazine on the plane?' Jemma asked. 'If you had, you'd have known that the British left in nineteen sixty. They'd kept the peace between the Greeks and the Turks for years. In nineteen seventy-four, the Greeks launched a coup d'état and the new military government voted to unite with the Greek mainland. That led to the Turkish invasion and the Turks in the south moved to the north and the Greeks in the north moved to the south. Follow it so far?'

As there was no response, she turned to find that everything had caught up with her daughter and she'd fallen asleep. Jemma tutted and went to stand with Brad.

'This watching and waiting is so frustrating.'

'All we need are a few photos.' He slipped an arm around her back. 'Then we can start the process.'

'I know,' she said. 'It's just that I feel like going down there, finding Kira and grabbing her.'

'We don't know for certain that she's there yet. I've not seen anyone, although the lights are on.'

Jemma brought the binoculars to her eyes and scanned the villa. 'Come on, Helen, show yourself, you bitch.'

Chapter 52

The following morning, Helen and Malek were roused by the builder's lorry pulling onto the drive. 'There goes our peace,' she groaned. 'But do you realise Ada slept through last night?'

'That's a first.' He shoved the pillow over his head.

'I'd like to take her out in the pool before it gets too hot, but I don't want the builders to see her in case they've got loose tongues.'

He removed the pillow and stuffed it back beneath his head. 'I need thirty-five thousand lira in cash to sort a birth certificate and passport in the name of Ada Aydin or Ada Fletcher, if you'd prefer.'

'Do it as Aydin,' she said. 'She might stay under the radar better with a Turkish name. What does Aydin mean?'

'I think it means bright,' he replied.

'So, in English, she'd be Ada Bright. That's funny.' She placed her hand on his chest. 'Now, what can we do until she wakes up?' She slid her leg over his naked body.

He grinned.

* * *

Jemma drove past the entrance to Helen's villa whilst examining the builder's lorry, which was now fully on the drive and no longer blocking the road. Brad took a photo of it as they passed.

'I know it's a long way around, but we might need to go that way occasionally in case we see them when we are passing.'

'I suppose so,' she replied. 'It's a bit of a frightening drive, though.'

'Do you think we might see Kira today?' Ellie asked.

'Hopefully. If she's there,' Jemma said. 'It would be good to send some photos off so the wheels can start turning.'

She parked in the same spot and Brad assembled the telescope. They'd bought some cheap folding chairs to make the surveillance more comfortable and by eight in the morning they were in position overlooking the villa. The scent of the surrounding pine forest filled their nostrils as the incessant sound of cicadas accompanied the long wait. During the next four hours, nothing happened.

'What a boring morning.' Brad yawned. 'It's not much fun watching a bunch of men building a wall brick by damn brick.'

* * *

Helen was standing at the windows holding Ada and watched the builders drive away for their midday meal and siesta.

'Can you pop into town, Malek, and get the bits I've listed? I need more baby vests for a one year old. I've no idea what they're called in Turkish.'

'OK.' Grabbing the keys to his Porsche, he kissed her and stepped outside. 'I don't like the gap where the gate used to be. It feels very open.'

She followed him outside. 'It's only temporary while they're working. When they've finished the whole wall, they'll fill that in as the last bit.' She peered around the garden at the progress on the new wall. 'Wow, look how much they've done already.'

He smiled through the car window. 'Bayram is a good worker.'

* * *

Ellie rubbed the sweat from her forehead and brought her eye back to the telescope's eyepiece. 'The builders have gone and Malek's driven off in his Porsche. Flash git. Wait! Helen's at the door and she's holding something.'

Brad and Jemma jumped out of their chairs and rushed closer, bringing their binoculars up to their eyes. 'What's she doing?' Jemma asked.

Ellie shook with tears as she gazed through the telescope. 'It's got to be Kira. She's holding Kira.'

* * *

Helen came out through the patio door carrying Kira. She slipped a pair of bright orange armbands on the child followed by a sunhat before padding towards the pool, slipping off her robe and stepping in the shallow end.

'Want a swim, Ada?' she asked.

The toddler waved her arms with excitement as they entered the water.

* * *

Ellie clicked furiously with her mobile phone against the telescope while Brad took repeated photos with his camera.

'Turn around,' he muttered, 'show us her face.'

They persisted until Helen climbed the steps out from the water and carried Kira back inside.

'Any joy?' Jemma ran her hands through her hair.

'So-so,' Ellie replied. 'It could be her, but I didn't get any clear shots of her face with that floppy sun hat. Oh, God, this is awful. I just want to run down there and grab her.' She ran to the edge of the trees. 'Give me back my baby you bastards!'

Jemma ran over and wrapped her arms around her sobbing daughter. 'Shush, Els, they might hear us from up here. It won't do any good if they know we're here.'

The sobs continued. 'I just want her back, Mum.'

'I know but come away from the edge.'

They walked back together with Jemma's arm around Ellie's shaking shoulders.

'Did you get any better pictures?' Jemma asked Brad.

'Not really,' he replied. 'We're not close enough to take any great photos but at least they prove she's got a small girl with her.'

Ellie's eyes glistened. 'It's her, Mum. I'm sure it's her.'

Jemma pointed her binoculars towards the villa. 'The builders are back.'

'Shall we go back to the Wi-Fi and email those photos to Amrik?' Brad suggested.

Ellie rubbed her eyes. 'But I don't want to leave her. She needs me.'

Jemma checked her watch. 'Let's send him the images we have. Hopefully, they'll trigger some action. We can come back later when the builders have finished.'

* * *

At the villa in Kyrenia, Brad emailed the last of the photos they'd taken to Amrik and closed the laptop. 'Over to the cops now. Let's hope they're good enough to send in the troops.'

Jemma hugged Ellie. 'It won't be long now. It won't be long. At least we've seen her and we know she's there.'

'This is awful, Mum. Knowing that she's there, so near but so far. What will we do if the police won't do anything?'

'We'll just have to go to the nearest police station, sit on the floor and refuse to move until they've rescued her.'

'If that doesn't work, we'll have to do it ourselves,' Ellie replied. 'Do you think any of the local pharmacies sell chloroform?'

Chapter 53

Amrik placed his coffee on the desk well away from the keyboard. After a disastrous morning a month before, he'd discovered hot coffee and electrical equipment did not happily mix so had set up a beverage exclusion zone around his computer.

His screen lit up and he spotted that his inbox was full of messages and attachments from Brad Jones. He opened the first.

'Bloody hell, they're in Cyprus.'

Hannah rolled her chair alongside him. 'Who's in Cyprus?'

'Brad and Jemma. Probably Ellie as well. They've sent a load of photos of a woman in a pool holding a child. Quick, can you call Laura while I download them all to the system?'

A few minutes later, with DI Day and DS Salmon peering over his shoulder, he had set up a slideshow of the best photographs. The final photo froze on the screen and Amrik turned to Laura.

'Well, what do you think?'

She frowned. 'I hate to say it but they're not sharp enough. You can just about tell an older woman is holding a young girl in a pool, but the woman's face isn't that clear and you can't make out the child at all. The floppy sun hat doesn't help.'

He stared at the last photo. 'I thought you might say that.'

'You can send them to the British High Commission in Cyprus, but I don't think they'll bother sending them on to the Turks. It doesn't prove anything.'

He tapped a few keys. 'I can ask Brad to try taking some better shots.'

'Please tell him to be careful. From what I've been told, Helen Fletcher is a vicious woman who's suspected of killing several people who got in her way.'

* * *

Later that afternoon, Jemma, Brad and Ellie were back at their vantage point overlooking Helen's villa.

Brad used his binoculars to scan the surrounding hillside. 'Amrik wants photos that are closer and which show Helen and Kira's faces clearly. I can't see any other places we can take photos without being in plain view of the house.'

Ellie pulled away from the telescope and pointed. 'How about that wooded patch over there? It might be a bit of a trek getting there but it's closer to the villa and has some cover.'

* * *

Hakan Yilmaz made himself comfortable in his green folding chair and took a series of photographs of Helen's garden. He checked the back of the camera.

They'll do fine for background shots. If I take some photos tomorrow of Helen with Sidika, that will be an easy five hundred euros plus more from Helen.

He couldn't help grinning as he picked up the binoculars and scanned the forest along the adjoining hillside. He jumped when he spotted three people with a telescope and binoculars looking back at him.

* * *

'Shit!' Ellie shouted. 'There's a man over there looking at us with binoculars. We'd better disappear.'

'Wait,' Jemma glanced around. 'See that vulture circling up there? Point the scope and bins at it so the bloke thinks we're birdwatching.'

Ellie adjusted the telescope as Jemma pointed to a speck in the sky. They continued watching it for five minutes before turning to leave.

'OK, let's go,' Jemma said. 'We can sneak back later.'

* * *

Hakan pulled his beaten-up Skoda onto the pull-in where he thought the birdwatchers had been. He locked his car and walked along the track, his feet crunching on the dried needles and cones. At the end, he could see down towards the villa and across the valley to the spot he'd chosen earlier.

Other than a few drag marks in the pine needles, there was no sign of anybody having been there, though the ground was dry so they wouldn't have left any footprints regardless.

He returned through the trees and drove down the hill to Helen's villa just as a large builder's lorry pulled out from her drive. The villa was quiet as he stepped out from his car and strolled towards the patio. 'Helen!'

She rushed out the house wearing a loose robe over a blue swimsuit and pulled it tightly around her. 'What?' she snapped.

'Nothing much happening up there. I saw some bird-watchers looking at an eagle, but they didn't stay for long.'

'Did you take any photos of them?'

He checked his camera. 'Only from a distance, and not very good as they were in the trees.'

She squinted at the screen in the bright sunlight. 'They're no use. If they come back tomorrow, you need to do better.'

He shrugged. 'I'll try, but I don't think they were suspicious.'

Helen turned away from the man. 'OK. I'll ask Malek to keep an eye out as well.'

* * *

Amrik received a swift reply to the email he'd sent to the British High Commission in Nicosia, saying the photographs were not clear enough to be used as evidence or to identify a child.

Amrik swore, snatched up his mobile and typed a message to Brad giving him the bad news.

* * *

The smell of takeaway food filled the kitchen of the villa in Kyrenia as the family demolished the kebabs they'd collected on the way back.

Ellie licked her fingers clean. 'The lamb skewers are brilliant. What are the chewy lumps?'

Jemma finished her mouthful. 'I think they're stuffed marrows, but I can't be sure.'

Brad's phone pinged, he reached for it but realised his fingers were covered in sticky sauce. He jumped up and washed his hands under the tap before drying them and checking the alert.

'It's a WhatsApp message from Amrik.' He read it and frowned. 'Damn it. The photos are no good. They need pictures where they can clearly identify Kira. We've got to get closer somehow.'

Ellie crushed the napkin in her hand. 'I'm never going to see her again. Why won't anybody help? They've stolen my baby.'

Jemma put her arm around her daughter's shoulders. 'Let's try getting some better pictures, Els. We've come here to do a job and we're not giving up.'

Ellie threw down the napkin. 'But they've kidnapped her. The police should just break down that bitch's door and fetch her out. I want my baby back!'

Chapter 54

The telescope's lens pointed out through the opening of the camouflaged hide positioned under the trees. Brad had bought the hunter's hide at a supermarket in Kyrenia to keep them hidden from the man on the other side of the valley while enabling them to move closer to the villa.

The only activity at the villa five hundred metres below was the tapping of hammers on stone as the relentless progress of the new wall moved along the property's boundary. Already, one side of the garden was shaded by the two-metre construction that would eventually block their view of the entire grounds.

Jemma stayed hidden under the trees and scanned the mountainside where they'd seen the man with the binoculars the day before. She tensed as, once again, she saw him on the hillside.

'He's there again, Brad. Be careful when you come out.'

'OK,' he replied.

'I'm worried they might be on to us.' Jemma told Ellie. 'It's a concern that he's there again. Maybe Helen suspects something, which would explain why she's having that wall built.'

Her daughter shrugged. 'It's probably just guilt and wanting to hide Kira away.'

* * *

Hakan stretched in his seat and took another pull from his beer. It had been cold when he'd slid it into his bag earlier but in the heat of the late morning, it was now warm.

As he reached for the binoculars, a lone vulture cried from high above, effortlessly circling and scanning for its next meal. Another sweep of the opposing hillside brought no sightings, so instead he typed a message into his phone.

Helen, my niece and sister will arrive in ten minutes. I'm in place for the photo.

A reply came straight back. *OK. Thanks.*

* * *

After a spell of inactivity, Brad jumped when a yellow Fiat pulled onto Helen's drive.

'Visitors at the villa,' he said. 'Looks like a woman and a young girl.'

Jemma peered through her binoculars. 'She's got to be five or six. Maybe she's come to play with Kira.'

Fifteen minutes later, Helen came out holding hands with the child and wandered over to the pool. She removed her robe before stepping into the water. The girl dropped her towel on the floor and jumped into the deeper end before splashing around with one of the bright green noodles floating in the pool.

Brad lowered his camera and squinted as he watched the child enjoying herself with Helen. 'Come on, come on. Bring out Kira as well.'

Jemma crawled over to the hide on her hands and knees to join him. 'What's she doing?'

'No idea,' he replied. 'It feels odd, though. Why isn't Kira in the pool? Do you think that guy yesterday was watching out for anybody near the villa and warned Helen?'

Jemma thought for a moment. 'I suppose so. We'll have to make sure we stay well hidden.'

* * *

Over on the other side of the mountain, Hakan snapped an array of photos from the activity in the pool, checking the camera display after each batch. After ten minutes, he packed away his equipment and returned to his car.

After returning to his apartment in Girne, he loaded the morning's work onto his laptop and sent a selection of images to the English policeman.

* * *

Ellie scrolled through her phone as she lay on a picnic blanket under the trees. Jemma crawled back over to her.

Ellie sighed. 'This is so frustrating, Mum. To know she's down there but I can't just go and grab her.'

Jemma lowered herself to lie next to her daughter. 'We'll get that picture, Els, don't worry. Then the police can come and rescue her.'

Ellie reached over and held her mother's hand. 'Why is this, another awful thing, happening to us? Can't we just play happy families without everything going wrong?'

'Soon, Els. We will, soon.'

* * *

As Brad observed the villa, Helen and the girl climbed out of the pool, towelled themselves off and returned inside. A short while later the girl came out with the woman who had brought her and together they left. There was no sign of Kira.

* * *

Amrik flicked through the latest transcripts of telephone calls received by the helpline.

Laura wandered over holding a cup of coffee. 'Any joy?' she asked.

He shook his head. 'Nah, all the callers seem to be weirdos or time wasters.'

She placed her drink on his desk. 'It's worse every time we do an appeal. Makes you wonder what's wrong with the world.'

Amrik's computer pinged as an email came in. 'Oh. It's from the Turkish PI. Let's see if he's earned his money.' His hand wobbled as he opened the first image. 'That must be Helen's villa. Looks nice. The rewards of crime and dodgy property deals.' He closed the photo and opened the next. 'You little beauty. Look, Helen's carrying a child.' He checked the other images but Laura frowned.

'This can't be right. That girl is too old to be Kira.'

'Bloody hell!' He opened the last file. 'A bill for ten thousand lira for taking photos of the wrong child.'

Laura sighed deeply and turned to leave. 'We'll write it off. We can't waste any more money though.'

After the door closed Amrik smashed his fist on the desk. 'What do we do next?'

* * *

The next day was overcast but, even without the sun, the temperature was over thirty degrees. Inside the camouflaged hide, Jemma dripped with sweat as she took a turn on the telescope, though it was hard concentrating with so little happening. She'd been surprised when the builders hadn't arrived to work on the wall but then realised it was Sunday.

Jemma felt something crawling up her leg and smacked her knee. 'Bloody ants,' she whispered.

Ellie smiled. 'You getting eaten?'

'Just a bit,' Jemma responded. 'Oh, keep a lookout, Helen's come out wheeling a large blue pram. Surely Kira's too big for that, isn't she Ellie?'

Her daughter watched through binoculars. 'She might stay in it if she's asleep but the moment she wakes up she'll be out.'

They held their breaths as Kira climbed out from the pram and landed hard on the ground.

Brad lunged for the camera and took multiple shots. 'Quick, Ellie. Stick your phone against the scope and get some photos.'

She fiddled about lining the phone up with the telescope's eyepiece but was eventually able to take some photographs of her daughter. She checked them on the screen. 'I got some good ones. They're really close up and in focus for a change.'

Jemma pointed. 'Look, she's crawling.'

Kira stopped alongside a sunbed and used it to pull herself up before taking a few tentative steps.

Ellie sobbed. 'She's walking, my baby's walking and I'm not there for her.'

Brad crawled over and joined her under the green, brown and black cover. 'Don't worry. Once Amrik sees these photos, he'll have to initiate some kind of action.'

Ellie pressed her eye against the eyepiece and gasped as her daughter took some more steps towards the edge of the pool. 'Stay back, Kira, don't go near the edge.'

Kira tottered across the patio until she reached the edge of the blue pool, took one step and disappeared beneath the surface of the wind-rippled water.

Chapter 55

Amrik stared at the major incident board with its array of photographs and statements joined together with lines of string. He narrowed his eyes in case anything else jumped out.

Laura came in and stood behind him. 'Any new ideas?'

He turned and shrugged. 'No. Everything points to Kira being in Northern Cyprus with Helen Fletcher, but without cooperation from their authorities, we're totally stuck.'

'I'll have another word with the ACC, but I can't see him allowing any more expenditure unless we get some definite proof.'

* * *

Brad, Jemma and Ellie could only stand in horrified shock as Kira failed to resurface.

'Oh, my God, Mum. She's drowning.' Ellie shouted. 'We've got to rescue her.'

'Let's go.' Jemma grabbed the car keys and they ran for the vehicle.

'Wait,' Brad called after them, 'Malek's jumped in the pool.'

They watched as Helen rushed out from the villa and took the dripping child from Malek as he climbed out the water. She wrapped Kira in a towel before carrying her back inside.

Jemma hugged her sobbing daughter.

Ellie shook in her mother's arms. 'Oh, Mum, what shall we do now?'

Brad joined them. 'Do you think the police would do anything if we gave them a call?'

Jemma frowned. 'I bet Helen has them in her pocket. That's her style.'

'Let me see if the signal here is good enough to send the photos I've taken. Maybe once Amrik sends those to the British Embassy, they'll be prepared to pass them on to the Turks.'

'Look,' Ellie said, 'they're bringing her back out. She seems ok.'

Helen waded into the shallow end of the pool holding Kira. She wore a bright blue bikini and the child a pink swimsuit. Malek wore his obligatory tiny trunks, or budgie smugglers, as Jemma called them.

'That's weird, Mum. Kira wants to go back in the water.'

Jemma smiled as she watched through the binoculars. 'Fearless, your daughter. Absolutely fearless.'

Ellie wiped away a tear. 'I'm fed up of all this watching. I want her back and I want to go home.'

'Soon, Els, these new photos have got to help.'

'But what if they don't? Or if it leads to a protracted international court battle to try to win her back?'

Jemma hugged her. 'Keep the faith. We'll get this sorted somehow.'

Still watching the events below, Helen pointed to the car and Malek left the pool, dried himself off and returned inside. After a few minutes, he came out and climbed into the black Land Cruiser parked beside a Porsche.

'Where's he off to?' Jemma muttered.

'I don't know,' Ellie replied. 'I wonder why he didn't take the Carrera.'

Helen played with Kira in the water until, half an hour later, the Toyota returned and parked beside the Porsche. Malek climbed out and Helen pointed at the cars.

He moved the Porsche in front of the Land Cruiser before opening the luggage compartment of the four-by-four and removing a large cardboard box. He then spent the next ten minutes assembling an old-fashioned wooden playpen.

'I'm sure you put me in one of those when I was little,' Ellie said.

Jemma nodded. 'Oh, yes. I thought child cages had gone out of fashion.'

Ellie thumped the nearest tree. 'This is so bloody frustrating talking about sodding playpens when all I want to do is grab her.'

* * *

Below them, Malek completed the playpen, dragged it into a shaded spot on the terrace and wheeled the unwanted pram into the garage.

Under the shade of a tree, Helen lay with Kira on a sunbed. She stroked the child's cheek. 'You're a little beauty, you know, Give Gran a hug.'

Kira put her arms out and hugged her back.

* * *

Up on the hillside, Ellie watched through the telescope. 'She's hugging Helen. My baby's forgotten me. She loves that bitch now. I can't take this any longer.' The tears started flowing again.

Feeling so helpless, all Jemma could do was clench her fists.

* * *

Helen turned the girl around to reveal the new playpen. 'Look, you've got a lovely new pen to play in. All nice and safe so you don't fall in the pool again.'

Kira stared at her. 'Mamma.'

'No, say Granny.'

'Mamma,' came the reply.

Helen shook her. 'Not Mamma, say Granny!'

Kira started crying so Helen plonked her inside the new wooden structure.

Malek wandered over and wrapped his arms around Helen, unfastened her bikini and let it fall to the ground. He whispered in her ear and she responded by cupping the front of his trunks before taking his hand and leading him inside with barely a sideways glance at the child in the playpen.

* * *

Ellie's hands shook as she watched the scenes at the villa. 'She nearly drowned so they've chucked her in a playpen and now they're off shagging again.' By now she was beyond the point of tears. 'I can't take any more of this. I keep expecting to see a squad of police cars roaring up with sirens blaring but there's nothing.' She stormed towards one of the camping chairs, dumped herself down and cradled her head.

Jemma crawled over to the camouflaged hide and knelt next to Brad. 'I'm worried about Ellie, she's getting stressed out.'

He turned and held her head against his chest. 'Remember how you felt when Zak kidnapped Rocky? You were inconsolable.'

'I was, but I didn't have to watch my baby with his kidnapper day after day.'

Brad held up his phone. 'These pictures have been

uploading for ages. I don't think the signal here is good enough to send files this big. Shall we pop back to the villa and forward them? We can come back later. Hopefully, by then, Amrik will have been able to pass them on and start some action.'

Jemma checked the time. 'OK. I'll let her know.'

She wandered over to where her daughter was cradling her head and touched her shoulder. 'We're going to go back in a few minutes,' she said. 'Brad needs the Wi-Fi to send the latest photos to Amrik.'

'Right,' Ellie said, 'but first I need a toilet break. I'll be back in a few minutes.' She took some tissues from the car and headed into the forest.

Jemma returned to the hide and knelt beside Brad. 'Anything happening?'

He stretched. 'No. The lovebirds haven't come back out yet and Kira's in the cot thing.'

'Playpen,' Jemma corrected.

'OK, playpen.' He touched the roof of the hide. 'Let me know when Ellie's back and I'll fold this down.'

She scanned the trees. 'Come on, Ellie. How long do you need to take a shit in the woods?'

'You better ask the bears,' he replied. 'Oh no!'

She turned. 'What?'

'It's Ellie. She's on Helen's drive. Creeping into the garden.'

Chapter 56

An olive tree in a large terracotta pot didn't offer much in the way of protection but Ellie crouched behind it anyway. Other than the incessant singing of cicadas and the hum of the pool filter there were no sounds in Helen's garden.

Ellie came out from behind the tree, her legs feeling like jelly as she moved across the edge of the patio towards the shady terrace. As she stepped closer, she could see Kira wide awake and standing in the playpen while fiddling with the beads on the abacus built into the side. She pulled out her phone and took some pictures of her daughter then, with a tear in her eye, she moved nearer until she found herself standing at the pen's wooden bars.

She knelt on the paved ground. 'I've come for you, Kira. I'm going to take you home.'

The child broke into an immediate smile, throwing up her arms. 'Mamma.'

Tears ran down Ellie's cheeks as she reached down inside the playpen and lifted her daughter out, making sure to scour the sliding doors to the house.

With Kira clinging on like a limpet, she gazed back up the

hill leading to the vantage point where she had spent the last few days. 'Let's go.'

She carefully trod back along the patio, behind the cars and out through the gate. When she arrived at the track, she sprinted up the hill as fast as she could carrying an armful of toddler.

* * *

Jemma watched the events unfold with an open mouth. 'Quick! Let's grab them and get out of here.'

Brad jumped up. 'I'll get the hide.'

'Leave it. We need to move quickly.'

They climbed into the Kia and reversed out of the parking space. As Jemma raced backwards, she made a quick decision. 'I'll reverse down the hill but then head over the mountain. We've got more chance of escaping over the top.'

He grabbed the handle above the door and prepared for a bumpy ride. 'You're the boss.'

She put her arm behind Brad's seat and peered around as she reversed at speed down towards the villa. When she was around fifty metres from Ellie, she slammed on the brakes, allowing Brad to jump out. He threw open the rear door just as the panting girl reached them.

'Holy shit! I've got her.' Ellie climbed in and slammed the door.

Kira gurgled with excitement, obviously enjoying the new game.

Brad slammed the door. 'Go, go, go.' He fastened his seat belt and held on tightly.

Jemma rammed the Sportage in gear, engaged the four-wheel drive, and tore off up the mountain road. As she wrestled with the steering wheel Jemma glanced in the mirror. 'No sign of them yet. Oh, Ellie, I wish you'd warned us.'

Ellie squeezed her daughter against her chest. 'I didn't plan anything. I just wanted to see her and when I did, I couldn't leave her for a minute longer. I've got her back, Mum. I've rescued Kira.'

* * *

Malek stepped out through the patio doors and lit a cigarette. He'd quit years earlier but on several occasions he'd stood out on the deck of the *Goke* to smoke as it helped him with the stress of what they were doing. He took a deep drag and savoured the smoke before blowing it out. With a yawn, he stretched out his arms and slid his feet inside a pair of black flip-flops. He slipped his box of cigarettes back inside the pocket of his shorts and wandered past the pool to survey the new wall, which certainly did its job because now he couldn't see over the beige stone edifice. A tiny brown lizard crept along the side, lapping up ants that had already made their home on the newly created habitat.

Malek strolled back towards the pool and dipped his toe in the cool water. He smiled and returned towards the villa. As he strolled past the playpen, he glanced inside and froze.

It was empty.

He ran to the pool and checked the water before searching the rest of the patio and garden. 'Helen! Ada's gone.'

She rushed outside barefoot and naked, except for a diaphanous robe. 'What do you mean she's gone? Have you checked the playpen?'

'Yes, it's empty.' He ran through the gate and out onto the road that passed the house. He saw it at once. 'Look at the dust.' He pointed up the hill. 'Somebody's taken her and driven off up that way.'

'Shit,' she screamed. 'Get some clothes on and get after them.'

They both rushed inside and threw on some clothes. Malek grabbed his keys while Helen disappeared into the kitchen. A few moments later she rushed back carrying an automatic handgun. Metal clicked as she pushed a magazine in.

Malek's eyes widened. 'No guns. I don't want to be involved in any shooting.'

'Just drive.' She ran to the Land Cruiser. 'Move the Porsche out of the way.'

He rushed around to the driver's door of his Porsche. 'No, let's take this. It will be quicker.'

She lowered herself into the sports car and slammed the door. 'Get after the bastards.'

Chapter 57

Clouds of dust billowed up behind the speeding Kia as Jemma raced along the track leading up into the mountains. Sweat slicked her palms as she grasped the wheel.

'Not too fast.' Ellie called from the back. 'Don't forget we haven't got a child seat for Kira.'

Jemma dropped a gear and the car surged forwards. 'Just keep her under your seatbelt and hold on tight.' The car hit a bump and for a second the wheels left the ground.

Brad's head hit the ceiling. 'Steady there, gal.' He kept an eye on the track behind. 'No sign yet but they'll realise at some point. The dust we're leaving is like a trail of smoke.'

Reaching a narrow section with a bridge, Jemma slammed on the brakes and skidded. She fought to regain traction on all four tyres and slowed as the road twisted around a set of hairpin bends with aluminium crash barriers. When the road widened again, the pedal hit the floor and the car bounced wildly.

'Wheee, upcoming breakfast,' Brad shouted.

'Don't joke,' Ellie said. 'It's worse in the back.'

Jemma checked her mirror. 'We might have lost them.'

'I doubt it,' Brad replied. 'But if we can put some time

between us, that'll help... No...' his voice sounded ominous, 'they've come around the corner.'

There was a loud crack as the back window exploded.

Ellie screamed. 'Holy crap. That was a gunshot.'

* * *

Malek accelerated up the hill, tyres spinning, and the Porsche's rear swung wildly as it fishtailed along. He glanced down at the dashboard. 'I think it has a traction control button somewhere.'

Helen screamed as they nearly hit a wall. 'Keep your sodding eyes on the road. What does the button look like?' She glared at the controls in front. 'Forget that, I'll be sick if I look down anymore. Just bloody drive.'

He wrestled with the wheel. 'I left it on sports setting, which will make it a bit lively but I'll manage.'

She grabbed the handle above the passenger side door. 'We should have used the Land Cruiser. This thing is useless on these crap roads.'

He hit the brakes as they met a car heading towards them. 'It'll be good when we get to the main road though.'

'We need to catch up with them before we get to civilisation,' she said. 'Easier to get rid of bodies up here.'

He accelerated and they shot off down the road.

Helen jabbed a finger. 'Look, there they are.' She leant out of the window and released a burst of shots, the noise from the automatic weapon was deafening when combined with the engine's roar. 'Bullseye,' she shrieked. 'Smashed their window.'

'Don't kill Ada,' he said.

She glared at him with a wild look in her eyes. 'I don't care. Nobody steals from me and lives.'

* * *

'They're still shooting at us!' Ellie leaned over her daughter in an attempt to shield her. 'That's it, Mum. Pedal to the floor.'

The four-by-four lurched forward as Jemma dropped a gear and hit the accelerator. 'You said it. How long to the border?'

Brad tried to unfold the map, but the car was bouncing too much to read. 'Probably over an hour away. I put the Nicosia border crossing in the satnav, but this track isn't on the system.'

'What will we do if we cross the border?' Ellie asked.

Jemma spun the steering wheel as she screeched around a bend. 'We could go to a police station in the south. Surely, Helen won't have bought off the Greek coppers too.'

Brad tapped the dashboard display. 'It'll be better when we hit the main road. The satnav should pick us up then.' The road had some tarmac stretches, but the smoother surface would suddenly turn into a concrete patch or, even worse, loose gravel in some parts. Most of it was just a single track with a few passing places.

Jemma tried to drive down the middle of the road to avoid the worst of the potholes but dreaded meeting someone coming the other way.

'Can't you go any faster, Mum? I still keep catching glimpses of them behind us.'

Jemma wrenched the steering wheel and skidded around another hairpin bend. 'I'll try.'

* * *

Helen screamed at Malek. 'You're losing them. Go faster. Now.'

He attempted to gain control over another spin. 'I'm doing my best. I'm not used to this yet and it takes some handling. It's not designed for off-road stuff on tracks like this.

It's got low-profile tyres and it would be easy to rip one of them off.'

She leant out of the window grasping the gun. 'Just catch up with them.'

* * *

Ellie glanced down at Kira, who was smiling massively. 'I think she's enjoying this.'

Brad frowned. 'I wish I was. Keep your head down if you can. Don't forget they just shot at us.'

Jemma reached a more open section of road with white limestone peaks on either side. The dashboard display showed one hundred.

'That's better,' she said. 'We're a ton up.'

Brad gulped. 'Just concentrate on the driving, please.'

The Kia screeched around another bend, but then a tractor rolled out through a gate pulling a large trailer which now partially blocked the road in front. Jemma slammed her foot on the brakes and the front of the car dipped under the pressure of the hard stop as they skidded towards the vehicle.

Chapter 58

Reaching a straight section with a smooth surface, Malek worked his way through the Porsche's flappy paddle gearbox. The car responded and surged forward.

He felt the power beneath him. 'Now we can catch up again.'

'That's better,' Helen said. 'It's so fast now we're back on tarmac. There they are. We've got them.'

'I told you it would be. They can't do two hundred. Why are they slowing?' He hit the brakes.

* * *

The Sportage skidded to a halt and Jemma blasted the horn. The tractor driver stopped and waved for her to pass. The overgrown shrubs on the bank scraped down the side of the car as she squeezed through the gap between the tractor and the edge of the road. Inch by inch, the big car crept past the obstruction while the farmer puffed on his cigarette.

Finally, she got through the gap and accelerated, racing through the gears as she rebuilt her speed.

The driver waved again and pulled out with the trailer completely blocking the road.

* * *

Being forced to brake, Malek could only watch as Jemma's four-by-four squeezed around the tractor, and he swore as the trailer moved in front to block his way forward. Malek gave him a blast from his horn and wound down his window to reel off a stream of angry Turkish. Ignoring the barrage, the driver slowly manoeuvred the massive trailer, carrying heavy bales of straw, back to the centre and continued along the narrow road.

Helen jumped from the Porsche and rushed towards the driver's side of the tractor. 'Can you move, please? This is urgent. We're chasing some thieves.'

The bearded driver shrugged and carried on down the road, pointing at a gateway two hundred metres further along.

She pointed her gun at the man and shouted. 'Move! Now!'

His eyes widened and the engine revved as the tractor lurched forwards.

Helen ran back and clambered in the Porsche.

Malek moved forward until he was close behind the farm vehicle, flicking his wipers to remove the build-up of straw from his windscreen. The revving of the sports car was drowned out by the noise of the agricultural machine and it took several minutes for the tractor and trailer to reach the exit so the driver could jump down to open the gate. He climbed back into the cab and drove cautiously into the field.

Malek wasted no time and slammed his foot against the accelerator.

* * *

Jemma sped by several farmhouses and small hamlets, the buildings flying past the car windows in a blur, and she hoped there'd be no more agricultural vehicles to test her brakes.

Brad peered at his map and waited for the satnav to wake up and find the road. He glanced back through the broken rear window. 'I think they got stuck behind that tractor. Try taking the next left up the mountain road towards the tank memorial. There's a chance they won't see us turn up there. It's coming up in a moment. Left, left now!'

Jemma wrenched the steering wheel and the car skidded through the bend. The road changed back to single track, forcing her to reduce speed.

Ellie sat sideways with Kira so she could see out through the hole in the rear window. 'Still no sign. We might have lost them. Maybe they drove past the last turn we made.'

The Kia raced up the mountain track and just when Jemma had reached a speed of seventy, she spotted the sign for another hairpin bend right ahead. She hit the brakes hard and the car skidded on the loose gravel before sliding perilously close to the flimsy wooden barrier.

Ellie screamed. 'Slow down, we don't want to end up like the coach in the Italian Job.'

Jemma removed a hand from the steering wheel and wiped her brown with her sleeve. 'Would you rather get shot at again?'

Ellie glanced back through the rear window. 'OK, Mum. You go as fast as you like!'

Chapter 59

Amrik had just finished reviewing a monotonous pile of witness statements when his phone rang.

'Hi, Amrik, it's Laura. Bad news, I'm afraid. There's been a shooting on an estate in Swanbourne and a suspected drug dealer has died. The ACC wants this cleared up pronto. You know how proud he is of the murder recovery rate on his watch.'

'Right, I'll finish what I'm doing and get the details.'

'No. That's the bad news, I'm afraid. He wants the disappearance of Kira Thorne put on the back burner and the whole team swapped over to the latest investigation.'

He shook his head. 'You're kidding?'

'No. I wish I was, but you know how important the crime figures are when there are budget decisions to be made.'

'OK,' he replied. 'I'll speak with Sarge, get the address and go down with Hannah.'

'Thanks, Amrik. One more thing...'

'What?' he asked.

'If you want to spend any bits of spare time on the search for Kira, I'm happy to look the other way. I'm sure you already know what Jemma, Brad and Ellie are up to.'

'Thanks, Laura, I will. Strangely enough, though, I haven't a clue what they're doing.'

* * *

Malek skidded up to the T-junction and looked both ways. 'Which way now? I bet they're headed for Nicosia. We can either go left over the mountains or right to join up with the main road.'

A car behind blasted its horn and Helen wound down her window to give the driver the finger.

Malek laughed. 'I say we head right and then cut back onto the main road. That will be quicker, especially in the Porsche.'

'Wait,' she said, 'they know we're in a Porsche and they're in an SUV with a smashed rear window. I reckon they'll avoid the busy roads and take the mountain road to get to Nicosia the back way. Go left, we'll have to follow them.' Her last words trailed off into a gasp as she was thrown back in her seat by the acceleration of the powerful car on the tarmac surface.

Malek slammed on the brakes, throwing them both forward against their seat belts. He slid the car around onto the single-track side road and hit the throttle, once again pushing Helen back into her seat.

'This better be worth it,' she said.

* * *

At that moment, Ellie was holding on to Kira in the back seat of their hire car as Jemma tore along the narrow mountain road.

Brad twisted around to look behind them. 'Crap. We haven't lost them. We've got no chance against a Porsche.'

'We might if the road gets any worse,' Jemma replied. 'That car can't be any good on rough tracks.'

They sped past an old vehicle with metal tracks that had been left on the roadside. Brad made a double-take. 'Was that a tank?'

'Yeah.' Jemma slowed for a van pulling out of a parking space. 'It's a war memorial. A Russian tank used by the Turks back in seventy-four. It drove over a landmine, which blew the tracks off, so they dragged it to the edge and left it there.'

Ellie shook her head. 'You're amazing, Mum. Only you could give a history lesson while screaming along in a getaway car.'

Jemma slowed as they reached the crest of the hill and the wheels briefly left the road. As they landed, she hit the brakes as they approached another hairpin. She fought with the wheel as they skidded and slid around the bend, almost hitting the crash barrier.

'Shit,' Ellie shouted. 'Did you see the bloody drop over that edge?'

'Nope. Concentrating on the road, Els,' she replied.

The Kia straightened and continued down the hill towards the next bend.

* * *

Malek wrestled the steering wheel, the rear wheels spinning and smoking, as he fought to keep the Porsche in a straight line. They flew past the tank following the clouds of dust thrown up by the Sportage and he pressed the paddle to drop a gear as they reached the brow of the hill. The engine screamed and red-lined as all four wheels left the road.

The noise from the engine drowned out Helen's shout of 'Bend' as they launched over the crest. She screamed as the car landed and bounced down on its shock absorbers.

Malek's eyes widened as they approached the hairpin with just a feeble wooden barrier between them and oblivion. He stamped on the brakes, but the Carrera's weight continued to carry it forwards and they hit the old barrier with a resounding thud, smashing it to pieces as they flew out over the edge of the cliff. The bonnet pointed downwards with the rear wheels spinning and the engine screaming as the momentum carried them away in a graceful arc like an Olympic diver. The vehicle disappeared into the ravine, a shuddering crash signalling the end of the car and its occupant's final journey.

Chapter 60

Jemma braked as they reached another bend on the hill.

Ellie screamed. 'They went over the edge. I saw them, they crashed.'

Brad twisted around to peer out of the rear window. 'What?'

'Th-that h-h-hairpin,' she stammered. 'They hit the barrier and flew over the cliff. You don't need to go fast anymore, Mum.'

Jemma took her foot off the pedal and looked in her mirror as the car slowed. 'You sure, Els?'

'Yes,' Ellie replied. 'On that last bend you skidded around, they took it too fast and went straight over.'

Jemma kept moving. 'Should we go back and check?'

Brad turned back. 'Just keep going. I can't see them either so maybe they did crash.'

Ellie frowned. 'I know what I saw.'

As they went around the next corner a herd of goats appeared from a gate followed by a teenage boy holding a long stick. Jemma hit the brakes, the car dipped and the boy waved as they pulled up and Jemma cut the engine. The boy headed into a wider opening opposite and they started moving again.

Brad folded his map. 'Do you think we can forget about them now?'

Ellie pouted. 'Why won't you listen to me? They've got to be in pieces in the bottom of the valley...unless they landed on the slope somehow.'

They drove through a small hamlet with a bar by the roadside. Four old men wearing hats and smoking cigarettes were sitting around a square wooden table playing backgammon. They ignored Jemma as she drove past at a more sedate pace.

'My heart is starting to slow down,' she said. 'That was a bloody adrenaline rush. How ya doing in the back?'

Ellie adjusted her hold on Kira, who continued to cling to her. 'We're good. She held on while we were being thrown about.' She smiled. 'I think she's just glad to be back with her mum.'

Brad unfolded the map as Jemma stopped at a junction. 'We're not out of this place yet. I can't see where we are on here.' He tapped the display on the dashboard. 'This crappy satnav still isn't working.'

An old man came around the corner leading a donkey and Jemma wound down her window to call him. 'Nicosia, please?'

The man revealed a toothless smile and pointed to the right.

'Thank you.' She headed that way.

Brad tried reading the map as Jemma drove down the single-track road. 'This must be the old military road. Stop, let me check this sign. Oh, that's pointing back where we came and says Turk Tanki. At least we're not going round in circles. It also says something at the bottom. No stopping or photos. Get moving. I don't want to get arrested now.'

She moved off and progressed along the tarmac road, only passing two vehicles, a delivery van and another tractor, but managed to pull over sufficiently to squeeze past. Finally, they arrived at a larger road with a metal sign.

‘Karsiyaka or Turkeli?’ Jemma asked.

‘Give me a minute.’ Brad pored over the names on the map. ‘It hardly helps when every town name is in Turkish, Greek and English.’

Jemma smiled. ‘I’m glad I’m not asking for rally directions from you. I’d never get out of first gear.’

He hit her arm playfully. ‘Shut up. I’m doing my best. Here we go. Head for Turkeli. That will bring us back to Nicosia. Stick to the speed limits and we should be at the border in less than an hour.’

Chapter 61

Ellie sniffed Kira's hair. 'I've missed so much about her but most of all I've missed her smell.'

'It's wonderful,' Jemma said. 'I still can't believe you just grabbed her.'

Her daughter shrugged. 'Well, there was no sign of the local police doing anything, I had to do something. I didn't think it through. I wanted to see her and hold her so badly. Once I'd picked her up, I couldn't put her down again. It would have been cruel.'

Brad turned and smiled at her. 'I'm glad you did. We had been messing about a bit. Have you messaged Dan at all?'

Ellie shook her head. 'No. Why?'

'It might be a good idea to let him know that, if all goes well, we could be back in England within a few days.'

'I'll send him a text.' Ellie pulled out her phone and tapped in a message. 'That'll confuse him coming from a different number.'

'What?' Jemma said.

'The sims we bought at the airport will have Turkish numbers,' Ellie replied.

Jemma frowned. 'Oh, right, I believe you.'

Five minutes later she received a response. 'Wow, that was quick.'

'Is he OK to fetch us?'

'Yep. He says just tell him where and when and he'll be there.'

'He's a good 'un, that lad,' Jemma said.

Ellie smiled. 'He is, isn't he?'

She sent another text. 'I've said I'll call him once I know what's happening.'

Jemma drove for an hour with no sign of any further pursuit.

Brad checked the map. 'We're nearly there. Satnav says it's half a kilometre away. I just wish the broken window didn't stand out so much.'

They joined a queue of traffic on the single track road marked out with orange posts. After every hundred metres, she had to manoeuvre around concrete blocks with bored-looking soldiers wearing military fatigues clutching assault rifles. Inching along, they followed an open-backed truck laden with football-sized watermelons. Pedestrians carrying bags of groceries plodded wearily past.

'Why are so many people crossing the border to shop?' Ellie asked. 'Seems a lot of effort.'

Jemma glanced at a woman with a heavy shopping cart. 'The magazine said lots of Greek Cypriots come across the border to buy food because the euro is strong against the Turkish lira. They get more for their euros and the locals like being paid in a currency that holds its value.'

Suddenly, half a dozen heavily armed soldiers rushed towards the back of their SUV.

'What's going on?' Brad asked.

As they watched, the guards surrounded the truck behind them and started gesticulating.

Jemma wound down her window for a better look. 'I don't know what that driver's done but they're not happy.'

Ellie watched through the broken rear window. 'They're arguing with him and pointing to the red fuel cans he has in the back.'

One of the soldiers climbed into the passenger seat and pointed down a slip road. The driver drove along and pulled up under a plastic-roofed compound where two men started unloading the containers.

'Maybe he's smuggling fuel across the border,' Brad said. 'I have a bad feeling about this crossing. Some of the guys with guns look about twelve and I bet they're trigger-happy.'

'That's a sign you're getting old.' Ellie gave a nervous smile.

'We're nearly at the kiosk,' Jemma said. 'No more talk about smuggling.'

A guard wearing a dark blue uniform with a holstered handgun pointed to a kiosk and Jemma drove towards it.

'Here goes.' She lowered her window and handed over their four passports, three of which contained slips of paper with an entry stamp.

The official checked the first passport and stared at Jemma before pointing to her face. 'Sunglasses off.'

Her hand shook as she removed them and gave her best 'roomful of first-year students' smile.

He stamped the piece of paper and put her passport to one side before repeating the process with Brad. He leant forwards and peered into the car. 'Bradley.' He compared the photo with the man in the passenger seat.

Ellie giggled at the name and Brad turned to her with a glare.

'Oh, American.' The officer stamped the paper.

'Yes, sir, born and bred,' Brad replied.

'Where is Ellie May Thorne?' the man said.

'I'm here.' Ellie slid over to the window.

He stamped her piece of paper and opened the final passport. 'Where is child?' he asked.

Ellie held Kira up to the window, who smiled at the guard with no response. The official flicked through the other pages of Kira's passport searching for the slip of paper with the entry stamp.

'Where is stamp from when you entered the country?'

'Er. It is...in th-there,' Jemma stuttered. 'No? Er... It must have fallen out.'

They all started searching the car and Brad got out to check the cases and rucksacks in the luggage compartment. The driver behind pipped his horn. 'Sorry. Maybe we lost it.' Brad walked back to the window.

'Not good.' The official twirled his moustache and shouted something in Turkish. A large man with a swagger stick and full military uniform came out through a door alongside the row of kiosks. He strutted over to the window and had a short conversation with the border officer. The officer pointed at the occupants of the car and handed over the four passports and three pieces of paper.

The military man pointed to a parking space after the final kiosk. 'Park there.'

Jemma gulped and inched the Kia into the space. She opened the car door.

'Get back in,' the man shouted.

She jumped back inside as if scalded and waited while the man walked around to the passenger door. He rested his elbow on the open window and touched Brad's arm with his swagger stick.

'You. Come to my office and bring passports.'

Jemma leaned over. 'What? All of us?'

The man shook his head. 'No. Just him. Quickly.' He pointed to Jemma. 'You stay in car.'

Brad took a swig from his water bottle and shrugged at her.

'Follow me, now.' The army officer spun and headed for the door he'd appeared from.

Brad flashed a glance at Jemma and stepped after him.

Jemma turned to Ellie and held her daughter's hand. 'Shit,' she whispered.

Chapter 62

A Jeep full of tourists pulled up onto the gravel parking area by the Turkish Tank Memorial. Long metal tank treads were stretched out beside the road, like mini train tracks to nowhere.

The tank itself was perched on the hillside by the road with its gun pointed back down the track. On the hill above, a tin sign with two flags fluttering alongside told the story of the fated vehicle. Behind the memorial, the stunning views of the coast acted as a contrast to the bleak reminder of a war fifty years before.

The tourists strolled up to the memorial for the obligatory selfies and the driver rolled his eyes at the lack of respect shown by one as he climbed up onto the turret.

'How long are we here for?' one of the tour members shouted to the driver.

He smiled and held up his cigarette. 'This long.' He took a long drag.

Two of the group, a young woman with brown hair and a bearded man, wandered off down towards the next bend. The side of the road was a mess of skid marks and some broken pieces of wood. They stepped cautiously down towards the cliff edge and gazed over. Down in the valley below, a plume of smoke was rising from where flames glowed in the undergrowth.

The woman shouted back to the driver. 'There's a fire down in the trees.'

With a last pull of his cigarette, the driver sauntered over. 'Forest fire, very bad.' He took his mobile phone from his pocket and dialled a number.

The bearded man gestured to the broken guard rail and tyre tracks in the leaf litter. 'I think a car has crashed through.'

* * *

Brad followed the Turkish official down a gloomy corridor clutching the passports in his sweaty palm. The door at the end opened into a brightly lit office that made him squint. The walls were covered in photos of the man he was with, posing alongside several other uniformed and suited people.

The man pointed to a plastic chair. 'Sit.' He pulled out a leather wheeled one for himself and lowered his corpulent frame into it.

Brad held his breath as the mechanism's piston hissed and complained.

'Passports.' The official held out his hand and flicked through them all. 'Where is entry stamp for baby?'

Brad shrugged. 'We must have dropped it. Sorry.'

'This is big problem.' He stared at the passport. 'Bradley, no stamp for the girl. The child could have been here for many months and you are trying to avoid an over-stay fine.'

'But why would Kira be here for months without her mother? We all travelled together. Maybe the border guy forgot to put a slip of paper in her passport.'

The man hit the table with his swagger stick, which made a loud thwack as it connected with the wood. He leant forward over the desk. 'My men do not make mistakes.'

Brad sighed. 'Everybody makes mistakes.'

The man sneered. 'Well, you made a big one when you lost the paper.'

Brad checked the time. 'We need to get to the south to catch our plane. How can we resolve this?'

The man stood and walked around the room.

Brad turned to face him. 'How about I volunteer to pay an over-stay fine as an apology for my mistake?'

The official's eyebrows lifted and he returned to his seat. 'That would cost a lot of money.'

Brad swallowed. 'How much?'

The man's lip curled. 'Five thousand lira.'

Brad made a quick mental calculation. *Almost one hundred and fifty dollars.* 'OK. I'll sort that out now. Then we can go?'

'Yes, my friend.'

Brad pulled out his wallet and counted the notes onto the desk. 'Teşekkür ederim,' he said.

The official grinned as he folded the money and slid it into the chest pocket of his crisp, white shirt with its straining buttons. 'You speak Turkish?'

'Just a little,' Brad replied.

The man brought a sheet of cream paper out from the drawer together with two stamps and an ink pad. He added two stamps to the paper, placed it inside Kira's passport and handed it back to Brad. 'Do not lose this one.' He smiled. 'You like Turkish coffee?'

Brad's eyebrows lifted in surprise. 'Yes, I love it, the stronger the better.'

'Stay here.' The man disappeared through a door behind his desk.

Brad glanced around the room. *What is going on? Am I in trouble?*

A minute later, the official reappeared with a tray

containing two tiny porcelain cups and some small square cakes. He handed one cup to Brad. 'You try baklava?'

Brad hesitated. 'Er...oh, yes, please, they look delicious.'

'My name is Mustafa, by the way.' He extended his hand for Brad to shake. 'Now, tell me all about America.'

Brad was hit by the coffee's strong smell. He took a sip. 'Well, I was born in Indiana.'

* * *

Jemma checked her watch for the twentieth time. 'What's going on in there? He's been over an hour and I'm starting to get worried. What if they've arrested him? How will we ever get home?' She shivered. 'I saw a film once called *Midnight Express* about a drug smuggler in a Turkish prison. It was horrible.'

'Calm down, Mum. They haven't searched our luggage so they can't be looking for drugs.'

'Oh, no,' Jemma wailed. 'They're torturing him! They'll keep us as hostages to try extorting money from our families, or the British and American governments.'

Ellie sneered. 'Good luck with that.'

They both jumped as Ellie's phone rang, the Turkish music tone echoing around the car.

'It's Dan.' Ellie answered. 'Hi, Dan. I can't talk now. We're trying to cross the border and there are men with guns.'

She listened for a moment and blushed. 'Dan! My Mum's sitting next to me. I know, I can't wait to get home as well. Hang on a minute.' She handed Kira to Jemma and exited the car before pottering away with the phone pinned to her ear and a coy grin on her face.

All of a sudden, there was a commotion, and a guard ran towards Ellie waving a handgun. 'No phones. No photos.' He pointed to a sign on the fence that gave the same message.

Ellie spoke into the mobile before turning it off, shoving it back in her pocket and scuttling back to the Kia.

* * *

The door opened and Brad stepped out smiling.

'He's coming,' Jemma said, 'and he looks like he's still got all his fingers.'

Brad shook hands with the uniformed official. 'Gule gule, Mustafa.'

'Goodbye, my friend. Safe journey with your family.' The man turned back into the building and closed the door.

Brad gave them a thumbs-up gesture before strolling towards the kiosk and waiting for the border guard to take the four passports from him. After he had checked the stamps, the official handed them back and pointed to the exit.

Brad walked back to the car and entered as Jemma gaped at him open-mouthed. 'OK,' he said, 'let's go. All sorted. Just keep quiet and drive.'

Jemma started the engine and crawled towards the exit. A smile flickered across her face but halfway towards the dusty ground, a different guard holding a rifle ran towards them. 'Stop! Stop. Problem.'

Chapter 63

'Bloody hell, now what?' Jemma said.

The guard knocked on the driver's window with the butt of his rifle. 'Out. Now.'

Jemma's mouth went dry as she twisted to face Brad. 'Do I put my hands up?'

Brad shrugged. 'Just ask what he wants.'

She climbed out of the car and followed the man as he strutted around towards the back of the Kia and pointed his gun at the shattered rear window.

'Illegal. You can't cross the border with broken glass. What happened?'

'Someone tried to break in,' she replied.

Brad wandered over to join the discussion.

The guard glared at Jemma. 'Where is the police report and crime number?'

She paused. 'Er. We haven't got one. We just need to be back in time for our flight.'

The man shouldered his gun and brought out a notepad. 'No crime report, big problem. You must call garage to fit new glass before you go through.' He wrote something on his pad and ripped out the page. 'This is number of garage,' he said. 'My cousin owns it. He is good.'

She sighed. 'Can't we sort it when we get to the car hire place? We have a baby with us and want to be back at our villa before it's dark.'

The guard raised his voice. 'Call garage now and buy new window.'

Brad stared at him. 'Ask Mustafa.'

The guard flinched. 'You know Mustafa?'

Brad's eyebrows raised. 'He is a friend of mine.'

The man pulled a radio from his jacket and spoke into it. He waited for a reply and then returned it to his pocket. 'We wait.'

The office door opened and the uniformed official sauntered over. 'Bradley, my friend. What is the problem here?'

Brad shook his hand again. 'Mustafa, I'm so glad to see you. Can you help, please? Your colleague here tells me we have to wait for a garage to come out and replace our rear window, which was broken when somebody tried to break in.'

Mustafa checked the ragged edges of the glass. 'Do you have a police report?'

Brad shook his head. 'No. Nothing was stolen and we just want to get back for our flight. We'll arrange it with the car hire company.'

'Well, my friend, the insurance will not cover the cost of the replacement if you do not have an incident number from the police. That is up to you to sort out with them.' He turned to the guard and fired off a burst of rapid Turkish.

The guard seemed to grow visibly smaller with the outburst. He shrugged, shouldered his rifle and strolled away sticking his chest out.

Mustafa smiled. 'I told him to let my friends go through.' He leant closer to Brad. 'I'll give him five hundred lira later.'

Brad reached for his wallet, but the large man held up his hand. 'No more,' he said. 'You have already been generous in paying the fine. Now, you go. I'll walk beside the car as far as the Greek buildings.'

Jemma smiled as they returned to the Sportage before driving at a walking pace over the no-man's land between the Turkish and Greek sides. As they arrived at the Greek side, Mustafa saluted them and turned back towards his office. Jemma pulled up to the next kiosk and handed over the four passports, which were soon checked and returned with a polite nod.

She pulled away from the border and Ellie whooped for joy.

'Welcome back to the E.U.,' Jemma said.

'Oh, Mum,' Ellie sobbed, 'I hope so.'

The traffic became heavier as they neared Larnaca and it took them nearly an hour to reach their first villa.

'Pull in right under the canopy,' Brad said. 'There are some black clouds about and I'd hate to return the car drenched with water as well as a broken window.'

They unlocked the villa and emptied the Kia so they could sort out what they'd need for the next stage of the journey home. Brad returned to the car with a dustpan and brush to try cleaning the fragments of glass. Jemma sorted and repacked the cases, and removed some food and clothes for Kira, while Ellie searched for flights on her laptop.

Brad wandered back inside carrying a small metal object. 'I'm glad the guards didn't find this.'

'What is it?' Jemma asked.

'A flattened bullet,' he replied. 'That might have been a bit trickier to explain.'

'Listen, guys,' Ellie said, 'I've found some seats on a flight from Larnaca to Heathrow that leaves at eleven am tomorrow. We'd need to be at the airport for nine.'

'That's great, Ellie.' Brad handed her a credit card to pay for the tickets.

Ten minutes later, she stood up. 'All sorted.'

Brad put his hand on her arm. 'Will you tell Dan we should land at Heathrow around two pm, and see if he's OK to collect us?'

She grinned. 'I'll call him from upstairs. Can you hold Kira for a moment please, Mum?' She handed her daughter to Jemma and the youngster smiled as she was passed to her gran.

After ten minutes, Ellie returned. 'All set up. He'll be waiting at Terminal Five at two-fifteen.'

'Right,' Jemma said. 'Fancy a walk to that restaurant?' She pointed outside. 'I think it's just back down the street.'

'I never say no to food,' Ellie said. 'OK for you, Brad?'

'Yep, I'm easy,' he replied.

They showered, changed clothes, and half an hour later were sitting in the cosy restaurant that served traditional Greek food. Kira perched in a highchair and merrily ate every treat they passed her way. It was nearly ten pm when they wandered back to the villa.

Ellie placed Kira in a cot and they relaxed with a bottle of beer each to watch some TV before heading for bed. Brad flicked through the available channels.

'Stop,' Jemma shouted. 'Go back to that Turkish channel, BRT.'

He pointed the control at the TV. 'This one?'

'Yes,' she sat up straight. 'That's the Turkish Tank Memorial.'

He squinted. 'So it is. That shot must be from a helicopter.'

As they watched the news programme, the picture zoomed in on a closer view of the charred wreckage of a sports car surrounded by firefighters damping down the smouldering grass.

'Oh, my God,' Ellie said. 'That's their Porsche.'

The picture zoomed out and a banner appeared at the bottom of the screen.

‘What does *Iki Olu* mean?’
Brad googled it and declared, ‘two dead!’

Chapter 64

Bayram reversed his lorry down Helen's drive and climbed out followed by the other workers. He knocked on Helen's door, which swung open of its own accord.

'Helen. Malek,' he shouted.

When nobody answered, he called them both but received no response.

Shrugging, he returned to his men unloading tools and picked up a trowel and mortar board. As he turned to walk down the garden, a white car with *Polis* written on the side pulled up outside the property.

He rolled his eyes and went to meet them.

* * *

Brad, Jemma and Ellie left the villa at six-thirty am for the short drive back to the airport. The traffic was light and they made swift progress. After unloading the cases at the car hire company, Jemma handed over the keys and paperwork with a smile.

The receptionist smiled back. 'Thank you, Mrs Thorne. I hope you had a lovely time.'

'A memorable holiday,' Jemma grinned. 'One we will never forget.'

'How full is the fuel tank?' the lady asked.

'It's on three-quarters,' Jemma replied.

'That's fine. Any problems with the car?'

'Ah, yes. We had a slight problem with the tailgate.'

'What problem?'

Jemma paused. 'The glass got a bit broken.'

'Oh. I'll need to ask one of our vehicle examiners to take a look with you.' She picked up the phone and shortly afterwards a smartly dressed young man came out from a door behind her.

'Mrs Thorne,' he said. 'Where have you parked?'

She led him back out to the carpark where an extremely dusty Kia Sportage was sitting with no rear window.

The man inhaled. 'How did that happen?'

'Somebody broke it but we didn't catch them.'

'Did you obtain an incident number from the police?' he asked.

'Unfortunately, not. We were about to cross the border and didn't have time. Nothing was stolen.'

'I'm surprised the Turks let you through with a broken window.'

'My husband spoke to the officials and said we'd just sort it out with you when we returned the car.'

He frowned. 'I'm afraid that without a police crime number, the insurance won't cover malicious damage.' He tapped his tablet's screen and took some photographs of the damage. 'There will be twelve hundred euros to pay.'

'OK, we'll pay that. Sorry for the trouble.'

'Don't worry, Mrs Thorne, these things happen. You should always get a crime incident report, though.'

'We know that now, but we didn't want to spend any more time on the Turkish side than we needed to.'

'It is rather different over there, isn't it?' he said.

Jemma nodded. 'Just a bit.'

He shut down his tablet. 'If you return to my colleague at the desk, she'll take your card details for the payment.'

Jemma went back inside the building. Even at eight am, it was scorching hot outside, and she was glad to be back in the air-conditioned coolness of the office. She paid for the damage and strolled back to where Brad and Ellie were playing with Kira.

'All sorted?' he asked.

'Yes, but I'm twelve hundred euros poorer.'

'What, for one window?' Ellie said. 'That's a lot.'

'I didn't want to make a fuss,' Jemma replied. 'I just want to get home and forget about all of this.'

'Do you think we'll be able to forget this, Mum?'

Jemma shrugged. 'I don't know, but hopefully Helen is the last of the Fletchers.'

'Good riddance,' Brad said.

They queued for immigration and the man behind the desk checked Brad's passport, staring intently at his photograph. He leant over to the edge of the counter. 'Well, did you find what you were looking for?'

Brad frowned. 'What?'

'A Cyprus Warbler.'

Brad released his breath. 'No. I never got to see one.'

'Shame.' The man stamped the passports. 'You'll have to come back again.'

'That would be nice.' Brad glanced at Jemma.

The plane was only around half full so was very quiet. Kira behaved impeccably and, after a meal of pureed fruit, she snuggled down on Ellie's lap and slept for most of the five-hour flight.

Ellie, Jemma and Brad all dozed for large parts of the journey and it didn't seem long before the pilot told the passengers to fasten their seatbelts as they commenced the descent into Heathrow. As they descended, Jemma gazed at the London suburbs beneath them until the plane bumped to a graceful stop on the tarmac.

While waiting for the doors to open, Jemma switched back to her old sim to find a deluge of text messages and emails, the latest from her ex, Dave.

Hi, Jem. Max tells me Helen Fletcher and a Turkish National called Malek Aydin died yesterday when the Porsche in which they were driving crashed off a narrow mountain road and burst into flames. An illegal gun was discovered in the wreckage. I spoke with Amrik and he thought you were still on holiday in Northern Cyprus. Nothing to do with you, was it? Cheers. Dave.

She typed a reply. *Hi, Dave. That's good news. No, nothing to do with us. The four of us have just landed at Heathrow after a thrilling trip. Speak soon. Jemma X*

They arrived at the Border Force turnstiles and Brad went through the non-UK/non-EEC gate while Jemma and Ellie queued at the UK kiosks. Jemma and Ellie's passports were both fine when checked by the immigration officer but when he scanned Kira's he frowned before tapping something into his keyboard. After a while, he picked up his phone, spoke quietly and returned to Ellie.

'Miss Thorne, there's a red flag attached to this child's passport. I'm afraid you'll have to accompany our officer.'

Chapter 65

Amrik peered at his computer screen as he put the finishing touches to the report for the prosecution in the drug dealer murder. The team had turned the case around in three days, mainly due to the stupidity of the fellow dealer who'd shot his rival in broad daylight in front of several witnesses. He'd then hidden the gun, covered in his fingerprints, under the seat of the black BMW registered in his own name.

DC Hannah Salmon wandered over. 'Want a drink fetching?'

'Coffee, please.' He reached into the drawer beneath his desk. 'Fancy a chocolate digestive to celebrate wrapping up the murder so quickly?'

Hannah's eyes widened. 'Yes, please. How have you managed to keep choccie bikkies in your desk without them getting nicked?'

Amrik peered around furtively and smiled. 'I wired the drawer handle up to the mains.'

Her eyes closed in bliss as she took a bite of the cherished biscuit. 'What are we on to next?'

'At the moment, it's full steam ahead back on to Kira's disappearance. I'm expecting some developments after I found out yesterday that Helen Fletcher and her boyfriend were killed in a car crash in Cyprus.'

'Oh, no, was there a child with them?' she asked.

'No, just the two adults...and an illegal gun.' The handset on Amrik's desk rang. He picked it up.

'Amrik, it's Alan.'

'Morning, Sarge. What's happening?'

'I've got someone on the line from Border Force England asking about a missing child.'

'OK, give me a moment to put it on speaker.' He pressed the button. 'Hello?'

'Good morning. Am I speaking to DS Hussain?'

'Yes. How can I help?'

'I'm calling from Border Force at Heathrow Airport. A young lady, Ellie Thorne, is trying to bring in a child by the name of Kira Thorne. We have a red flag alert on the system for the child and you are the contact to call.'

Amrik grinned at Hannah and held up his thumb. 'Is Ellie with you?'

'Give me a moment and I'll put her on.'

Amrik grabbed Hannah's hand and squeezed it hard. 'She's been found.'

'Hello, Amrik, it's Ellie.'

'Ellie,' he said. 'Have you really got her back?'

'Yes. She's here in my arms. We're back safe.'

'How did you get her?'

'Er...I sort of picked her up and brought her home.'

'In that case, put the immigration officer back on and I'll explain.'

'Thanks so much,' Ellie said.

He squeezed Hannah's hand again. 'One thing though, Ellie. You must come and see me when you're back and give me the full story, off the record, if you like.'

'You're on, Amrik, and thanks for all your help. Here, I'm passing you back to the Border Force man.'

'Hello, DS Hussain, is it OK to let her through then?'

'Yes, she's clear to bring Kira into the country. I'll notify the authorities to remove the alert on the system.'

'Thank you and goodbye.'

Amrik put down the phone and looked at his hand, which was still holding Hannah's. He blushed and snatched it away. 'Sorry. It's such good news.'

She smiled. 'Don't worry. I'm just happy she's been found.'

Amrik grabbed the phone again and dialled an internal extension. 'Laura, can you come to the incident room, please? I've got some fantastic news.'

* * *

Ellie left the interrogation room holding Kira and followed the signs for baggage collection. She checked the screen for the carousel number and, as she headed for belt five, spotted her mum and Brad waving furiously.

Jemma ran over and hugged her. 'All OK, Els? We were getting worried but they wouldn't let us wait in there, so we came and collected the cases.'

'Yes, I'm fine. There was an alert out for Kira but they rang Amrik and he cleared it.' She sighed. 'Is that it, Mum? No more false starts and questions from bloody officials? Are we actually back in England and safe from Helen Fletcher?'

Jemma smiled. 'Unless the bitch comes back from the dead to haunt us.'

Brad wheeled the final suitcase over to where they were standing. 'That's it, we're good to go. Where's Dan meeting us?'

Ellie checked her phone. 'He says go to the arrivals hall and we'll spot him there.'

'This way.' Jemma led the way through the *Nothing to Declare* channel.

Ellie glanced at the mirrors on the wall. 'I'm getting paranoid about self-important officials running out and saying *just one moment. Please come with us, we have a problem*.'

The customs post seemed deserted as they wandered through to arrivals.

Jemma walked alongside Brad wheeling the cases as they followed Ellie and Kira through to the crowded hall.

Ellie suddenly pointed to a large white card with *ELLIE & KIRA* written in black handwritten letters. She ran over with Kira and moved it to one side to reveal a smiling Dan.

'Love the card.' She hugged him and planted a big kiss on his lips. Kira held out her arms for a hug as well, which Dan duly obliged.

He went over and hugged Jemma before shaking Brad's hand. 'Great to have you all back safe and sound. Which is Ellie's case?'

'This one,' Jemma said.

He grasped the handle, along with Ellie's hand, and set off towards the short-stay carpark. 'This way. Let's go.'

Brad hugged Jemma. 'What a relief. Love you.'

'Love you, too,' Jemma murmured. They each grabbed a suitcase and followed the young couple.

Brad smiled at the sight of Ellie and Dan walking hand in hand and bumped Jemma's hip. 'As Humphrey Bogart said at the end of Casablanca, "I think this is the beginning of a beautiful friendship".'

Acknowledgments

I'm extremely grateful to Randall Krzak, Amy Fearn, Clare Kimble, and Kate Thomas, whose feedback on early drafts was invaluable, and to Tim Bartlett, Erin Byrd, Lucy Lyons, Deb Allen, and Donna Sundblad for their help as beta readers.

Thanks especially to Pauline and Sara for their constant reviews, insights, help and typing.

Thanks for the professional assistance of Shaun Baines (structural editing), Damian Jackson (copy editing, proof reading and formatting) and Ken Dawson for the book cover design.

Thanks also to Steve Hunt for the information and videos of Brixham Harbour and to Sophia Moseley for the cover photo of Lyme Regis cliffs.

* * *

Thank you for buying this book. I hope you enjoyed it. If you did, may I ask a small favour please?

As an independent author reviews are important for getting established so, if you could leave a review on Amazon and Goodreads, I would greatly appreciate it.

Thanks for your support.

Printed in Great Britain
by Amazon

51185685R00196